HE'S A PLAYER

SPECIAL EDITION

STACY TRAVIS

CHAPTER 1

*J*ordan

Click, clack.

My shoes sound like a metronome on the parquet floors. A noisy wristwatch counting down the seconds. Counting down my fate.

No, not fate. I don't believe in fate. Or karma. Or destiny. I don't think life operates according to some karmic sense of justice. Karma doesn't have it out for one person or another based on a past slight or insult. And a good deed doesn't earn extra points in life's big swear jar.

Please.

Calling on fate always feels like putting the blame someplace else when it's more likely that life is a big random happenstance. Because a large stellar explosion yielded anxious little life forms looking for explanations.

People cross paths randomly, not because it's meant to be. And if it happens twice, it's just more dumb luck or similar taste in movies or food.

That's it.

I'm a scientist, after all. Sports doctor, but a scientist none-theless. That means there's no reason to get ruffled over inconvenient events or people. Things just happen. Or don't happen.

Science is the backbone of all things. Want to know whether it's okay to play tennis with a torn labrum? Look at the science.

Want to know whether whole milk or skim milk leads to stronger bones? Science.

Everything that happens has a cause, every cause has an effect, every effect has an explanation. Living with such an impassive, unemotional outlook has served me well. Everything is just one tiny data point in a constellation that will make perfect sense later.

Even if that data point turns out to be my unrequited crush—the guy who led me to make impulsive decisions in the past. If he's the first person I see in a giant room full of people, it's just a big, big coincidence. Tim Cheltenham won't fluster me. My heart won't race in his presence. Even if it's racing now.

For all I know, as the resident newbie, I'm heading into a den of debauchery, hazing, and torture from the team's stupidly handsome defender. My fault for taking a job on his home turf.

Click, clack.

But it's a dream job, and I want to succeed. I don't start work for a month, but my new boss wants me to meet the players in an informal atmosphere. Hence the invitation to a casual post-game gathering at the stadium. "Easy crowd. And I don't like crowds, so trust me on this," the Strikers' owner, Charlie Walgrove, said when he hired me. The awkward genius billionaire famously avoids the spotlight, so if he finds this sort of event manageable, it works for me.

"Sounds good. I don't love crowds either." Not that my previous job at a sports medicine clinic dropped me into a lot of crowds filled with professional athletes.

A nervous butterfly jazz band marches through my chest at

the thought of tall, muscle-bound jocks who view me as the enemy. Yeah. About that…

Charlie just fired the prior team physician for mishandling the health of his athletes. It wasn't as bad as doping, but the good doctor was apparently keeping injured players pumped up on prescription pain meds to keep them in the game, even if it led to worse injuries and other wear and tear.

He kept them bandaged and iced just enough to numb them up, but Charlie, king of data and stats, noticed that some players weren't recovering from games and workouts the way they should. Their speed was slowing. The time it took for them to launch from ready to a full run was a split-second off, which made all the difference when it came to fighting for a ball. And winning games.

The head coach was in on it as well, so Charlie cleaned house and brought in a new coach and a new medical team, with me leading them. I assured him my ethics would never allow for abusing the health and safety of players.

"I don't doubt you at all, Doctor Page," he'd said. His confidence boosted my own. How intimidating can a bunch of jocks be? They'll be like more talented versions of the amateur athletes who came into my old clinic with sprains, tears, and broken bones. Only instead of getting back to spring skiing, they'll be heading back to million dollar contracts to play pro soccer.

I've been preparing for this job with all my heart and soul for more than ten years. Not only is it a chance to work with top athletes, but I'll get a front row seat at my favorite sport. A shot like this comes around once in a career.

Yes, Alexander Hamilton, I know what to do.

Following the signs inside the San Francisco Strikers soccer stadium, I walk past the luxury boxes toward the fancy members-only clubhouse, where a cacophony of voices and music blasts from a hundred yards away.

Click.

Clack.

Not like Charlie gave me much wiggle room when he invited me to the event tonight. "Come meet a few folks and get your bearings before you start instilling fear in the players."

I laughed and nodded because at five feet, three inches, and with what people refer to as "doe eyes," I rarely instill fear in anyone.

I'm busy mulling that over when I trip over something invisible and almost face plant on the floor. Steadying myself, I glance around to be sure no one saw my near-fall from grace.

Damn these two-inch heels. They're not even high, but I want the added stature as long as I can avoid my usual clumsiness.

Slowing my pace, I want to be sure I can walk the last few yards without taking a bite out of the hardwood floor. My stomach churns with a flutter of nerves the closer I get to the stained oak doors that flank the clubhouse entrance. I stop and lean against the wall, fortifying my nerves.

I've always made it my goal to blend into a group. To disappear. My mother would have a lot to say about this. "It's why you're still single. You're a bystander. No one notices how pretty you are when you're hiding behind someone taller."

A whole other issue, my mother. Her goal is to see me married, pregnant, and feathering a nest. My goal is to make a difference in the world by working hard. I'm good at that. I'm *bad* at dating, evidenced by making terrible, impulsive decisions around men.

Starting when I was sixteen. Starting with Tim Cheltenham.

Glancing down at my gray pencil skirt, pink silk blouse, and sensible heels, I look like I dressed for a day at a law office, not a night on the town.

Ugh.

I pull my russet hair out of its clip, so it falls over my shoulders. Bonus points for the loose waves from having it twisted into a bun all day. And I wipe off the pale pink lipstick with the back of my hand and rifle through my purse for a brighter, darker shade. Extracting a tube of red, I feel my party cred notch up a tad.

Then I flick the button just beneath my throat on my blouse, giving me a hint of cleavage that wouldn't pass muster during a workday. Not exactly nightclub-worthy, but less uptight. It will do.

When I reach the door, I don't have time to process my unexpected panic when I see that the couple dozen people I anticipated are easily a hundred. Panic is panic, and mine has just ratcheted my heart rate over a thousand.

A hundred people drinking, talking, laughing. Having fun. They're in groups, smiling and socializing. Some wearing dress shirts and ties, others in casual T-shirts and jeans.

No one wears a pencil skirt and sensible pumps.

"Oh, Jordan. Greetings." Charlie extends his hand. "Welcome to the team. And the post-game madness, as it were. Always nice to have a win." Charlie's easy manner belies the truth—he wants more than just a win. The man didn't build his billion-dollar virtual reality company with modest goals. He wants the Strikers to be the best, and he's put faith in me and his new coach. No pressure.

None.

I try to ignore the sudden stifling warmth in the room. A rivulet of sweat dribbles between my shoulder blades.

"Congrats on the win. I'm thrilled to be here." I compensate for my knocking knees with the biggest smile in my arsenal. Confident. Savvy.

Before I can come up with more empty pleasantries, Charlie is buttonholed by a tall, broad man with slicked-back hair and a navy suit. Probably an agent, manager, financial partner. Doesn't matter. Charlie smiles apologetically as he's whisked away to a nearby table.

With my safety net person gone, I make my way toward the

bar, passing through groups of men and women standing at tall cocktail tables. More groups sit around four-tops and in black leather banquettes. It's standing room only around the four-sided bar in the middle of the room, but I slip between people without being noticed.

The sealed concrete floor and high industrial ceiling make the acoustics extra loud. The only items to absorb sound in the room are some throw pillows with the blue and black Strikers logo on them, and this place would need four thousand of them to blunt the noise.

"What'll you have, miss?" A bartender who looks young enough to be carded grins at me beneath round wire glasses and spiky brown hair. Leaning my forearm on the heavy oak bar, I survey the liquor on well-lit glass shelves.

"Margarita, rocks, no salt, thanks." I watch him pour a jigger of expensive tequila into a shaker with triple sec and lime juice before giving it a shake. He drizzles it over ice and adds another healthy pour of tequila. He winks as he hands it to me.

I'm buzzed after one sip of his strong cocktail and cringe as it burns my throat. Relaxing a bit, I scan the faces in the crowd. Mostly men—trainers and coaches, office staff, and players who look a little different from their roster photos now that they're showered and dressed in street clothes. One pretty brunette in leather pants and tall heels throws her head back and laughs. Another wears a short blue dress, dirty blond hair trailing down her back. They huddle together, easy in the crowd, comfortable with themselves.

"Hello." The voice is accented. Gruff. Deep.

Even amid the din, I recognize the voice as huskier than Charlie's. My stomach drops to my feet, and I fight back a surge of adrenaline mixed with nausea.

I turn, and I'm met by broad shoulders under a tight black Henley with the Strikers logo on the front. Even in heels, I have to look up to see Tim Cheltenham's face.

It's gorgeous. Undeniably gorgeous—angular jaw, olive-colored eyes under criminally long lashes, lips that inspire fantasies among virgins. And everyone else.

Except right now, those beautiful eyes are squinting in confusion, and his luscious lips are pressed into a line. The only thing harder than this man's muscles is the intensity of his stare, and his muscles could tear holes in his shirt.

My eyes go rogue, taking a slow tour of his frame, starting with his ripped, low-slung jeans and those sculpted soccer player thighs, hugged tight by the denim fabric, which is probably having its own orgasm from the contact.

Lucky-duck jeans.

His shirt is tight enough that I can clearly see his six-pack abs, right below carved pecs that have me swallowing hard, so I don't open my mouth and take a bite out of his bicep. It would be embarrassing but so worth it.

"Tim." That's all I can muster.

Bringing my glass to my lips, I feel a tremor in my hand, which I hope he doesn't notice. Fifteen years since I've seen him in person. Same damn reaction.

I take a long sip. Then another.

Thank you, bartender. I'm drunk now.

Just looking at him brings back age-old hurt coupled with memories I've pushed down hard and tried to forget. Tried and failed.

Tim had burrowed in deep, affected me in ways I couldn't fight and couldn't fathom. I stopped thinking about him eventually out of pure self-preservation, but I never forgot about him.

Besides, it's pretty hard to forget when his name and face are plastered all over the sports news, which I started looking at when I applied for jobs as a medical director. And for years before that, right about the time I met Tim. Coincidentally.

"What are you doing here?" His eyes flicker under the dark blond hair that falls across his forehead before he pushes it back with a large hand. His gaze bears down on me, and he jiggles the sudsy remains of a beer in a pint glass.

You've earned this. Own it. Just breathe in and out, in and out.

I choke halfway through my inhale. I sputter my exhale. I don't own a damn thing.

"I work here. Or at least I will in a month." I feel a tic in my cheek.

He stares at me like my words make no sense. Like I make no sense. "Doctor Jordan Page."

"Yes?"

He shakes his head. "You went by Danny. Back then."

"Nickname. Jor-dan. Dan-ny. No one calls me that anymore, except my mom on occasion, and even she mostly doesn't because I've asked her not to. Of course, I think that makes her want to do it more. Or maybe old habits die hard." I'm oversharing. Or under-explaining? Or rambling because he makes me nervous—that hasn't changed at all.

But he still seems flummoxed. "Doctor Jordan Page. Fuck me for thinking it was a bloke," he mutters, raking a hand through his hair. My eyes track the motion, fixated on how much better he looks in person than in recent photos. Pure masculine virility radiates from him.

And yet…

"Because you assume all doctors are men?" My sexism radar flares to life, my bottom lip jutting out with my retort.

"No, I—"

"Good. You shouldn't."

"You're the team doctor?"

"Director of Sports Medicine. Yes. I'm—"

"Part of Charlie's new brigade. Coming to fix what isn't broken. Right. I know all about it. Don't think much of the plan." His accent makes him sound so much more polite than his sharky smirk suggests.

My confidence shrivels like a sunburned grape. I feel my attempted smile pull down into a glower.

Is that what all the players think?

I tell myself I don't care what he thinks, that I'm a professional. But I do care. And I *have* worked hard to get this job. I *should* own it. I'm tethered to my resolve by a fraying thread.

As I try to kickstart the syrup in my brain to find a witty retort, I'm jostled from behind by someone big—big enough to send me off-balance in my stupid two-inch shoes.

I lurch forward toward Tim, who puts his hands on my shoulders to steady me, but not before his entire beer spills down the front of my blouse.

His eyes go to the spill, which makes my shirt virtually sheer. And now it's sticking to my bra, which has demi-cups made of thin baby blue lace—a stupid gift from my mother, who hoped I'd wear it on a date. Instead, I wear it on laundry day when all my plain cotton bras are in the wash.

After a mortifying second or six, Tim wrenches his eyes upward and releases his grip on me. I close my eyes to blot out the image of him. Of everyone.

Tonight was supposed to be the beginning of my future, the culmination of everything I've worked to achieve. It was supposed to be proof to my mother and anyone else that I don't need a boyfriend to be happy. I was supposed to drink and celebrate and meet the players who'd be grateful to have me on their team.

But apparently not. They're not all grateful, starting with this one.

I must have stepped on a puppy in a past life.

Because karma's acting like a little bitch.

im

I'M TRYING SO hard to force my eyes upward I'm giving myself a migraine. If Danny—I mean "Jordan"—doesn't do something about her wet T-shirt contest wardrobe quickly, my resolve may slip into foul territory and get me into serious trouble.

I should just walk away. That would save her the agony of dealing with me when I'm in a mood. And let's face it, lately, I'm always in a mood.

That's what a badly tweaked knee and other aches and pains will do, especially when one wrong move could land me on the injured list and on the bench.

I guess I'm an asshole for thinking Jordan, the new team doctor, would be a bloke. The old medical director was a man, so that's where my mind went. It never occurred to me to consider that Jordan would be the same person I knew years ago as Danny.

She was shy, sweet, cute. "Doctor Jordan Page" sounds impressive, serious, and hardly cute.

Nor does she look that way. That's because the teenage girl I knew has been replaced by this impossibly gorgeous woman with wide eyes fringed by long dark lashes, a pouty mouth that is ripe and luscious while communicating that she doesn't suffer fools, and endless curves under wet scraps of silk and lace which I'm trying my damnedest to ignore.

Her long, auburn hair makes my heart beat faster, imagining it splayed out on a crisp white pillowcase. To be clear, it's my pillowcase. And it's just-fucked hair.

Bottom lip jutting out, fire in her eyes. The flushed glow on her cheeks, pink and round as she glares at the spilled liquid, makes her look even prettier. Her features are as delicate as she is feisty, and it's a lethal combination for me.

I have a type, and smart, sassy redheads bring me to my knees every time.

Well, not this one. Not now.

Jordan Page may set my heart hammering, but if she's the new medical director, we are not going to be friends, not if I want to keep playing soccer. The last thing I need is a new doctor trying to prove herself by looking hard at my medical clearance and finding issues.

"Here, let me help you with that." The voice, gruff while still managing to sound whiny, belongs to Gus Reilly, the second to last person I want to see right now after a new team doctor.

He's the aging club president who got himself in hot water last year for sending paparazzi to take pictures of our striker, Donovan Taylor, and his girlfriend at the behest of Donovan's publicist. Reilly should've been booted from the Strikers front office, if you ask me, but Charlie let him off with a warning since Reilly is barely social media-savvy enough to realize what he'd done.

If it were me caught on camera in a stunt that almost cost me my relationship, I'd have been nowhere near that charitable. But Dono didn't ask me what I thought about it.

Reilly's of a different generation, a man in his sixties who stoops over his paunch and waddles through the Strikers headquarters each day on the way to a cigarette break in the courtyard. He's the only one around here who smokes, and he spends most of his time currying favor with deep-pocketed fans who spend big on the luxury suites in the stadium.

"Oh, I'm okay, really." Jordan crosses her arms over her chest to block the view.

"You don't look okay," Reilly says, continuing to ogle her as though he can see through bone.

Somehow, Reilly is always one step away from something that will get his ass handed to him—hints of harassment and talk of him trading favors with business owners to get sponsorship money, but never anything overtly unethical. So he gets to stick around, year after year, puffing his feathers as the team's biggest rainmaker. At the end of the day, it's always about the money.

I guess every team needs guys like that, but I was really hoping Charlie would get rid of him instead of firing the medical director and our coach. We had a good system with those guys, and it was working fine.

Reilly annoys me and always has, partly because it seemed a little too convenient that the revelation about the medical director came right after the Dono incident, almost like Reilly was trying to deflect attention away from his shitty behavior by throwing someone else under the bus.

Charlie's been scrutinizing my game since then and finding fault with it. Not like it takes a genius. All my stats are off, and they have been ever since I slide-tackled a fourteen-wheel truck of a striker in the game against the Seattle Sounders and sprained my collateral ligament, aka my knee.

I can't let our backup left back, Jordy Steiner, take my spot, even temporarily. He's young and hungry, and all he needs is one sign of weakness from me to challenge my starting position. So far, I've hung on by the shred of a worn bandage.

But if Jordan tells Charlie I'm too injured to play my A-game, I'm as good as traded or sidelined. Like a horse in the slaughter truck. Door closed, no way out.

That means I either need to avoid the new medical director or curry favor with her. And I remember Danny Page—she's smart and principled and won't let me get away with any of my shit. So I'm choosing Plan A. Right after I help her get away from old man Reilly, who looks like he's about to feel her up.

He can take his connections and his deep-pocketed friends and bugger off.

"Here, let's just—" I place my hands on Jordan's shoulders and turn her around, so her back faces Reilly and me. Then I glare at Reilly, willing him to catch my drift that he should take a hike. He doesn't move, so I signal to the bartender for a towel or two, and the kind gentleman in the black uniform shirt obliges without a word. He also tilts his head at my empty glass, and I nod for a refill. I'm going to need it.

Reaching around, I hand the towels to Jordan so she can try to dry her shirt. "I think we're good here. Your services aren't needed," I tell Reilly, who, for some unknown reason, moves his hands to Jordan's waist, just a few inches above her ass. His small fingers squeeze. I swipe them away and lean into his face. "She's good. Thanks for your concern."

Reilly pulls his hands away before I'm forced to remove a limb from his body and stuff it down his throat.

"Just trying to be helpful to my new hire."

Swallowing hard, I try to unhear what he's just said since my fists are still feeling twitchy. *His* new hire? When the team owner told us he'd hired a new director of sports medicine, it sure didn't sound like she'd be working for Reilly. Not that I paid much attention at the time because I had my own problems to worry about. And because I didn't know it was *her*.

For now, I'm happy that Reilly is moving away with his hands in the air as though I've held him up at gunpoint. I nod as though we have an understanding, when really, I understand nothing about how he gets away with half the nonsense he pulls.

I have to check myself for my response to an old man who probably just got his jollies for a month by touching a woman.

But this isn't just any woman.

It's *her*.

Danny…Jordan…whatever name she wants to use—it's always been her.

Casting a glance over her shoulder, Jordan meets my gaze, which has been focused on her back. I'm dangerously close to burning a hole through the fabric with the heat of my stare.

When she turns, towels draped over her shoulders like a shawl, I see she's done a good job of covering up. "Thanks for your help there." Her words sound nice enough, but the way her mouth turns down and her brow furrows, I can feel her discomfort, and I can't help but wonder how much she remembers about me. How we left things over a decade ago.

I nod. "Sure." Now that we're face to face again, I feel the jagged pangs of regret take up residence in my chest. I'm not even sure if apologies need to be made. Maybe there's some sort of statute of limitations on feeling bad about complete disasters from over a decade ago.

I should be an expert by now. I'm good at disappointing people—started doing that back in England and continued that streak when I met her. Common sense says to back away from her before I do it again. Better to have people lower their expectations all around.

Too bad my physical reaction to her is the same all these years later. I still see her mane of dark red hair and want to run my fingers through the strands or grab it in a fist while I crush my lips to hers. Those full, sweet lips.

Can't. Do. That.

Nope, not by a long shot.

Now is hardly the time to send my teetering career even further off the rails. Even if just looking at her lips makes me dream of tasting them, and a part of me—a really large, pushy part—urges me to make it a reality.

"You're welcome. Are you really working for Reilly? If not, I don't recommend it."

I get a surprised laugh for my trouble. "Not technically, but when I start next month, I'll report to Reilly when Charlie gets pulled away to his company. I don't know the specific hierarchy here. I don't know anything, really. Or anyone. Hence the invitation to show up here tonight. Only now"—she gestures to her soaked top beneath the bar towels—"I'm not feeling super social. I might just cut my losses."

This is a lot longer than I planned on talking to the new team doctor. My feelings about her job haven't changed in the five minutes since her shirt got soaked. Even if we knew each other a hundred years ago. Even if I can't stop looking at her. Never thought I'd get another chance, so my eyes are soaking in the sight of her like raindrops on parched land.

And now I need to walk away. "Sounds like a plan."

I could be a better guy, offer to introduce her to people—hell, I could probably even find her a dry shirt—but I don't want her mistaking me as a friend, someone she can send to the slaughterhouse because I was dumb enough to trust her.

She nods. "Um, yeah. So anyhow, guess I'll see you next month when you come for your physical."

With that, she turns on her heel and is headed out of the room before I consider whether I should apologize for not being more welcoming. I watch her walk away, feeling like the asshole I am for keeping my eyes on her tight ass as it sways through the crowd until I can't see her anymore.

"What was that all about?" Danny Weston, our center midfielder and my best mate on the team, suddenly appears by my side. Or maybe he's been there the whole time. There's no way for me to notice my surroundings when Jordan is in my sightlines. It's been that way since the moment we met.

We were an accident waiting to happen. A gorgeous bookish girl with big eyes and a tender heart. And a big, bad wolf who was bad for her reputation and her future. Bound to disappoint.

In other words, the perfect storm of attraction—a gin-soaked rag, a jerry can of lighter fluid, and a flame.

Match. Strike. Boom.

Unless one of us took the high road. Since I had more to lose, it had to be me.

If I say I haven't thought about her over the years, I'd be lying. If I say I didn't date anyone because I held out hope of seeing her again, I'd be lying also. I dated. Plenty. If empty rounds of sex with jersey chasers over the years counts as dating.

The memory of her hung in the back of my mind like an ever-present beacon that reminded me of a place I hoped to revisit, even as my boat drifted farther from shore every year. When I moved back to the States as an adult, I had every intention of looking her up, but then the shameful memory of how I'd hurt her kept me from following through.

"Nothing. We used to know each other. That's it." I grab the fresh beer off the bar and bring it to my lips. I can feel the weight of Weston's stare as I start to drink down the amber liquid and realize I have a choice. I can down the entire pint and hope he gets tired of waiting before I hit bottom, or I can behave like a sensible man, put the beer down, and be honest.

Since Weston and I are legit friends, I opt for the latter, cringing at the grilling I can already see he has planned.

"Right, but how do you know each other? I don't recall you mentioning anyone named Jordan."

"No, probably not."

"So was it before, then? In England? What?"

He looks as eager as a puppy with a new squeaky toy, and I

want to boop him on the nose to calm him down. I fix him with a stare that I hope will tell him to back off, but it seems to only encourage him. And despite my recent moods, my teammates don't generally fear me.

Maybe that's part of my problem. The reason the coaches and team owner seem quick to put me on the injured list. If they were more afraid of me and my temper, maybe they wouldn't mess with me.

Meanwhile, Weston orders each of us another round and puts mine in my right hand, even though I have most of a pint in my left. "Here. Finish your drink. From the look on your face, you need it."

I put my other glass on the bar and scan the room for any sign of Jordan. Maybe she was only bluffing when she said she wanted to leave. Maybe she just wanted to get away from me. Not that I blame her since I wasn't particularly welcoming.

I crane my head over the crowd, still hoping to see that gorgeous red hair, but as my eyes scan the faces, my spirits dim. But I didn't get to be a starting defender on the team by giving up when the odds are slim, so I take a final sweep of the place because I don't want to overlook a dark booth where Reilly might have her cornered.

Then I turn back toward Weston, who's drumming his fingers on the bar with a grin on his face. "She left already."

"You could've told me that ten minutes ago and saved me the whole Lewis and Clark expedition."

He snickers. "I'm impressed you know your American history."

"I spent a half a year in the States in high school."

"That where you met her?" Weston gestures over his shoulder.

"Jordan. She has a name." I feel a strange warmth in my chest when I say it.

I shouldn't be taking my irritation out on him, but giving each other a hard time goes with the territory on our team.

"Wow, someone's a little touchy."

I rake a hand through my hair and roll my eyes to the ceiling. "You would be too if you were gonna end up on the injured list."

He knows the pressure I'm under. He also knows I'm barely keeping my game together.

Weston shrugs. "You *are* injured. So, you sit for a bit. Happens all the time." He downs half of his beer and wipes the suds from his lips with the back of his hand, then wipes his hand on the leg of his jeans. Reminds me that I'm still holding the beer he handed me and haven't taken a sip.

I don't really want it, so I turn to put it next to my other one on the circular bar. I always liked coming here after games and celebrating with my teammates, but everything feels different now. I have no idea what having Jordan around will look like, but I know she'll complicate things that have already gotten quite complicated with my insistence that I'm fit to play.

The dangers of playing while injured give every game, every interaction with my teammates, every decision on the field a feeling of inevitability. Almost like each time I'm here could be the last.

"No one can play well under that kind of pressure," Weston says as if reading my thoughts.

He's right. Playing scared is the one surefire way to assure a crap performance on the field on top of everything else. "Probably my own doing, then, if I can't get my head straight for a game."

He perches against a vacant wooden barstool. Folding his arms over his chest with the beer still in hand, he regards me. "Naw, man. It's the complete opposite. I'm saying…you've gotta relax. Give your body a chance to heal. Have faith in what will come of it. Maybe go get the girl." He gestures in the direction of the exit.

"Yeah, not happening."

"What's the deal? Why does she have your fancy British trousers in a twist?"

"You got an hour?"

"I've got all the time you want if it's a good story."

"It's a bloody good story." The bartender wordlessly replaces my now-warm drink with one fresh one and puts Weston's on a coaster next to mine. I don't know if he's been eavesdropping or if some unknown signal passed between Weston and him. Doesn't matter. I'm going to need the full drink to get through this story.

Weston guides us through the team photogs who are always snapping photos for the organization's various feeds. We walk past the guys in jeans and suit jackets who work in the front office. Those guys rarely dress down, even when they come to games. Makes me glad I don't have their jobs.

When we reach a low glossy black table in a corner, Weston gestures to me to take the black leather chair facing the wall, and he sits on the overstuffed Strikers-blue sofa, in view of the room. I put my coaster on the table and position the glass right in the center, staring into the amber liquid as I recall the events from eons ago that led me to this moment.

"So, I was an exchange student a year before university, came to the US and lived in the Bay Area with a family. Went to their local high school, played for an academy team here."

Weston hangs his arm over the back of the booth and nods. "We had a kid at my high school from Japan. Music student, super nice guy, from what I remember." He grins. "'Course I'd have liked it much better if he was a soccer player."

"Sure, yeah. I got the high school coach pretty excited until he realized I couldn't play for his squad since I was playing for the academy."

Weston chuckles. "Oh, man. I can imagine some high school coach strutting around in his Adidas track pants bragging to his buddies that he was getting an English kid with mad skills, and then you show up and can't even come to a practice."

"I came to practices," I correct. "So that helped with some player development, at least. But yeah, Coach lost his bragging rights straightaway." I take a long sip of beer and place it back on the coaster. "Anyhow, I enrolled at her high school. Ended up staying about six months." I take another sip. "And I lived with her family."

I wait for this information to land. "Yeah. My host family. Obviously, their sixteen-year-old daughter was off-limits."

"How'd *that* go?" Weston can't hold back his laughter, thinking he knows me. He does. And yet, he doesn't.

"I behaved myself."

"Why do I not believe you?" Weston grins like a jack-o-lantern.

"Nothing happened with her. I made sure of it. I was all sorts of crazy about her, but she was sixteen and the daughter of the family putting me up so I could play here. She mostly ignored me anyway. Then one night, she came into my room and pretty much offered to let me take her virginity."

Weston smacks me on the shoulder. "You didn't. Come on, man."

"No, I didn't. But needless to say, I was on the first plane back to jolly old England."

He shakes his head. "Got it. Well, gotta give you props. Never a dull moment around you."

"Yeah. Great." Now that I've spilled some tea for his amusement and gotten the boulder off my chest, I sink down in my seat and wipe the sheen of sweat from my forehead. Feels good to tell someone, and I know Weston's got my back. The less the rest of my teammates know about my weak spots, the better.

Now I just have to figure out how to hide them from Doctor Jordan Page.

CHAPTER 3

$\mathcal{J}$ordan

I HAD a full month to rethink my decision to take the job with the Strikers. One full month to talk myself out of it.

I could have. Could have found a job with no strings attached to my past, no drama lurking just out of sight. Could have cut and run at the sight of a certain player's scowly face.

But my so-called past was fifteen years ago, and this is my dream job. I'm not about to give that up over a guy. Especially when life has taught me that guys only want one thing from me.

No, not that thing.

Okay, sure, that thing—of course, they want sex.

But I'm talking about help. They want me to help them study, help them ace their science labs, help them figure out whether to shave the goatee (hint: yes, always) like a good gal pal. And the guys on the Strikers team want—and need—me to get them healthy so they can play their best and win games. That's my core strength. That's why I'm here.

So I double down and do more research on the Strikers season, watch more game footage to see how the players looked after injuries. I notice some patterns, and that sends me down a rabbit hole of watching more footage, making more notes, comparing them with the notes from the now-fired coach.

There are discrepancies. Big ones. Errors of omission designed to keep the players on the field despite the wear and tear on already-injured bodies. I can see that Tim Cheltenham favors his sprained knee, and I can see his speed and agility taking a hit.

Game after game, he goes back on the field and looks worse for the wear. A coach who wants to win so badly that he'll do it at the expense of his players' health is…probably pretty common. I suspect that Tim's growly attitude toward me that first night had less to do with awkward memories of high school and more about fear of doctors.

So I plan to meet the challenge head-on at my first team meeting.

After spending too much time this morning sweating what to wear, I cave and put on a safe work outfit, one I've worn dozens of times before—black pencil skirt, pale blue blouse, two-inch pumps—sensible, doctor-y.

Over that, my white coat.

Same thing I wore for six years with the Oakland Orthopedic Group, lovingly known as OOG, where I mostly tended to weekend warriors with torn ligaments, meniscus tears, rotator cuff injuries, and tennis elbow. Twice a week, I'd put on scrubs— the pajamas of the medical world—and spend the entire day in the operating room performing surgeries. Loved those days.

But for my first official meeting with the players, I want to look like a medical pro.

Everyone seems restless, and I'm ready to give them my short, prepared speech about how I'm looking forward to making them better on the field by taking care of them off the field.

"Doctor Page," a voice intones behind me. I turn to shake the hand of Grayden Jaynes, the new head coach, mentally berating myself for not staying at the team event last month so I could get to know him and everyone else. Amateur move, and now I'm walking into the lion's den like the fresh kill I didn't want to be.

Jaynes looks genial, at ease with himself and his stature with the team. He should. He's the boss. The fact that he's a former soccer player helps. He still walks with the swagger of an athlete, and at well over six feet tall, he has an imposing presence I can't quite muster in heels that threaten to trip me up if I hit a strand of carpet the wrong way.

I smile through the thought salad in my head and try to project confidence by not slouching. "Hi, Coach. Great to see you again."

Jaynes and I met for about five minutes after I was hired because the team was getting on a plane for an away game. It took even less time for Charlie to convey his expectations. They were simple—clean up the mess.

"You ready to put these guys in line?" He gestures around the locker area, where the players are in various versions of the team's practice gear, some guys in black hoodies over their training jerseys, others in just the red jersey, others in the black zip-up jacket.

The lockers behind the blond wood benches are painted blue, and the wall to my right bears a giant Strikers logo above a well-used whiteboard.

All the players look antsy, happier on the soccer field than in a room about to get a talking to by a coach and a doctor. Or maybe that's me projecting. Then there's Tim, arms crossed over his chest, looking more skeptical than the others. Just makes me want to break down his resistance.

Yeah, some things never change, I guess. It's exactly how I felt back in high school, and that didn't end well.

"Always ready," I tell him. He claps me on the back in the same way I've seen him do with players. His broad smile carries me along. A rescue boat on top of a wave.

He has an older brother quality mixed with fierce lone wolf vibes. With his close-trimmed beard and piercing blue eyes, he exudes a brooding masculinity that conveys to the players that he's been in their shoes, knows a lot more than they do, and expects them to listen. His professional career ended a decade ago, but he's still physically fit, and he's all over social media scrimmaging with the team. Rumors swirl around his personal life—supposedly, he went through a nasty divorce—but he's notoriously closed-lipped about it.

I'm hoping the respect the players have for him will somehow extend to me by association. We're both part of the overhaul, and Jaynes has a reputation for turning teams around and getting the most out of his players. Maybe they'll assume the same of me.

I don't know how Charlie managed to keep the drama behind the changes under wraps, but I haven't seen even a glimmer of speculation in the media about the reasons.

There's a chorus of "Hey, Coach" and "G'morning."

He waves his hands to quiet the remaining chatter amongst the players. "This isn't my meeting, but I want it clear that I fully support the new way things are going to work around here. Doctor Page will run each of you through physicals, and you will obey her directions. I trust that's all that needs to be said on the matter."

Jaynes has a presence that screams, "don't mess with me." He's taller than several of the players, and when his deep voice rolls out, it has an authority I appreciate.

"Thanks, Coach. Hey, guys. I'm Jordan Page, really happy to be here. My only job is to help you. That's it. I'm your first line of defense when you even feel the hint of pain or a pull or a tear. If we can address these things early, put in the work, you'll get back on the field faster and be better for it."

I see some players nodding, as they should. This is good news for them. I need them to understand that I'm not looking to sideline them. "I know what I'm walking into. I know some of you have been encouraged to play through pain, and maybe it worked for you. It does work for a while. That's the operative concept here—a while. Playing through injury is only a temporary solution, and it leads to something chronic. You guys are pros. I know you know this."

Pausing to take in the faces in the room, I try to get a bead on their response to what I'm saying. Donovan Taylor nods, but I'd expect that. He's a veteran, and he's lost time to injury in the past. He knows the drill. A few of the other guys seem agreeable as well.

Then there are those like Tim who sits stony-faced and unreadable. Maybe they're playing through injuries. Maybe they just don't like a regime change. Charlie warned me that players were loyal to the last guy, regardless of how things shook out.

Earning their trust won't be easy, but I have no other route. I know this. If they don't trust me, I can't help them. They won't come to me with injuries if they believe I'll cost them precious game time when they need those minutes on the field. I know this too.

It will take time, and I'm not afraid of the challenge.

"We'll get into it individually when we meet, but I can smell the menthol from down the hall. If you're bathing in topical analgesics—or abusing over the counter pain meds or gummies or anything else—in place of actual medical attention, we're going to change your protocol and get you healthy. I can't emphasize it enough—I am here to help you. I've spent my career helping athletes get past injuries, so please trust me to get you back to full strength. Your game stats will show for it."

Jaynes's baritone gives my words more gravity. "If you need

any convincing, that alone should do it. You play better when you're healthy. No heroes on my squad." There are a few muffled words of agreement from throughout the room, but I have my eye on Tim, whose grim expression doesn't change.

Coach Jaynes continues for a bit, outlining the week's practice schedule as the team heads into the final matches before playoffs. I watch the faces of the players, trying to ascertain who's going to challenge me and who appreciates having me there. Probably too soon to tell. They've turned their attention to Jaynes, but I continue assessing them.

I can tell a lot from how players act when they think no one's looking. Some of them have their eyes on Jaynes; some look at the floor or fidget, but they're still listening. Then there are a few who are exchanging looks with each other, half listening, half doing other shit.

They think they know what their coach will say, so they don't need to focus like the other guys.

Tim Cheltenham falls into that group, mouthing words to a player across the room, probably sharing a joke. Color me unimpressed.

The meeting doesn't take long—its main purpose accomplished, letting the players know we're done messing around, and Jaynes has my back. I wrap up with my own logistical plans, getting each player in for a full evaluation so I can compare what's in their charts with their current fitness to play.

"I know it seems like overkill since you've been monitored and the notes are in your files, but under the circumstances..." I don't want to belabor the team's issues with the prior medical director. "And since we're heading into playoffs, we need to know where we are."

Coach Jaynes shoots me a look, and I know it's a warning to stay in my lane. Player tensions are always high, with talks of trades and players worried about losing their spots in the lineup.

I know where my lane is, and I don't need to say a word about the starting lineup. It's implicit in me signing off on each player's fitness to play.

Lockers slam, and players start gathering their gear to bring out to the practice field, so I look once more at my brief notes to see if there's anything I forgot. In big letters at the bottom, I'd scribbled, "Go Strikers!!"

I decide against any fangirling. They don't need to know how excited I am to have this job. It will only give them the impression I'll do their bidding in order to keep it.

As I said, not going to happen.

im

No sooner has Coach left the locker room than the chatter begins.

Actually, it began as soon as Jordan stopped talking. Across the locker room, I could see Caleb Schmidt, one of our keepers, make a lewd gesture behind his sports bag. Unmistakable—he was eyeing Jordan and letting everyone know he wanted to bang her.

I mouthed some choice words to try to shut him up, and then I saw Jordan staring at me like *I* was the problem. If she only knew.

"Not gonna be a hardship to have her examine me, all I'm saying," Jordy Steiner pipes in, taking a little extra time pulling up his socks and making sure both hit just beneath his knees.

"You want me to get out a tape measure, make sure they're even?" I snap at him.

"Whoa. Does someone want to wedge ahead of me in line to

get felt up by the good doctor?" Jordy laughs, and normally, I'd indulge his infantile banter in a heartbeat. We're guys. We talk shit to each other on the daily. And it wouldn't be the first time someone in the locker room made a comment about a woman.

I'm not saying I'm proud of our behavior—I know it's appalling that we act like emotionally-stunted horny assholes, but despite the objectifying, there isn't a guy on this team who wouldn't stand up for a woman and defend her. It's all just stupid talk.

So why are you taking it personally?

I know why, but I don't want to admit I'm attracted to her, even to myself. So I dump on Steiner some more. "I don't want to wedge myself anywhere near you. I just think you should act like a grown-up. For once."

"Not likely to happen," he sing songs on his way out to the practice pitch.

I follow him out, disinterested in hearing the guys continue to talk smack about Jordan and her "examinations." I shouldn't give a rat's fucking ass what my knucklehead teammates say in the locker room. It's meaningless posturing.

It just bothers me that they're saying it about her.

I CAN'T FOCUS.

An hour into today's workout, I should be in a zone. It's a process my brain and body understand from years of the same drill. Thirty minutes for me to stop fighting the harsh bite of air entering my lungs when I force more speed than the day before. At least, it feels that way. Another thirty of brutal warm-up drills that nearly sap the strength from my quads—box jumps, ladder drills, and in-and-outs with cones.

Then a brutal peacefulness takes over, the hard-earned endorphins circulating in my system. That's when I can go farther, run harder. That's when the real workout begins.

And I fucking love it.

But not today. Today, everything hurts. It's like my bum knee has spread its injured love to my other muscles and joints. I cut right, my left shin hurts. Take a header and somehow feel it in my hip. I'm thirty-fucking-three, and I'm sagging like I'm sixty.

We're running a circuit, passing to another player as we run up the line, then one of us makes a cross, and the other shoots against Schmidt.

My pass to Danny Weston, our center mid, is clean. Straight to his left foot, giving him a wide space for a shot. He shoots, Schmidt dives and misses. Weston knocks a fist in the air as we both jog back to the lineup.

I look up to see Jordan sitting on a folding chair on the sideline of the practice pitch. She's maybe ten yards from where we're finishing up drills before the real work begins. In her sunglasses with her lush hair trailing behind, she could be on a sundeck at a resort, except that she has a notepad in her lap and she sits ramrod straight, biting her lip in concentration.

The impossibly bright grass pales next to her wild auburn hair, which somehow picks up the rays of sun. A light wind swirls flyaway strands into an angelic halo effect.

Day one on the job, and she's perched herself in our space— my sacred space—with plans to wreak havoc. I can just tell. I remember how she was as a teenager—quiet, observant, whip smart. She never said it out loud, but it always felt like she understood a situation from the moment she entered a room. Her eyes would dart around, taking everything in, and she'd nod to herself. Never let anyone in on her thoughts. Like they were her superpower.

She intrigued me because, for as smart and pretty as she was, she didn't seem to notice. She hid in corners, let other people take the spotlight, even though she could have outshone any of them.

Well, she hid until that one night—the night that ended up either being the biggest mistake of my life or the night I avoided making one. Best not to think about that right now if I don't want to trip over my own feet and injure something else.

And…it's all I can fucking think about—the sixteen-year-old Jordan, auburn hair trailing down her back, standing in my room in boy shorts and a tank top, eyes glistening with hope and promise. I'd spent several long months ignoring her curvy figure in that outfit by looking at the floor, the ceiling, or any available corner when she walked down the hall before bed.

Strike. Flame…

You did the right thing.

I glance her way again, wondering what she's thinking. I never could tell. "Healthy players," she said earlier. Sure. We'd all love to be fit and healthy like we were at twenty. We'd love it if we could practice for four hours and have it feel like twenty minutes, scrimmage all day, drink our weight in ale at a pub, and feel great in the morning. No harm, no foul. Younger bodies could handle any stressor and come out stronger for it.

Now, we're under a whole different kind of stress. There's money at stake. Big money.

We need wins, the kind of peak performance that gets us to the playoffs. Healthy is just a pipe dream when we're staring down the post-season. If we're alive, we're playing hard, plain and simple.

My turn comes up, and I pass the ball to Weston, then sprint up to receive his pass back. It's my turn to shoot, but his pass is slightly farther than I expected, so I have to pour on the gas to get there. That's when I feel knee pain that's gotten worse since the last game. It's like a metal butterknife trying to pry off my kneecap. I feel a wave of nausea at the pain, but I can't let that show. I need to take a clean shot, but I'm just off-balance enough.

I kick the ball hard, feel a gripping pain in my knee that rolls down my shin, and watch Schmidt catch the shot easily in his fat goalie gloves.

I don't dare look at Jordan. Better just to believe she took that moment to check a text on her phone and didn't see my bobble. Doing my best not to limp, I jog back to the line.

Our last medical director understood how to tape me together and keep me going so I could push myself past the point of pain. Jordy Steiner has been gunning for me since he came to the team, but he's not getting a minute starting time until I retire or take a trade. No room to debate there.

He's watching me. I can see it; we all can see it. That's the game. But I got here first, and the rookie has nothing on me when I'm in fighting form.

I'll get back to full peak condition as soon as playoffs are done, and I can really rehab the way I ought to. The temporary fixes with pain meds and wraps and ice are only that—temporary. Players do it all the time.

Even the taped-up version of me is a better player than him, but he's younger and meaner, and he wants his shot, even if he has to get it by banking on another guy's injuries. I don't blame him—I'd do the same thing if I were in his shoes. I'd just be less cocky about how much I think I deserve it.

End of the season's almost here. I just need to play through the pain a bit longer, and then I'll let my body do its thing. The thoughts churn through my head over and over again like a mantra.

If I can't outright avoid Jordan and her "get 'em healthy" mandate, I'll just have to convince her to do things my way. She can look like a hero after the season when my sprint speed improves because of her rehab recommendations. Just not now.

Dropping into a set of pushups, I shoot one more look in Jordan's direction, just a glance to see how seriously she's taking this. Maybe she just wants to observe us training because it's a whole lot nicer out here than inside the team offices. The morning fog lifted early, and the air still feels clean, but the dampness is gone.

My eyes instantly dart to Jordan's legs beneath that tight skirt, crossed at the knee and showing enough thigh to make my brain wander where it shouldn't. Her skin is a sun-kissed golden color that conjures some tropical vacation.

I should really warn her against wearing short skirts. The Strikers don't have a dry corporate culture, and the good guy side of me hopes she dresses in something more comfortable for her sake. The possessive side hopes she does it so the rest of my teammates stop gawking at her.

In her lap, Jordan has a sheaf of paperwork spilling out of a folder. As she looks down and shuffles through the pages, the wind chooses the moment to kick up and tear a few sheets from her hand.

I could get up and help her gather her shit. I should.

But I don't.

Because maybe she'll lose the page that has my running stats from the two months, and she won't notice my speed has notched down.

Coach calls us over to chat before we start the next round of punishing drills. I turn my attention away from Jordan and her paper mess. Can't worry about it when my knee is screaming at me to take today off. And tomorrow.

Can't do that either. Mind over matter.

A few more games until playoffs, then however many weeks we stay in it. I just need to push through without anyone noticing too much.

Then I'll take the proper recovery time, I will.

Until then, I need to stay as far away from Jordan Page as I can possibly get.

CHAPTER 5

 ordan

"THEY DON'T TRUST ME." I hate saying the words out loud, and there's only one person in the world I'd allow to hear them. That man is sitting cross-legged in the dirt wearing holey faded jeans and a large straw sun hat that looks like a dog ate half of it.

"That's normal, isn't it?" my dad asks, pulling up a dirty bulbous thing from the makeshift garden bed behind the house where I grew up. He built it himself out of timber he scavenged from a neighbor's roll-off dumpster, so it leaks in places and sits crooked on the dirt. Which makes it a perfect garden box, according to my dad.

Dusting off a surface layer of dirt, he chucks the plant into a red sand pail.

"What is that?" I ask, unable to identify it under the dirt.

He laughs. "That, my dear, is known as a parsnip. They're easy to grow, and they taste pretty damn good pureed with cheese on top, so I have a lot of 'em out here."

That, he does. Most of the garden bed consists of small bunches of leafy tops like the one he just pulled. "How do you know when they're ready?"

He brushes the dirt away from beneath the leaves of a plant. "You can check them without pulling them out. But they tend to ripen at the same time. Most of these will be good if you want to dig in here."

I don't. Not because I object to getting my hands dirty, but because the garden is his baby, and I know he really wants to tend to each plant himself. "I'm good. I'll just watch you do it. Watch and learn." My dad smiles and exhales. I sense relief.

He takes a moment to stretch his back before bending over the plants again. When he does, I notice his vintage Grateful Dead shirt, which he proudly told me he acquired at one of seven Las Vegas Dead shows he went to before he met my mom. His hair is a little gray at the temples but still mostly brown under the hat. It's his beard that shows his age—almost entirely white—along with the bifocals he calls his "old man glasses."

But don't let the glasses fool you—my dad is more physically fit than I am, even though I bike in the neighborhood a few days a week and hike on weekends. And his pale blue eyes still light up when he talks about work—mine or his.

He's a doctor as well, but as an obstetrician, he's always had little control over his schedule. I spent most of my childhood hearing explanations about why he missed family dinners or my gymnastics meets or my brother's orchestra performances. "Babies come when they come," he'd say.

Now he's semi-retired and mostly sees gynecological patients who have more regular schedules. Even then, he only works a couple days a week.

It was no accident that I pursued the pre-med track. I saw how much he loved his job, and I worried for how my mother seemed to have given up on career aspirations to raise kids. I never wanted that. Maybe I worked a little too hard to bend myself in the opposite direction, but both parents encouraged me to pursue my love for science from a young age, and I know I make my dad proud now. My mother…well, she's complicated.

Which is why I intentionally came through the wooden side gate to hang with my dad before going into the house.

"Why do you think they don't trust you?" I love that my dad never loses his train of thought.

I explain how my predecessor did things and how I'm supposed to right the ship. "Doesn't make for a big ole welcome wagon."

"Give it time. What's it been, a week? Let them get to know you, and I'm sure they'll see what you're made of. They'll respect how dedicated you are to helping them stay healthy." He shrugs. Simple.

My dad doesn't like to belabor conversations when he thinks they're done, so he picks up the bucket of parsnips and starts for the house. I trail behind him, holding a bakery box and readying myself for part two of the fam bam. It's always unpredictable, depending on whether my mother feels satisfied with mild hints about how she'd like me to meet a nice man or fancies an all-out assault on my life choices.

As if she knows I'm thinking about her, my mom whips the back door open, drying her hands on a dish towel featuring a cartoon slice of cake in a fighting stance and a speech bubble, "You want a piece of me?" Her hair is red like mine but shorter and pulled into a ponytail. She wears red lipstick every day, even if she's not leaving the house. I've almost forgotten what she looks like without it.

"How's the new job, sweetie?" Her question sounds innocuous, but it translates into, "How are you going to find a husband if all you do is work?"

Instead of following in my dad's footsteps, she wishes I'd followed in hers. Wishes I cared about coffee table books and orchids. Wishes I cooked instead of eating takeout. Wishes I wasn't a Martha Stewart code violation waiting to happen. My clumsy streak has taken its toll on her shelves of decorative trinkets over the years.

Now I outright avoid the areas of the house where she has excessive knickknacks. Which pretty much relegates me to the kitchen and the yard. Even in the kitchen, I try not to touch anything that isn't food.

"Fine. Great," I say, hoping to put an end to the conversation if I keep moving past her toward the kitchen. She closes the door behind us, and I hear her kitten heels on the wood floors as she trails behind, her thoughts about the dirt on my dad's hands loud enough to be heard in New Zealand.

Without needing to be told, he washes them in the kitchen sink after handing my mother the bucket and kissing her on the cheek. "These will make a nice side dish to go with the brisket. Do you have time to stay and help me make the marinade?" she asks me, already knowing the answer.

"I can't. I need to review a bunch of charts and stats for work." I don't really have to do that, but I don't feel like marinating a brisket and hearing about her latest mahjong partner's sister's son, who happens to be single. At some point, I stopped wondering why my mom shifted from cheerleading me through med school to bemoaning my singlehood. What's the point?

My eyes sweep around the kitchen as though some detail may have changed since I last came here for dinner. It's been a couple weeks, so there's always a slim chance.

But no, even the stack of newspapers on a yellow-painted telephone table in the corner looks about the same size as the stack that was there last time, also on a Friday—six days before the next recycling day. My parents are nothing if not consistent with their routines.

I hand my mother the cake. Her brown eyes warm under raised eyebrows. "What have we here?"

"Are those new glasses?" I ask, pointing to the red rims on the plastic readers she unfolds to examine the box further.

Waving a hand dismissively, she shakes her head. "I don't even know which ones these are. I have a bunch. They come in a pack online." She slips a manicured fingernail under the tape holding the box flaps down and lifts the lid. "Lemon?" She looks at me and smiles.

"I know you like lemon." I can't help but enjoy our ritual, where she pretends to be surprised, and I pretend to have made a lucky guess in choosing her favorite flavor.

Pulling one of the barstools out from around the kitchen island, I scrape the legs on the parquet floor. I hear my mother's disapproving *tsk* at the sound, indicative of perceived damage to the wood.

"It's a floor," I mutter. "It's supposed to get worn."

"You're not a caveman. You don't need to drag things around."

I don't bother to respond because she has a ready list of other transgressions that made her perfect house look shabby—the day I pushed the living room chairs against a wall so we could play family charades and they nicked the paint, the time my dad thought it would be cute to build a mailbox and put the gawky, unpainted thing outside our house, the time I spilled red wine on her white couch.

I'm sorry, but who buys a white couch and expects it to stay clean?

I look down to see if maybe my mother has replaced the red gingham seat cushions with something more contemporary, but there they are. It's both reassuring that I can come to a home where nothing ever changes and a bit disheartening because I fear my mother lives a little bit in the past.

I can't really blame her because the past was a happier time for her, a time when she had two teenagers with bright eyes and big potential.

Now, they have me, still trying all the time to make her proud with my career accomplishments, and they have Chet, my older brother, who bolted as soon as he finished high school. He spends most of his time driving his van from campsite to campsite, playing guitar, and living off of the proceeds from potholders and tea cozies he makes out of recycled yarn.

In some ways, his lifestyle seems blissful. He works only as much as he needs in order to buy food and purchase yarn. He has a longtime girlfriend who shares his interest in crafts and music, but she's the real breadwinner. She grows a strain of cannabis in a hydroponic setup in the back of their van and sells it to several dispensaries that have become reliable clients.

Their "whole lifestyle," as my mother refers to it, doesn't sit well with her dream of him being some sort of white-collar professional. And she never misses an opportunity to tell me about it.

"Have you spoken to your brother?" She always asks in a formal way like this. Never calls him by name, as though they're estranged. Meanwhile, with his career flexibility and love for meals not cooked on a Bunsen burner, he comes over more often than I do.

"We talked last week when he was in Arizona."

"Oh? I hadn't heard about that trip."

"That's because they're nomads. You can't be a nomad if you go around planning your itinerary and telling people about it. They're hiking through the slot canyons for a few days and then driving to Sedona for a meditation retreat."

The snort that erupts from my mother startles me. "They need a retreat for that? Meditation is just thinking. Your brother can't think without making a vacation out of it?"

"Guess not."

"And then there's you," she continues, shaking her head. "You're beautiful, you're smart, and you could have any man you set your eyes on, and yet you're determined to work yourself to the bone."

"I like my job. I'm good at work." I don't bother to tell her the other part of that truth—that I'm not good at relationships. I don't read social cues that well, so it's safer for me to stick to work, where I'm proficient in science and facts.

"I don't suppose you met a soccer player on your first day there," she says, tapping her teaspoon on the cup. She probably doesn't even know she's doing it, but the sound makes me antsy.

I manufacture a laugh and twist my hair into a knot on top of my head. "I met a lot of players. They're basically my coworkers since it's my job to take care of their health."

The tinkling in the cup stops, and she sips some tea from the spoon before dropping it into the big white farm sink, where it clatters against the unwashed dishes. "I don't know why you do that."

"Do what?"

"Wind your hair into a ratty bun like that. You look...like those tweens I see on the Internet."

I laugh. "Why are you looking at tweens on the Internet?"

"Cultural literacy. I want to know what the next generation is thinking."

"How's that going for you?"

She shrugs. "There are a lot of selfies, which is why I know about the hair. Do you really want to look fourteen?"

I fight the urge to roll my eyes. "I look the way I look, and it's too hot in here to wear my hair down." She never turns on the air conditioner, even when it's above eighty degrees in the house, which only happens for a few weeks a year, usually in the late summer or early fall.

It's been beastly hot for a week now, and half the conversations I've had with players have been about waiting for the weather to break. No one likes playing in blistering heat, and the practice schedule grinds on no matter how hot it is.

"I hope you don't wear it like that at work." She gives me sad eyes and a droopy mouth.

I don't say that I almost always wear it exactly like this. "Why would it matter?"

She exhales a long breath which tells me she's nearing the end of her List of Ways My Children Disappoint Me.

Mercifully.

"Anyhow, I hope you'll find time in your schedule to come to the birthday party we're having for Dillon." Dillon is Chet's two-year-old, and I know the only way Chet would let my mom throw a party here is if he needs money. Which means he'll probably let my mom throw a party. Chet isn't dumb.

"Just tell me when, and I'll be here."

Her frown turns upside down. "It's two weeks from Saturday. That would be great. And you remember my friend Grayson from the tennis club?"

"I don't know anyone from your tennis club, Mom, since I've never been there." I poke through the pantry, looking for a snack I can eat in the car because I'm definitely leaving now. Talking to my mother drains me of energy more quickly than a workout at the gym. I find myself needing sustenance within twenty minutes of entering the house.

"Grayson's son just moved back to town. He's a *lawyer*." She says it importantly, as though just hearing his occupation will make me swoon.

"That's nice." I refuse to take the bait. I start walking toward the door and yell goodbye to my dad. He yells something back.

My mom follows me through the living room, no doubt looking for things I'm about to knock over. She mentions the lawyer once more before I manage to make it out the front door with a box of purloined Wheat Thins under my arm.

"When we send invitations to the party for Dillon, I'll ask Grayson to come and bring her son."

"Please don't," I say, heading down the path that leads through overgrown rose bushes my mother refuses to deadhead until every last scrawny stem has been given ample chances to grow and bloom. More disappointing offspring to *tsk*.

"Love you," she calls from the porch before I hear the door close.

I know she does. That's the problem. That, and having a friend named Grayson, whose son is single.

im

ON MONDAY MORNING, I decide to take the bull by the horns.

Or the messy bun, as it were.

It's an about-face from my decision to avoid her. Better to be cheerful and welcoming. And then, hide in plain sight. Which is why I show up two full hours before practice.

Two hours will also give me a bit more warm-up time before my teammates arrive. They don't need to see me grunting as I stretch and ice down aching body parts. My knee starts to loosen up after running a few extra miles, taking my anti-inflammatory meds, and rubbing a balm into the joint. The less other people know about the pain and agony I'm putting myself through, the better.

But first, Jordan. I'm not waiting for her to come to me with big ideas about how to fix something that isn't broken—at least, it's not so broken that I can't handle it.

The problem is that she already has me distracted, which,

unfortunately, makes me do stupid things. Anticipating her arrival, I ran an extra six miles one day and did a set of sprint repeats the day after that. I pounded my quads with bench presses of so much weight, they were screaming by the end, but I'm hoping stronger muscles will stabilize my knee.

That's what our old director told me to do. If I keep going like this, I'll push my already-injured limbs too far, so I need to manage her properly.

I walk down the hallway of the Strikers offices, a drab set of cookie-cutter boxes which overlook our practice pitch. I don't know if Jordan will be there or down in the exam rooms, but my gamble on offices turns out to be correct. I inhale the scent of gardenias before I arrive at her door, which is open, revealing the wall of Strikers posters and banners leftover from the prior director. I hear quiet blues music, which immediately calms my jangled nerves.

Then I notice the tightly coiled mass of red hair peeking over the screen of a laptop on the blond wood desk. The computer sits in between two large stacks of papers, messy and disorganized with file folders shuffled in and Post-it Notes sticking out at all angles. I kind of love that Jordan is disorganized. It makes her seem less likely to be a stickler for rules, or at least that's my wishful perception.

"Morning," I say, flashing a smile. I'm eyeing the tall piles, which list just enough to the side that they'll tumble under a modest breeze from the A/C.

She looks up. "Oh, hey." Playing with the arm of her dark-rimmed glasses, she gives off such a hot librarian vibe that I snap my mouth shut to keep from drooling on my shirt. I barely know her anymore, and she still has this effect on me.

It's going to be a problem.

Which is why you're here. Put out the fire.

When Jordan removes the glasses, a few tendrils of hair come loose and dance around her face. I fight the urge to reach over the desk and brush them out of her eyes. She takes a swipe at them, moving them to the sides, though they look ready to spring free again. My fingers twitch, and I tell myself to stop looking at her.

I can't stop.

She seems to search her piles for something and gives up a moment later when one of the piles tips over and papers fan across the desk.

"So, hello." I wait for more words to work their way free, but apparently, that's all I've got.

"Hi."

I don't want to stare at her, so I look at her desk. She follows my gaze to the messy papers and bites her lip. Like she's debating whether to dive into the chaos. Instead, she reaches for a blue water bottle on the desk and unscrews the cap. After she takes a sip, her eyes return to me.

"Hi," I say again. Like I'm a computer programmed only with banal greetings.

For some reason, I then look straight to the front of her shirt and picture her wet blouse from a month ago. I linger there a bit too long and glance up to find her head tilted at me, entertainment in her eyes. "So…did you need something?"

I choke out a laugh that sounds ridiculous. "No. I mean, yes. Wanted to say a proper hello."

Which you've done three times.

I put a hand on the desk and lean, hoping for casual. "What's new since high school?"

She gasps a laugh. "Since fifteen years ago?"

"Yes. That. All good?"

"Sure. A lot's happened, but yeah. You?"

"Great."

"Good."

I'm losing the thread here. And sounding idiotic.

"Nice catching up," she quips.

"Yeah. Speaking of… I was just…remembering that teacher we had for history, what was his name?" I flash a grin, hoping to convince her I remember a single iota of high school. In fact, I only remember one regrettable bit.

"Um, we were two grades apart, Tim. We didn't have history together."

My new attempt at a laugh sounds like I'm gargling marbles. "Right. Silly. 'Course."

Shifting from one foot to the other, I try to think of anything else I can remember, but the only image that comes back to me is her in a tank top and shorts and me closing the door in her face.

And the regret. So much regret.

"So…is there anything else?" she asks, pushing her chair back and crossing her tanned legs. Making a concerted effort not to fix a stare on them, I force my eyes up once again and meet hers. I catch a glimmer of amusement on her face at my complete lack of subtlety.

So I tell her why I'm really here.

"Yes. I wanted to talk about the medical clearance. Mine. You know, it's just a formality."

"What is?"

"The exams, the precautions. I feel fine, I'm game-ready and there's no reason for me not to start. I plan to give it my all, same as always. Letting you know so you can…focus on the other players, not waste your time." It's total bullshit, but at least I'm producing words.

"Okay. Glad you feel ready. But I'd like to run tests and do a full workup all the same. Since it's my job and all."

"Yes, but it's silly to worry about me when I'm fine. I know my own body."

"You don't."

"Excuse me?"

"You're playing on an injury." She pulls a page from the pile and reads from it. "Sixty-three days ago. Sprained collateral ligament. No MRI done since then."

"Right. Because it's fine."

She looks back at the paper, and I have no way of knowing if it's a random page from the messy pile or the exact document that spells my doom. "You're avoiding medical help, but I think I can help you. I'm kind of a fan of science."

"Well, I'm a fan of staying in the game. The team needs me if we're going to make playoffs."

She gives me a rueful smile, nodding slowly. "Team needs you healthy."

"I. Am. Healthy enough."

"If you don't mind, I'd like to see that for myself."

Why is she so damn stubborn? And why am I stupidly attracted to it?

She squints and slowly closes the laptop. "I'm sure you understand. I need to do better than the last guy, so we should get right to it. I'll do a workup ASAP if that's all right with you." Her round eyes sparkle with enthusiasm for her job, and I wish I could stop focusing on how her lashes brush the tops of her cheeks like pretty fans. Each time she blinks.

I need to look away before I agree to her running tests that will show injuries I don't want her to know about. I can handle them. So I run my mouth without thinking. "You don't need to do better—you need to do the same. You don't need to shake things up just to prove something."

Pressing her lips together, she nods. "Okay, well, thanks for the advice."

"It isn't advice. It's fact." My aggravation overcomes my attraction to her. Finally. This is useful. If I can't be sweet and welcoming, I'll just be a regular old asshole as long as I get my way. This is my career and she seems unconcerned about fucking it all up for me. I can't have that. "You can't just come here and put people on the injured list. That will ruin careers. Don't you get that?"

"Tim, I get it. I promise I'm on your side here."

She's so…patient. While I spit nails.

Clearly, she's not on my side. She's looking to make her mark at a new job, impress her bosses, and her objectives and mine are diametrically opposed. Her good nature in the face of my pissy attitude is only making me madder. Like a pat on the head from a parent.

"No, you're on *your* side. How do you even have this job when you don't know a damn thing about footie?"

She laughs. "Footie? You're in the States now, pardner. We call it soccer here." She has the nerve to put on a western twang.

"Have you got a lasso to go with that accent?"

Her eyebrows bounce. "You want to be hog tied?"

I want to respond, but the words die on my tongue. She seems to realize what she said and her cheeks bloom pink. "Sorry. Shouldn't have said that."

"Shouldn't have mocked me calling the game by its proper name."

"Somehow, even though I 'don't know a damn thing,' I doubt that footie is the proper term." She air quotes me, and I feel prickles of heat on the back of my neck.

"Not. The. Point."

She scoots her chair back toward the desk so I can mercifully stop jockeying for a look at her legs while I pace in front of her desk, getting more worked up with every heavy step.

"What's your point, then?"

"I'm a starting left back. My game is solid, and I belong on the field. Playing."

She raises an eyebrow and gestures to the chair in front of her desk. Reluctantly, I lower myself into it, not really liking the way the spindly arms on the sides fence me in. It feels like chair jail.

Like she's locking me in here to gain some sort of tactical advantage.

It's hard for me to trust people.

Myself.

It's hard for me to trust *myself* around her. She almost derailed me once, and people don't change all that bloody much.

"If you're healthy, you'll play. Simple." She tilts her head and gives me a closed-mouth smile as though it really is simple.

"Great. I can tell you right now I'm healthy. Save you valuable time you can spend looking at the rest of the team."

I get a hollow laugh. "This isn't a negotiation."

She pops the top on a tube of Burt's Bees lip balm. I can smell the pineapple scent from across the desk as she swipes it over her lips and rubs them together. And now all I can focus on is the plump swell of her bottom lip and how it would look around my dick.

Which gets me even more riled.

She holds up a hand. "Look. Tim. I can see when a player's favoring one leg to hide pain in the other. And I'm not the only one. Your coaches have all seen your performance lag."

I exhale an irritated breath at that and feel my body coil, ready to say something I'll regret. She stops me with a hand. "I'm not saying I can't help you. It just can't be done if you come in here with attitude."

"There's no attitude," I spit out.

"Yeah. I can tell." She laughs.

I feel like a frustrated toddler who just wants a cookie. And she's doling out kale. "How can you do this job if you don't know the game of soccer?" That fact sticks in my throat like a skinny chicken bone swallowed whole.

"I was kidding. I know soccer. Quite well, in fact," she says calmly.

I feel my gut twist into an uncomfortable knot. She's not going to budge. And I'm just as drawn to her as I was as an unpolished lad, lovesick over a girl that was too good for him. I'm well and truly fucked.

I exhale a long breath and push a hand through my hair. Watching my anguish seems to soften some bit of her insistence on being a hard-ass.

"Tim. Tell me what's really going on. What are you afraid of me finding out?"

I have an opportunity to be honest. I can just tell her what's at stake for me if I can't finish the season as a starting defender. I could start things off on the right foot and maybe she'll go a little easier on me. Maybe she'll even help me.

Be honest. Just tell her.

But I don't tell her. And it's something I have a feeling I'll regret.

"Just being a good guy, saying hello." Hope dies with that lie.

She looks at me suspiciously before nodding. "Hello." She looks at her watch again. "You sure there's nothing else you want to talk about? Seems like a person doesn't show up two hours before training starts just to say hello."

"I came to get a little extra warm-up and cardio in before we start."

"Okay, well, don't do anything dumb. Not worth burning yourself out by going crazy in training only to have it bite you later. That's *my* friendly advice. Also a fact."

I feel myself deflate from lack of spine. I should just tell her what's up.

Guess it's not just myself I don't trust.

"Not interested in your facts."

She shrugs. "Fine. Have at it."

"I will."

I don't say goodbye on my way out the door. If I'm going to act like a surly grouch, I'm all in.

Except for the part of me that wants to glance over my shoulder for one last look at her.

CHAPTER 7

Jordan

Wow.

So much for separation of church and state. First week of work, and Tim is in my business, distracting me while I get my bearings.

Not to mention that he looks like a dream I shouldn't dare to have. When he leaned on my desk, I couldn't take my eyes off his large hands, the sexy tattoo snaking up the underside of his forearm, the hot-as-sin way his lips crook to the side when he's annoyed with me.

Which seems like all the time.

We were always like this. From moment one. He was gorgeous, provoking, sure of himself. I was a rule follower, nerd girl, dying to walk on the wild side with him. Only now, it's not just a matter of showing up in his room in my underwear. Now we're adults and I have a job to do.

Back when my parents first let me know we were hosting a

foreign exchange student, I dreaded the intrusion into my teenage world. What sixteen-year-old wants to babysit a mousy kid from another country who doesn't speak a whiff of the language and needs a constant chaperone at school to get from class to class and find the cafeteria?

Not me. Not anyone I knew.

I remember how I groaned and complained that it wasn't fair that they'd waited until my brother moved away to bring in a stranger. If he'd still been at home, at least we could have complained about the new interloper together.

Or better yet, with two rowdy teens already creating havoc in the house, my parents wouldn't have dreamed of bringing in a third kid.

I was so busy blaming my brother for going off on his Jack Kerouac expedition and my parents for springing the exchange student on me two weeks before classes started, that I didn't stop to ask a whole lot about her.

Turned out *she* was Tim Cheltenham—not a mousy girl from a country I couldn't find on a map, but an eighteen-year-old soccer player from England.

Jackpot.

Except not.

We bantered and fought, only in no way Chet and I had ever fought. With Chet, it was dumb things like who left barely a handful of Lays potato chips in the bag—him—and put it back in the pantry because he was too lazy to throw it away. Or who took so long blow-drying her bangs over a brush in the bathroom—me—that he barely had time to brush his teeth before school.

Having Tim down the hall was different. When he wasn't ignoring me, he acted like everything I did irritated him—my music was too girl power-y. I rarely had friends come over when he wasn't at soccer practice, so he teased me about being antisocial.

I hit back, criticizing his music for having too much base. And his heavy steps on the hardwood floors kept me from falling asleep, wondering why he needed to go downstairs three times for snacks before bed.

We went for the same chair at the kitchen table, reached for the same last carton of yogurt, grabbed for the TV remote at the same time, only I wanted to watch cooking shows, and he wanted Premier League soccer.

We may not have had anything in common, but that didn't prevent Tim from weighing in on every guy at our high school and telling me why I shouldn't be dating him. That older brother trait annoyed me more than any other.

"That kid Forrester is a twat," he'd say. "Don't know why you'd bother with Davidson."

"Don't know why you need to cock block my dating life," I'd say, only to earn his superior smirk. He didn't need to know that I really didn't have a dating life.

He also didn't need to know that I wasn't interested in Forrester or Davidson. As soon as he walked through our front door, I only pictured myself with him. Only wanted him. Only dreamed about him. If he knew it, he ignored it.

My hormonal friends may have dreamed of dating him—and they gave me a hard time about why I wasn't—but he could not have been less interested in me.

Even if I dreamed that he might be.

My eyes briefly fall shut at the pain and embarrassment that resulted from thinking I could ever mean anything to Tim Cheltenham, the gorgeous athlete with the chiseled physique and smirky smile. The one night I got up the nerve to offer myself up, he turned me down without a moment's consideration. "I'm sorry. No. We're not doing this."

I'll remember his words until my final breath.

The pain still feels as raw as it did when I walked back to my teenage bedroom, red in the cheeks and teary-eyed over the guy who I wanted so badly I was willing to give him anything. Everything.

He couldn't have made it more clear he didn't want me. Didn't even have to ponder it. He knew.

And now, I should feel confident, accomplished. I do, of course, and the past is the past. But dealing with his swollen ego all over again is knocking some wind from my sails.

He still has the same effect on me as he did back then. My insides turn to jelly at the sight of his forearm porn, the stubble on his hard jawline, the beautiful olive eyes veiled in cool disinterest.

The longer he glares, the better he looks.

I'll just have to keep reminding myself to look away.

CHAPTER 8

ordan

I HAVE zero chill when Charlie stops by my office. It's the first time I've seen him since I started my job—rumor has it there are some issues at the virtual reality company he owns, and he's been away putting out fires.

But right now, he's here. In my office. Baggy jeans, hair half in his face, bright eyes leaving no doubt about his inquisitive intellect.

I've always been at home around nerdy, bookish people. They don't think it's weird when I'd rather read a science book than go to a party. I'm fangirling my new boss hard, and I hope I'm not a disappointment as I stand in front of my ever-growing desk mess.

I hope Charlie won't notice and think I lack organizational skills. Tipping his head toward the piles I can't fully block, he smiles. "You and I have a similar filing system. Bet you know where each and every player profile is in within that stack."

That makes me smile, happy to be with like-minded people who talk about things like player profiles. "It's imperfect, but it works for me."

He nods, and I ask if he'd like a seat on the couch. He declines, backing toward the door, cutting to the point of his visit. "No, no. This is a quick thing. First, I want to reiterate that I think of you as an equal partner with our coaching staff in terms of decisions about players. I know that may sound unorthodox to some coaches, but Jaynes shares my philosophy and will defer to your judgment about their fitness to play. You have my complete support."

Hearing that gives me chills. I didn't think this job could come any closer to a dream situation, but having someone I respect as much as Charlie offer that kind of support makes up for any resistance from the players. Charlie's giving me authority. I need to own it.

"Thank you. I'm thrilled to hear that."

He nods and smiles. Then his smile fades. "That was the good news. On the flip side, I'm afraid I've been pulled away again. Expect a visit from Gus Reilly sometime later. Things have gotten more complicated with ViviTech, so that's going to require a lot of my energy right now. In tech, we do what we have to do—we pivot. I'd like to think we can do that here as well. If you have any questions, ask Reilly. He's been here longer than anyone, so he should be able to answer in my stead."

"Um, okay." I don't want to complain, though I was really hoping to work with Charlie. I'd be crazy to tell him I can't do what he's asking, so I try not to let my disappointment show.

"Sure, Charlie. Whatever you need. I'll pivot. It's all good."

"Thanks, okay, good." Charlie turns on his heel and almost runs right into Reilly as he strides into the room, but they side-step each other. On his way out the door, Charlie calls out, "Reilly, you two take it from here."

Reilly waddles into the room. He doesn't sit in either of the chairs opposite my desk. Instead, he makes his way to the side table that sits next to a navy blue couch with the Strikers logo on two well-fluffed pillows. Perching on the edge of the table, he crosses his arms over his paunchy belly and regards me through smallish dark eyes.

I don't like him, and I can't pinpoint why. He's shifty. Self-important.

"We didn't get a chance to talk at the event last month due to your wardrobe malfunction." Reilly grins at me, and I stare at him, trying to telegraph that he should stop leering at my breasts. Matching his stance, I fold my own arms over my chest, blocking his view. Not that he has one since my beige cotton sweater has a crew neck.

Reilly is easily twice my age, judging from his salt and pepper hair and the creases around his eyes. He wears round glasses that give him an owlish vibe, and I notice he doesn't have a wedding ring even though his bio on the team website says he's married to his high school sweetheart.

Most of the front office staff seems to dress in business casual, if not extremely casual in Strikers gear.

He wears an expensive-looking navy suit, as though he's one business lunch away from closing a multimillion-dollar financing deal. He probably is. He's convinced companies to pony up so much money for luxury boxes and sponsorship opportunities that the club coffers have doubled over the past couple of years.

That's good for the team—more money to pay salaries for some top players, and I know Charlie intends to clean house there too. He wants a winning franchise.

Given Reilly's stature around here, I don't want to alienate him. I also don't want to give him the impression I want daily visits from him.

Fine line.

"So I hear we'll be working together." I ignore his comment about the party.

"I hear the same. That makes me happy, Jordan." His smile feels more like a leer than a show of happiness. This guy is creepy, and I've spent many years finely tuning my creep radar. Alarm bells are going off all over the place.

"Great. It shouldn't take me too long to get up to speed, and if I need anything, I'll let you know."

He doesn't answer, just keeps staring. It's a little strange.

"Are you in a relationship, Jordan?"

"I'm sorry…?" More alarm bells in the distance, but I'm still trying to give him the benefit of the doubt.

"Do. You. Have. A. Boyfriend?" He says it slowly and loudly as though he's accommodating a dumb person.

"I-um, is that relevant to my job?"

He laughs. "Isn't everything?"

"Um, I guess at some level, sure."

"So…do you?"

I stall, taking a sip of my coffee as though I need it to formulate my thoughts. "It's just such an interesting thought now that you bring it up. Everything *is* relevant, isn't it?"

He relaxes into his perch and leans back, looking at the ceiling. "I tend to take a wholistic view."

"Okay…"

"You know. An employee's personal situation becomes part of the big picture, the fitness to do a job."

"Hang on. I'm not following. A boyfriend makes a person more fit to be a physician?"

"A boyfriend makes a person's life more stable. Stability leads to higher productivity. The research is clear. Women in relationships make better employees."

My jaw must be somewhere south of my knees. I want to respond with some choice words about his chauvinistic attitude, but the words escape me. And I dislike that even more than I dislike him.

"I'd like to see that research," I grit out.

His face falls, but he catches himself and forces an even bigger smile, waving a hand dismissively. "I'm just trying to get a bead on you. I'm a night owl, so I tend to come in late, work late. I'd really like it if you could accommodate that. Are you okay working nights? Long hours?"

"Um, sure. Whatever it takes."

"I really hope so. The last two women who worked for me flamed out. One met a guy online and ended up moving to New York for him after six months on the job. The one after that only stayed three months before leaving to travel the world. I know it's not PC to talk about gender and things, but I don't want to go down a road with someone new and have it not work out. Again."

I can't decide if I hate that he's basically asking me if my relationship status is going to get in the way of my job, or if I respect him in a weird way for being upfront about it.

"You don't have to worry. I-I do have a boyfriend." The lie comes out before I consider whether it's a good idea to introduce a fictional significant other.

"Great. That's the sweet spot. When you're in a relationship but not looking to have kids anytime soon, that's best for me."

I find myself looking around the room on the chance some bystander has appeared who can referee this situation, tell Reilly his questions are inappropriate, or suck me into a vortex that will spit me out of the nightmare I'm surely having. People don't actually say things like this out loud, do they?

Unfortunately, my quick scan reveals that we're the only ones in the room, and the conversation hangs in the air like the *Hindenburg*, ready to fall on my head.

It's still not too late to retract the lie, pretend I got confused about the conversation, and admit that I'm single and proud of it. I'm a hard worker, and my track record speaks for itself—I've never chased a boy across the country.

No, you just spent fifteen years fangirling soccer because of a boy and made it your professional goal to work for a team.

I hate to think Reilly knows me better than I know myself.

"Okay, so boyfriend it is." I nod enthusiastically, though I'm inwardly squirming at the lie and when it's going to come back and bite me.

His eyes dance with amusement. "You sure about that?"

Then I make it even worse. Dig a deeper hole.

"Yes. I mean, he's not technically my boyfriend because we're engaged, so I guess that's why it threw me a little at first, and I said the wrong thing."

What are you doing?

"It's funny, in corporate America, which is where I cut my teeth…" He pauses like he's waiting for me to acknowledge that I know how successful he is. I simply nod. "We found that women who were in stable relationships like yours are so much better than married women."

I feel the bile rise in my throat. "Why's that?"

"Oh, you know. Married women want to start a family, they take maternity leave." He waves a hand as though dismissing the stench of sexism from the air. It lingers, pungent as a broccoli fart. "That's all well and good, of course. We love babies. But I've found that motherhood leads to a certain…reprioritizing."

"You mean women figure out that there's more to life than working all the time?" He's caused me to parrot my mother, and that infuriates me.

He nods. "Exactly. You understand. The work suffers." He studies my face, which has morphed into a wall of stone. "I'm just saying what we all know is true."

He's speaking like I'm not a woman who could have similar proclivities someday. Or maybe that's the point. A preemptive strike so I'll know not to do something so career-defeating as having babies.

The horror.

"Nope. Just engaged. Not planning on getting married

anytime soon. Like I said, long engagement, we're just enjoying that phase for now." Just digging a ditch for myself.

He nods slowly, digesting the information. He's looking at the ceiling again, so I can't tell if he believes me. I'm tempted to look up there as well and see if there's some sort of lie detector among the acoustical tiles. If so, it's tipped so far into the red, it might as well be turning me in for engagement fraud.

"Ah, okay. Well, that certainly bodes well, according to the research."

"Yes, well, I do love research. Scientist." I point to myself with both thumbs. I hate this conversation. I hate him for making me have it.

"Anyhow, I've got piles of work to get to. Need to be productive so I can get home at a reasonable hour, spend time with my fiancé."

Dig, dig, dig.

The strange thing is as soon as the words leave my mouth, I'm overcome with a sense of calm I've never felt before. Maybe all my mother's nagging has worn off on me, but the idea of having a fiancé at home makes me feel warm and comfortable.

Hmph. Gonna have to unpack that one later.

Later. When Reilly isn't staring me down with his mouth open. He's looking pointedly at my ring finger. "No ring?" he asks.

I grab the finger with my other hand, as if to confirm that it's bare, all the while smiling like a loon because words keep coming out of my mouth without my apparent ability to stop them. "It's being sized. The engagement was a recent thing, so…"

Have to stop talking now before I blurt out anything else I can't take back later.

"Nice. Well, we'll have to get him in here, meet everyone." He pushes up from the corner of the table and stands, surveying my office, which has no personal touches save for my piles. But if he has any observations to make, he keeps them to himself. "Or you two could come to dinner one night. My wife is a very good cook."

"Sounds good." I'm certain my face is blooming a shade of pink only seen when my mother asks her embarrassing questions. Great. Now I have two people in my life who can make me cringe and lie in tandem. "Anyhow, I've got tons to do. Still getting up to speed."

Sitting behind my desk, I pull a folder from the stack of pages to my right and flip it open. Thankfully, Reilly is too far away to see its contents because the folder contains magazine spreads with kitchen ideas I hope to implement someday.

Reilly looks so pleased that I've confided in him that I find his big grin contagious. So we stand there smiling at each other until my phone mercifully rings, and he backs away so I can get to work.

Right.

Like I'm going to work now that my career aspirations have landed with a thunk in a smelly dumpster, and I've gotten myself engaged.

"Say no more. Don't want to keep you." Reilly steps closer and glances at the two pages of country chic kitchen shelves. His expression clouds, and he nods. He keeps nodding as he makes his way out of my office.

After closing the door behind him, I return to my desk, put my head in my hands, and try to figure out how I went from having a secret nonexistent boyfriend to having a nonexistent fiancé in a matter of minutes.

Then I pull out the players' medical charts and dive in. Because I have no idea what to do about the other part.

CHAPTER 9

im

I OVERDO IT AT PRACTICE, and it's going to bite me in the ass.

I should know better after the number of years I've been playing, and I'm not getting any younger. Just dumber.

There's no way that throwing more hours of training at an injury is going to help me play better, but some part of my brain thinks that if I can just improve my fitness, it will compensate for the sprain.

The extra hour and a half of sprints and drills I put myself through earlier didn't help. I'm more dead tired than I was the first day I made the squad back in England and went from two hours of training per day to six.

It's my own fault, and I know I need to be smarter. We have a fleet of trainers who've already given me regimens designed to up my physicality without damaging my game readiness. I ignored all of them in the hour-plus I spent pushing past my own limits before practice.

Coach called me on it right away. "You're lagging, Chelty," he said more than once. And I could see him paying a little extra attention to me during the passing drills and the one-v-one match-ups where I made sure I dominated. Every. Single. Time.

And now I'm gassed.

I'm also annoyed that Jordan was right in her assessment of me—just a dumb jock who pushes himself too hard at practice and now stands to pay the price.

I'm so tired that it takes me longer than my teammates to collect my gear and stuff it into my bag before heading into the locker room. I'm shuffling like an octogenarian, and I can only hope no one's around to witness it. So far, so good.

Most of my teammates have already hit the showers by the time I arrive, so there's no one to hear my grunts at how my muscles ache when I sit on the bench in front of my locker. And no one hears me curse a blue streak when I realize that in my haste to have a sit-down with Jordan, I left my street clothes in my car.

Fuck it. I don't need to eat with the team. Better to head home anyway and get into an ice bath, so I toss my sweaty workout towel in a bin and head out.

It's how I end up in the parking lot at an hour when no one else is there. No one, that is, except for Jordan.

And she looks unhappy. Her faraway expression is complicated—she's not absentmindedly staring into space; she's working out something troubling.

It shouldn't affect me as much as it does, but seeing her frowning tugs at something deep within me. I want to fix whatever's bothering her, and I have no idea why since logic should have me avoiding her as much as I can.

Her car sits two spots over from mine, but when I draw close, she doesn't react. She stands motionless by her driver's side door, open wide. A coffee cup wobbles in her hand.

From our brief interactions so far, I can tell Jordan is as solid and unflappable as I remember her. But something has her spooked.

"Hey." I slow my stride when I approach so I don't startle her, since she seems oblivious to everything around her.

We're the only ones there. Just us and a bunch of Teslas, their fans revved high to keep their batteries cool in the sun.

My pulse rockets in her presence, revved up like the car fans. And I know it's not from the suicide drills Coach had us run at the end.

I marvel at how I can be wary of a person and feel attracted to her at the same time. I'd like to pretend I'm feeling something else, but being an athlete my whole life has taught me not to lie to myself about what my body feels—even if I'm lying to everyone else. It doesn't serve me well in a game situation.

It might serve me well now, however, because I genuinely don't want to be noticing how her eyes look aflame. Flecks of gold in the deep gray irises. Glowing despite themselves. I don't want to be affected by the way she's chewing on her plush bottom lip. I am, though, and if my training shorts weren't so baggy, it would be embarrassingly fucking obvious.

But it's the crease in her brow and the look of defeat that gets me.

It hurts me. It's always been that way. I can't understand why my body and some stupid steadfast flame in my heart react to her the way they do. It's been fifteen years—let it fucking go.

I can't.

I reach a hand out and gently lay it on her shoulder. She flinches as if noticing me for the first time. "Oh. Hey." She blinks a couple times and forces some composure over her features. It seems like the effort costs her.

"What's going on?"

She shakes her head slowly but doesn't answer, still focused on a point in the distance. I look in that direction but only see cars and the tops of trees beyond the lot.

Her dazed expression worries me a little. Gone is the confident smile, the heat-charged banter I'd really fucking dig if it didn't come while she was telling me to get my knee checked. She seems…lost.

"Jordan, you okay?"

My voice seems to shake her out of her daze a bit, almost like she's noticing I'm still here. "Oh. Um, not really." She winces after she says it. "I mean, I'm fine. All good."

"Liar."

Her eyes lift to mine, challenging. I see a tiny bit of her spark return, and even though it almost looks like a glare, I welcome it. "Do you need something?" Even as rattled as she is, the offer sounds genuine.

"I need you to tell me what's up."

"Why? Why do you need that?"

"I just do."

She doesn't argue. Just blinks heavily.

Gingerly, because I don't want to unnerve her more than she already seems to be, I reach for the coffee cup and take it from her hand. Wordlessly, she lets go of it, but her eyes follow what I'm doing with it.

I take a sniff through the hole in the lid to make sure it's actually coffee. If she's slugging down tequila in the middle of the afternoon, it seems worth knowing.

It doesn't smell like coffee, but it's not alcoholic, either. "What the heck is this?" I ask her as I pop off the lid and inspect the contents, which are pale pink and smell like some kind of sour fruit.

"The dregs of a smoothie I had for lunch."

"That's all you had for lunch?"

"It was a busy afternoon. I had players' careers to ruin." There it is—it heartens me that her sass is back even if it reminds me what an asshole I was the last time I saw her. She inhales a deep breath, then puts a hand on her chest and exhales like it hurts.

"Tough day at work?"

"It was all right." She can barely choke the words out without flinching at the lie. We'll get to that in a minute, but first, there's the issue of this warmed-over fruit drink in my hand.

"You should eat a real lunch." She probably doesn't want to hear it from me, but the fruity swill in that cup doesn't have me convinced she knows about proper nutrition.

"I'll keep it in mind." She puts a hand out and waits for me to hand the cup back. I don't.

I walk it over to a nearby trash can and toss it in. "Hey," she protests.

"It was warm, and it smelled rotten. Come on, take care of yourself. You can do better."

"Says someone who hasn't scheduled his physical with me."

"Apples and oranges."

"Sounds like a bad smoothie."

"No worse than that rot. Where'd you get it?" I move so I'm leaning against her car, which effectively blocks her ability to get in and drive away. She seems antsy.

"I brought it with me. It was breakfast."

"Ah. So you're capable of procuring food, but you made the choice to let a warm smoothie fester on your desk all day instead of eating a proper lunch. That is what you're telling me?"

"Not that it matters, but yes. And I'm going home, so I'll eat there." She realizes that I'm blocking her access to her car and tips her chin up. "Anyhow... Thanks for bossing me around and throwing out my dinner." She cracks a smile, and I'm a goner.

I don't trust her as a doctor, but it doesn't matter right now. I want to keep talking to her.

So I don't budge.

"Excuse me. You're kind of in the way." She makes a move as though to get around me, but I've got her good and blocked. "Why are you standing here?"

"Because you haven't told me why I found you staring into the distance like someone sucker punched you. What's going on? What happened at work today?"

I cross my arms over my chest. She puts her hands on my forearms as if to dislodge them, and I feel her suck in a tiny breath. Ever so slightly, I feel her fingers dig in. This woman likes my forearms, and I'm here for it.

I bite back a grin.

Teammates have given me shit over the years for spending extra time doing weight drills that bulk up my upper body when soccer is all about the quads. But I never liked the idea of being quad-dominant and skinny from the waist up. My extra workouts even things out and give me extra power when I take a throw-in. At least, that's how I've always rationalized it.

And now I have another point in the win column. "Not moving until you tell me what happened."

"I did something really stupid." Her shoulders drop after she says it. Relief? Resignation?

Raking a hand through my hair, I move away from her car and pace a little. "Look, I'm not so great at reading people or figuring out the meaning behind things. You're going to need to be more specific."

Her quiet laugh surprises me. "Oh, I can be very specific. I told Reilly I'm engaged."

Maybe I took a few too many headers during training because I can't have just heard her correctly. "Hold up. I feel like you just said you told Reilly you're engaged."

My stomach knots up instantly, and my heart hammers so hard I can't hear anything else. Not that anyone told me Jordan was single…not that I should have assumed…but hearing that she not only has a boyfriend but she's getting married to him, I feel my face pale.

She nods. "I did." Her eyes glaze with tears.

I take a step back, holding up a hand. "Wait, stop. No crying. I'm still unpacking the other thing. Can't handle tears too."

"Well, I'm sorry. I can't just turn them off like a faucet." Her voice quivers, and I see her trying to steady a trembling chin. If I wasn't so bloody confused by what she's saying, I'd feel bad that my only thought is how damn beautiful she looks, even on the verge of tears.

"Why are you crying? Are you not happy to be engaged? Or did you just not want Reilly to know?"

I may not be the sharpest knife in the drawer, but I don't get it. Why does she care what Reilly thinks?

She drops her forehead into her hand and shakes her head. "No. I'm not engaged. I'm not in a relationship at all. And that's a problem, apparently, and I didn't want to flunk Job Security 101 in my first week at work. So I lied."

Warmth spreads through my chest at the knowledge that the engagement is a lie.

Placing a hand on her shoulder, I get her to look at me. Her eyes are still watery, but she's steadied her chin, her mouth turned down into a frown I don't like. "Start from the beginning."

She explains why she said what she did, and it sort of makes sense. The first thing that strikes me is that Reilly would never dare say it to a guy. Confirms all my worst instincts about the slimy turd.

"You know what he's telling you is not okay. You could file a discrimination lawsuit or some such," I tell her.

She shakes her head. "I know it's not okay. But I'm not rocking the boat on my first week at a new job. It's fine. It'll be okay."

"How will this be okay? Are you going to run out and get engaged to the first guy who crosses your path?"

"Of course not. I-I don't know what I'm going to do. Maybe... maybe I'll meet someone?" she says hopelessly, rolling her eyes.

"Really? Meet someone and marry him just to get Reilly off your back?"

"Gah. No. I don't know what I was thinking. I froze, then I

unfroze and started babbling nonsense that started and ended with a fiancé I don't have. And now Reilly wants me to bring the fiancé to dinner with his wife."

I can't help it. The image of that makes me laugh.

Jordan looks at me aghast, then quickly comes around and starts laughing quietly too. "I know. I'm ridiculous. This is a ridiculous problem to have. I'm a physician, for crying out loud. A clumsy physician with piles on my desk that I pretend are organized, but they're not, and now I have to make a fiancé materialize before the next team event."

"That's happening in two weeks, you know. The cocktail thing before the post-season."

"I know! And now I've really cooked my goose." She's pretty distraught, so I make a point of ignoring her expression, though it strikes me as funny. All this time in America, and I still hear new things every day.

"You don't have to bring anyone. Your fake fiancé can have a work thing that night. What does he do for a living?" I can't help smirking at her predicament.

"Haha."

"Come on, you have to have a little fun with this. It'll be fine. It's not like Reilly will do a home check or anything."

She doesn't look convinced. "He might. At the very least, he's going to expect me to show up with an engagement ring and some cute beach pictures on my desk, or he'll know I lied."

I can see that she's not taking this lightly. And fuck me, for some reason, I want to help her.

"I-I could be your fiancé." The words are out of my mouth before I can edit them or even think about how stupid they sound. "I mean…not your real fiancé. Clearly. That would be bloody awful. For you, I mean. I'm bad about doing dishes, and I don't cook. Or…you know, whatever. Not the point—"

"What?" Thank fuck she cut me off because who knows what was coming out of my mouth next?

I don't blame her for being confused. I'm baffled myself, trying to sort out how a flicker of a thought made me blurt out such nonsense.

"Nothing. Ridiculous thought, obviously."

"No, wait. I mean, yes, it's ridiculous. But it wouldn't be real, so we wouldn't have to spend any actual time together. You wouldn't have to, you know, do dishes."

My brain is trying to play catch up. Is she…agreeing to this?

"You're not serious. It was meant to be a joke."

Was it?

Her cheeks go a deep shade of pink, and she takes a step away from me. "Of course it was. Of course. I know you don't want to be my fiancé."

"Wait, hang on." She agreed a second ago, so a part of me is stuck on this. A very rogue, reckless part. Gently, I reach for her and pull her back to where she stood a moment ago. Reluctantly, she lets me. "Maybe we could do this."

"We couldn't."

"Why not?"

"What are you saying, Tim? We tell everyone at the Strikers club that we're engaged? No one would believe it."

"I feel like I should be offended by that."

She smacks my shoulder with the back of her hand. "No one would believe that you, with your infamous reputation for dating…everyone…would get engaged to a nerdy doctor and not tell anyone."

I tap a finger against my lips. She's right, and I should drop the entire idea, but some crazy part of me wants to make sense of it. I should have my head examined right after she finishes checking out my knee.

Instead, I look up at the waning blue afternoon sky and start spitballing.

"Well, that's why I didn't say anything. I didn't want the guys giving me shit about being dick-whipped or what have you. To protect you and the integrity of our blossoming relationship, I kept it a secret from everyone."

Her eyes widen, and there's a hint of a spark within the gray. Just enough to tell me she's considering it. "Go on…I'm starting to see it. You felt that protective of our relationship?"

Raking a hand through my hair, I scramble to make more shit up. "Yes. I did it all for you, love."

"Don't call me that."

"Relax. It doesn't mean what you think it does."

"What, that you love me? Don't worry. I get that."

"Good."

"Great."

"Perfect. So do we agree? We're going public now with our relationship because it's progressed, and now we're so mad for each other that we've gotten engaged?" I can't keep the sarcasm from my voice. The words sound so absurd coming out of my mouth, but I don't hate saying them.

"Wow, you sound so sincere."

I raise a hand. "I'm still getting used to the idea. We've only been engaged for five minutes, love."

Her aggravation loses its stronghold on her, and she laughs. "Fair enough." Her eyes trace over my face before looking me up and down like she's sizing up my physical fitness for this mission. "You think people will buy it?"

I nod. "If we sell it, they'll buy it. It's not even that crazy—we knew each other years ago, we always carried a torch for one another, so all these years later, we meet again at the team event and…kaboom."

"Kaboom." She nods. "Okay, maybe I believe kaboom."

I shrug. "Crazier things have happened."

I'm still blocking her car, so I shift to give her access to her door if she wants to leave. Her eyes narrow.

"What's in this for you?"

Taking a deep breath, I realize I have no easy explanation. I can't say that she has an undeniable hold on me that makes me do crazy things. Even if it's the whole damn truth.

Besides, there is something I want from her. I just know there isn't a snowball's chance in hell I'll get it.

"Clear me to play until after the season. It's only a few more games."

She shakes her head. "I can't send you out there if I know you're injured, and I can see that from watching game footage and observing practice. Not going to do what the guy before me did, if that's what you're asking."

"It doesn't have to be like that, exactly."

"How exactly can it be?"

I'm so shocked that she's even open to discussion that I have to force my brain into motion. What am I asking for? If I'm saving her hide with a fake engagement, I need to make it good.

"We play with injuries all the time. Maybe that's all this is. There have to be things that will keep you busy, so you don't have time for my physical just yet. Just put it off. Please."

Her face softens at the word *please* and she blinks those doe eyes at me. Then she shakes her head. "Most I can wait is a week. Especially since it's obvious to me who needs to be evaluated the most. You're at the top of the list."

My jaw clenches so hard I feel a muscle start to spasm. I have to open my mouth to work it free. She notices.

With my back against the wall, I have no choice. If I want her to ignore medical protocols, I need to put it on the table.

"How about we do it the other way? Bring me in ASAP, do all the tests, and if it's not a massive threat to my well-being, you clear me to play, take it week by week. You know I've been doing it for months. Just let me get through playoffs, and then, I promise, I'll do whatever you medically advise."

The words grate at my throat as I push them out. I hate having to basically beg her to let me do my job. After all these years of leading the team, it's embarrassing.

"Ethically, I need to do what's right for you and your health."

"You will. We're just talking about timing."

I wait while her brow furrows, and she thinks it over. Then, I let all the words I've spewed in the last five minutes permeate my brain. I have to be fucking nuts. I shake my head in disbelief, wanting to roll back time and recant half of it before she can tell me I'm deplorable.

"Okay." She gives me a plastic smile that looks anything but certain about this whole plan.

I feel dizzy. "What?"

"Okay. If you agree to come to my office first thing tomorrow, so we know what we're dealing with, I'll see if I can clear you to play for a bit longer. But I can't promise anything until I see a fresh MRI."

"You're serious."

"Are you?"

"Um, yeah. Of course. It's just…so we're also engaged, you didn't forget about that part?"

She nods and exhales a long breath. "I will probably—definitely—live to regret this, but I don't know what else to do now that I've lied my way into five minutes of job security."

"Reilly's a twat. You could still just report him."

Another long exhale. "Not when I'm new on the job. No. I need to prove my worth first."

I don't bother to point out that the other part of our agreement might not exactly do that. From her grim expression, I can see she knows exactly what I'm thinking.

"Okay, then. I guess I'll see you in the morning."

She nods, her eyes faraway and unfocused. She opens the car door. "Yeah. I need to go digest all of this." But she doesn't move, doesn't seem capable of it.

"You okay, love?" I venture. Her eyes close for a long blink, then she shakes herself back to reality.

"Yes. Fine. Okay? Probably not, but I have plans for getting drunk…I mean, dinner. Well, probably getting drunk at dinner, given all of this. It'll be fine. And if not, I'll be out of a job by the end of the week and probably set some kind of record, so that's a good resume-builder, dontcha think? Um…"

She drifts off again, staring into space, leaving me with that jumble of words. "You don't seem fine."

As if realizing she's been holding the car door handle in the vise of her fist, she releases the metal and stretches out her hand. "I will be." Her eyes clear and she nods, resolute.

I nod. "Okay. Okay, good."

I feel like our agreement deserves a handshake or something, but I don't dare reach for her and risk knocking away her tenuous grip on being fine. Instead, I take a step back, then another, before turning to my car.

"By the way, I think you're decent at it—reading people," she calls. I turn around and give her a small nod. "Give yourself some credit…hubby." Her crack of laughter drives home the craziness of everything I've suggested. And the fact that, inexplicably, she agreed to it.

Before I can digest her words and their implications, she slips into the front seat and slams the door.

I hear her gun the engine, then she's gone. Just like my sanity.

ordan

"What are those shoes?" Sofia points accusingly to the black pumps that have become a regular part of my work wardrobe. I know I look more like a lawyer than a sports trainer in the pencil skirts, but I haven't figured out a "work casual" that feels comfortable and still gives me some authority. I need authority.

The two players who came in for physicals today didn't exactly speak to me with disdain, but that's because they didn't really talk to me much at all. Caleb Schmidt, one of the team's keepers, broke a rib six weeks ago and has been coming to practice all this time. No wonder it hasn't healed. He's a backup keeper, so there's no reason he should have been training like that.

The mismanagement blows my mind.

Harry Gunderson, the right midfielder, did a lot of stern-faced nodding while I checked the tendonitis in his knee. He could barely sit still while I prodded and looked for tender spots.

The level of pain he endured during the exam was nothing compared to what he must have been dealing with during games.

He's the first player to be pulled from the starting lineup for a strenuous course of physical therapy, and I don't think he'll be the last.

I can hardly wait to see what the exam with Tim will turn up tomorrow. Tim. My new fiancé who wants me to let him play through his injuries.

And with that thought, I drink down about half of the lemon drop from the sugared martini glass in front of me on the marble-topped bar. This job seems to make my alcohol intake go up.

Meanwhile, Sofia is still glaring at my shoes like they've attacked her personally. I look down at them. They seem fine to me. "What's wrong with them?"

"They're…what are they, orthopedic high heels? Like, stripper shoes for clumsy doctors?" She laughs at her own joke, and I wish I'd never told her about how many times I've tripped in them.

"They're from the Walking Store. They're comfortable, and they help with back alignment."

"Oh my God, they're an insult to shoes. Please give them to me so I can burn them."

"I'm not letting you burn my shoes. But I will let you explain to me why I keep making terrible impulsive decisions where men are concerned." I take another long, long sip of the lemon drop and tell Sofia what Tim and I agreed to in the parking lot. By the time I'm finished, she's forgotten all about the shoes.

"Yes, I believe I've lost the official count. There was the original attempt to seduce Tim…"

"Then the lab partner I slept with in college."

"How many times?"

I put my head in my hands. "A bunch. Every time I didn't want to share my results with him, I vowed to have an honest conversation, and somehow we'd end up in bed."

"And the guy in med school—"

"Enough already. Yes. Exactly. And lying to Reilly and saying yes to a fake engagement. This is why I stick to science and facts and work. Emotional decisions send me off the rails."

"Um, yeah, I'd say so."

She leans back on the leather-topped barstool and almost tips over. I grab her arm to catch her and can't help but notice the difference between her forearm, which I can wrap my fingers around, and Tim's muscular arm that I gripped earlier. That was all roped, sexy strength. I'd have needed both hands to encircle one forearm. My fingertips still tingle with leftover lust.

Shaking my head, I put a halt to that train of thought. It's bad enough I agreed—too readily, I now realize—to his offer to be my fake fiancé, but I agreed to see him first thing tomorrow to run tests. I need to stay focused on medicine, health, work. That's it. No impulsive decisions that cost me later.

"I know. I'm ridiculous. But the fake engagement does get me out of a bind."

Sofia puts her elbows on the white marble and leans her chin on her fists. "No, it puts you in a new one. Now you're lying to your boss, who, by the way, had no right to make any comments whatsoever about your relationship status. It has no bearing on your ability to do your job. And do it well."

Sometimes I wish Sofia wasn't so principled.

Or so right.

Sigh.

"Are you really telling me you've never had to cave to what some guy thought about your ability to do your job? You, of all people, should understand." Sofia runs her own company, Buckingham Pals, which matches families with nannies in Europe who want to work in the US.

She got the idea when she studied abroad during college and stayed an extra two years working as a nanny for a family in London. Betting that American families might want to have their very own Mary Poppins taking care of their children, she started a business. And it grew into a mega-successful empire. She's dealt with bankers, lawyers, and pushy people all over the world.

"Of course I understand. I live the same nightmare. But it doesn't mean I want you to live it too." She swivels on her barstool and hops off. "Be right back. Gotta pee."

I watch her move through the dark bar, which is attached to a trendy hotel in the Oakland Marina, across the San Francisco Bay from the Strikers stadium. When we made the plan to celebrate my first week at work, it made sense to meet here, only a short drive over the Bay Bridge from work to a spot we both like.

Now, however, with a perfect view of the stadium visible through the tall plate glass windows, I feel like my new job is mocking me and my poor decisions.

Slurping down the rest of the lemon drop and licking the sugar from the rim of the glass, I tip my head at the bartender. He appears a moment later, a bar towel over his shoulder, and leans his elbows on the bar between us, clasping his hands. "You doing okay? Another round?"

I look at Sofia's glass of chardonnay, which has barely been touched, and blink back mortification at how quickly I drained my glass. "I guess just one for me. Thanks."

He nods, and I take in his features—soft green eyes, high cheekbones, and the kind of wicked smile women probably find irresistible as he gives me a wink and goes off to fetch me a fresh drink. But he's no Tim Cheltenham. In an instant, the pretty face of the bartender is replaced by Tim's, and it pains me to admit that I'm still thinking about him.

My fake fiancé.

Sofia swings her leg over the barstool before I can think of ways to get out of my mess. If I even want to.

No, I do. At least, I should. Because I don't want to admit that something about having this strange tie to Tim excites me a little bit.

"So let's talk about this. Practically. How's it going to work?"

I lean away from Sofia so I can look her in the eye and admit that I have no earthly idea. "It's not like I thought this through. That's the problem with an impulsive idea. There's no logic to it, and it pretty much can't work."

"And yet you agreed to it."

"I'm still trying to figure out how that happened. Desperation, confusion…?"

"Hot guy brain melt?"

"Yeah, that. I didn't think that was a thing for a thirty-one-year-old professional who doesn't do relationships."

"I don't know if you need to get that dramatic about it. Think about my situation. If we can work, pretty much anyone can."

"Ha. You don't have a situation. You have a hot next-door neighbor who comes over for booty calls. Your only common interest is sex." The bartender returns with my second lemon drop, and I note Sofia's raised eyebrow when I take a long sip. "Are you judging my drinking?"

"Hardly. I'm judging your judgment of my booty call. Does Tim know *why* you share a common interest in soccer?"

"No, and I don't plan to tell him. It's bad enough I was fangirling his teenage muscles when he lived with my family. He doesn't need to know how much soccer I watched after he left the country."

Let's just say I watched a lot of soccer.

"Well, he is your fiancé and all. You might as well get to know him." Sofia laughs at my expense, and I can't even get mad at her. Hearing her say the words out loud makes me groan and drown my stupidity in more of my strong drink. I feel myself wobble on my barstool and reach to steady myself before I topple off.

"How did this even happen? For two months, I've been working out the details with Charlie Walgrove, who's so brilliant anyone would give a kidney to learn from him. For two months, I've been looking forward to the chance to combine my two favorite things in one awesome job. And now…" I can't even finish the thought. It's too depressing.

"Now you can't fangirl Charlie on the daily because you're working for some asshat who's afraid you'll chase a boy across the country or go on a seventeen-month babymoon. I still say you should report him. That's sexism. It's sexual harassment. It's-it's—"

"It's not worth losing a great job over."

"But it's not a great job. Not if you have to pretend to have a fiancé to be taken seriously."

"It's still pretty great." I can't help my giddy smile. "I know, I'm such a soccer dork, but I love being a part of the team. It's what I've trained to do, and I'm finally getting my shot at it. There's no way I'm jeopardizing any of it over some old dude who plays by rules no one lives by anymore."

Sofia swirls her drink. "Hold on. I'm not saying no one lives by those. Plenty of people still do, even women. Some of the ones I know are harder on other women than men are."

"That's terrible. Shouldn't be that way." I notice that the bartender has delivered a tiny white dish of olives and another with sticky-looking almonds. I don't want to get sticky, so I pick up an olive. The salty brine tastes good after the sugary lemon drop.

"Well, it is. Good news is, we can be part of the new guard of women who don't put up with it."

"Really? Would you quit your dream job over some antiquated ideas from an old guy?"

"No, but I wouldn't fake marry a guy for it either. Though he's really hot, so maybe you should."

"We're not getting married. It's temporary. Once I get situated at work, we'll break it off."

"Why is he even willing to do this for you?"

"He's hoping I'll let him play through a pretty serious injury."

"Which you won't do."

"Which I've taken an oath not to do. Do no harm."

She shakes her head and finishes her drink. "What about harm to yourself?"

"There won't be any."

"No? You're not gonna fall for him?"

"Oh, good God, no. Been there, done that, heard his rejection loud and clear, experienced a world of hurt. Not revisiting that feeling again, thank you very much."

That is what's going to keep me on the straight medical path— the memory of how awful it felt to be rejected when I hoped he felt the same way I did.

And with that, I feel sorted out.

"I just worry about your tender heart," Sofia says.

"It's not that tender anymore. It's mature and practical, and it's buried under a white coat. I just need to get him to trust me so I can help him get healthy, and by the time the new season starts, he'll be back on track, and we'll be fake broken-up. It will all be fine."

It will be.

"Okay, if you're sure." She hoists her purse from the hook under the bar and signals to the bartender for the check.

I nod and slug down the rest of my drink because I'm not so sure about any of it.

im

I HAVEN'T SPENT this much time in the Strikers offices in my entire career, and yet here I am again, looking for Jordan in her office.

It's early, a good hour earlier than I need to be here for practice, and the hallways are surprisingly quiet. Passing by the framed posters of my teammates on the walls, I know exactly where I'll find the one with my mug on it. I barely spare it a glance, not wanting to see the power behind the penalty kick I was taking when the team photographer got the shot. Just reminds me I don't have that power or accuracy right now.

But I'll get it back. I will.

I find Jordan behind her desk, holding a ceramic Strikers cup and staring at her computer screen. Hair pulled into a high ponytail, the ends of which dust one shoulder. My eyes fix on a small paper bag on the desk. "Breakfast, lunch, and dinner in a paper bag?" I point to it from my spot in the doorway, where I brace my arms on the jam.

Jordan looks up and takes off her sexy glasses. Her gaze lazily rolls over the ink on my forearm, and she swallows hard.

"Hi, wifey." I take a step into the room and watch her cringe at the term.

She shakes her head. "Don't do that."

"Why not?" I can't deny that I enjoy teasing her. Especially when her discomfort causes a deep blush to spread across her cheeks, turning them carnation-pink.

She fans her hands around her face as though she can wave away the heat, but it's as useless as trying to bring a Mack truck to a skidding stop in the rain. Her eyes dart around. "I changed my mind. I'm going to tell Reilly I got nervous and lied."

I follow her eyes around the office and notice she's ditched the generic Strikers swag in favor of a stack of coffee table books on human anatomy and a vintage-looking black and white photograph of a soccer game. I point to it, recognition dawning. "Is that Wembley?"

She smiles. "It is. Look at the crowd, all wearing suits and hats. I love it."

I take a closer look. "It's awesome." Scanning the rest of the office, I'm struck by a suspicious lack of greenery. "Maybe a plant or two, you'll be all set in here."

She holds up a hand like a stop sign. "Whoa there, none of that. I kill plants, even the supposedly hardy ones."

I'm about to suggest some that are practically murder-proof, but I'm distracted by the array of piles and papers, which has grown by threefold since the last time I was in here.

"It's like they're breeding."

Confusion clouds her face. "What?"

"Your piles. There are even more of them now. If you feed them after midnight, do they turn evil and try to take over the world?"

She smiles at my *Gremlins* joke. I count it as a win.

Why are you counting anything? She could still bench you if you don't pass her physical. Get to the point.

But I don't. I rake a hand through my hair, concerned that she wants to break our engagement. Our fake engagement. "You're going to tell Reilly? Why?"

"It's the smart thing. I never should have lied."

Plopping into the chair in front of her desk, I don't feel as hemmed in as I did the last time. I rest my elbows on the arms of the chair and tent my fingers in front of my chin. "Are you sure? Will that be awkward?"

"Yes, it will be horrible, and I'll probably get fired, but it's better than pretending to be engaged to you." As soon as she says it, her eyes go wide. "Wait, I didn't mean it like it sounded. I meant it mainly for you. I shouldn't force you to lie for me. About this. To your bosses."

"Whoa. First of all, it was my idea. You didn't force me. Second, they're not my bosses. They're yours."

"So what?"

"So I say we think this through before you run off and pull the plug on our engagement."

"We're not engaged," she says through gritted teeth. Just makes me want to keep saying it. Engagement. Fiancée. Wife. All the words that will get me a feisty reaction.

"Whatever you say, love. But this says otherwise. Put out your hand." She looks wary but extends a graceful palm while I extract a small box from my pocket. Popping it open, I show her the pretty ring with a very large rock.

She recoils, pulling her hand back, eyes widening. "Wait, what? You bought me a diamond ring?"

I dismiss her worry with a wave of my hand. "It's a pretty good imitation of a two-carat solitaire if I do say so."

Like a timid turtle edging out of its protective shell, she extends her hand again, and I place the box in her palm. Her hand quivers a tiny bit as she stares at the ring, and I'm transported to a parallel universe where I'm actually asking her to marry me.

The thought sends an unexpected jolt of adrenaline through me, dead-ending at my dick.

I know, I know. Donkeys will circle the sun on wings made of butter before that happens. And yet…my thudding heart doesn't get the memo.

But she looks touched, which stirs a stronger tide of emotion than I want to acknowledge. Her gratitude makes me nervous, and I shift from foot to foot.

"I can't believe you're serious about doing this."

"It serves both our purposes. It just makes sense." I shrug and push away the feeling that it makes sense for any other reason. It doesn't. Jordan stands to be a direct threat to my career if I don't handle things the right way, so I'm handling them.

Delicately, she extracts the ring from the box and holds it up. The refracting light through its faceted surface dances across her cheeks, pretty like a smattering of snowflakes. But she places it on the desk instead of putting it on.

"I thought you were here to set up your evaluation appointment. You know, like we discussed." Her voice is quiet. I worry that she's disappointed, maybe thinking I'm trying to pull a bait and switch.

"I'm here for that, too," I reassure her. "When should I come in?"

She moves a handful of papers from the top of one pile. When she doesn't find what she's looking for, she starts thumbing through the pages in another pile. It amuses me that she's this disorganized.

A moment later, she finds the object of her search, a day planner that's covered in purple chicken scratch. I lean in for a closer look and find the writing illegible. "You're the cliché of a doctor with impossible handwriting."

"It will be very legible when I write a note telling Coach you can't play," she taunts, a smirk on her lips.

"Right. Sorry. Your writing is beautiful. Please schedule my appointment."

She looks at the tiny squares, each of which is crammed with writing. It can't possibly help her stay organized.

"You do know they make these marvelous little things that help organize your life," I hold up my phone. "You can see your calendar in a nice neat little app."

"I like it this way."

"Messy."

"Old school."

I laugh, earning a suspicious look. "Friday, first thing before training. Plan on three hours. I want to put you on the treadmill, run tests, get an MRI. We're going to do this right."

"Do you really think it'll require such a big workup?" I'm worried the harder she looks, the more she'll find injuries she can't ignore.

"And then some. We're not cutting corners, footie player." Grinding into the paper with her purple pen, she adds me to her schedule in tiny letters. I stare as she writes my name, liking it until I remind myself we're not going on a date.

"Fine," I grunt. "Let's talk about the team event in a couple weeks. Is that where we're coming out as a couple, or should I tell the guys beforehand, take some pressure off?"

"I liked your other idea, saying my fiancé is too busy for the team event."

"That was before it was me. It's either the team party or dinner with Reilly and his wife, though that could be fun in its own way."

Her eyes go wide. "Yeah, no. Team party it is."

"Great. Done."

I start to get up, but she waves me back. "Hang on. About the other part—definitely tell the guys beforehand. I don't want some big reveal at the event."

"Should I say you're pregnant? Shotgun wedding…"

"Um, hard pass. I'm on birth control. I'm a planner."

I can't stop my cheeky grin. "Good to know."

The flush blooms on her cheeks and extends down her neck. "It wasn't meant to be a guide."

So she says. I push up the sleeves on my Henley and cross my arms over my chest for effect. She makes a concerted effort to look away, but her eyes sneak back.

Coming around to her side of the desk, I perch on the corner, getting in her space. She locks eyes with me but leans away ever so slightly. "You can guide me whenever you want, love."

She doesn't flinch, but her pupils dilate enough for me to know I've nicked her resistance. It's a dangerous game, but I'm playing.

"No pregnancy. But Tim, let's be honest. Your reputation precedes you. Any ideas how to convince people we've been working on a solid relationship while you were out with jersey chasers on the regular? I don't really want to look like a jilted bride."

"I wasn't planning on leaving you at the altar. What kind of man do you think I am?" I glance at the bag on her desk, interested to know what she's brought for breakfast and lunch and wondering if it's more questionable fruit drinks.

She watches my eyes wander and pulls the bag toward herself protectively.

"Look, I already told you. You're the one who got away. The one I always compared everyone else to. The fantasy. And when I saw you again…I was outmatched. Couldn't control how I felt about you."

One hundred percent true.

Her gaze softens, voice quieter. "Yeah, okay."

"Too much?"

"No. I think it's…it's good."

"Right? I'm reckless. People will believe that in a heartbeat," I venture.

"But I'm not reckless. People won't buy that at all."

"No? You made up a fiancé."

"That's impulsive, not reckless."

"Same thing. Besides, people don't know you well yet. They don't know you're uptight and rigid and bound by rules."

"Hey."

"Isn't that what you just said?"

"Not even close."

"Okay. You're not rigid."

"I'm not. I'm very chill." She folds her arms across her chest, schools her expression, and looks about as not-chill as a person could be.

"You might need to work on your chill."

She rolls her eyes. "Great."

I see the wheels turning in her head as her eyes dart around, so I nip her other preconception in the bud. "And as to your other concern about my reputation, I haven't 'cheated on you.' There are no jersey chasers in my life. Haven't been for a while."

"Any since we've been together?" She's so serious I almost have to check myself to make sure this is all a fabrication.

"No. Not for years, actually. And I'm sorry for my behavior in the past if you think it reflects badly on you."

Jordan doesn't answer immediately. She hits a few keys on her computer until some low volume hip-hop music rumbles out of her computer speakers. I feel like I'm in the middle of a real argument with a real girlfriend. And I want her to forgive me for real. Which is nuts.

"Jordan."

She startles and looks at me. I'm dying to know what's going on in her head, but her grip on all of this seems tenuous, so I don't want to push her.

"What will you say to Reilly when he asks why you didn't tell him I'm your fiancé?"

She answers quickly, as though she's already thought this part through. "That's easy. I'll just say I was trying to keep my work life and personal life separate because I'm a professional. That will speak to his whole thing about wanting a woman in the office who's here to work."

I eye the bag on her desk again, wondering why she isn't eating whatever's inside it. My mind drifts to the possible contents. Looks like a brown bag lunch, but that might be wishful thinking for someone carrying around a rotten smoothie at six at night. Whatever, it's probably a crustless cucumber finger sandwich or a lone plum.

"Great. So…it's official, then. We're engaged." With a flourish worthy of royals, I hold out my hand for the ring, which she places in my palm.

As her fingers graze the skin, I feel an electrical storm that shouldn't surprise me at this point. But it does. Because I'm in denial about what this woman does to me and what it could mean.

When I slip the ring on her finger, there it is again. The brush of skin. The nerves on fire. This is a different kind of twinge deep inside me. Something that feels very un-fake. I swallow back the tremor in my jaw.

"So when's the wedding?" she asks. So innocently that I doubt she felt anything resembling what I did. Maybe she had those feelings once—when we were kids—but I put a stop to that straightaway. Serves me right that I only got one chance when I handled it so poorly.

I shrug. "We haven't planned it yet. We'd like to enjoy being engaged for now."

"And are we planning on moving in together?"

"Nope, not until after the wedding. You're traditional like that."

She bites her bottom lip and fights a smile. "I am traditional like that. Do you have an answer for everything?"

"Not everything. But when I don't, I make something up."

"Good to know." She opens the bag on her desk and, takes out a donut hole covered in rainbow sprinkles, then offers the bag to me. "Want one?"

"Donut holes? I would not have pegged you for a donut girl. Fat-free, sugar-free granola, some kale, maybe, but not donuts."

I take the bag and glance inside to find a half dozen or so donut holes, a few with sprinkles, others with different toppings. I extract one covered in powdered sugar and coconut and pop it into my mouth. Her face falls. "What?" I ask through the donut bite.

"Just…that one was my favorite."

I stop chewing and debate what to do. It's not like I can spit it out and hand it back to her, so I swallow the thing whole. "I'm sorry. I didn't—"

And now she's laughing her ass off. "Gotcha." Her smug smile tempts me in new ways while reminding me why she irritates me.

"Nice."

She hands me a napkin from a pile I didn't notice on her desk and points to the sugar on my lips. "Serves you right for the kale comment. Sorry if these put a kink in your straight-laced perception of me."

I can't help waggling an eyebrow. "See, you say we don't know each other anymore, and then you start talking about kink. Just proves we're…" I make a V with my fingers and motion between our eyes. She rolls hers and starts gathering papers.

"Okay, footie player. We're done here. I have a meeting.

Thank you for the ring, and I'll see you and your swagger bright and early in the medical suite on Friday." She looks down and pretends to focus on what she's typing, but I can see her smile.

It's all I need to keep showing up in her office with all my swagger.

im

ON DAYS LIKE TODAY, San Francisco reminds me of home. It's the chilly, foggy weather that eases in with little innocuous whisps that turn into larger sheets and eventually become a cloud blanket. But it happens so subtly that it feels like one minute there's sun, the next dank cold.

I never mind the weather here, maybe because it lets me fool myself into thinking I'm not an entire continent away from my family. I miss my sisters. Don't miss my dad. Can't waste emotions on a man who thinks I'm a failure for not being just like him.

But the early morning sheet of fog and my nostalgia pushes me to ring my sisters, who are roommates back in Saltney, our hometown. They run a pub in nearby Chester. "So you've gotten yourself in a bit of a pickle," Linnie laughs after I recount my fake engagement and worries about the medical exam. "Not particularly surprising."

"Dunno why I called you two. I expected support." I switch our call over to Facetime so I can see them both. Two sassy blondes who look more like the pictures of our mum each time I see them. Linnie is the older one, twenty-eight going on fifteen. She'd rather be hanging off the back of her boyfriend's motorcycle and living on Cadbury Flake than cooking meat pies for the pub and waking up at a reasonable hour.

"Not gonna find it here," Mary pipes in. Spitfire, that one. Bossier than her sister and fiercely intelligent—reminds me a bit of Jordan. She's been dating the same bloke for five years now, the one who owns the pub where they work, but there's no mistaking that she's the one running the place, from the business side to the decor. She loves big and hates bigger if someone wrongs any one of us. "Not when you're living like royalty, and we've got to listen to Dad harp on how you've abandoned us."

She isn't saying it to make me feel guilty. And I'm not about to change up my life to make my dad stop harping. It's just the family dynamic. We all know it like we know it will rain in November.

"Yeah, that's an old song," I gripe.

"Keeps threatening to sell the shop, you know," Linnie says. "Telling us he just wants to clock in as a mechanic and leave before dark to join us at the pub." Same old tune.

"You think he's bloody serious this time, then?" My accent gets stronger when I talk to my sisters.

"Doubt it. You know him. He'll run the place till he runs himself into the grave." Her voice has a lilt of humor, but I worry. Even if he doesn't want me as a son, I can't stand the idea of him working himself to the bone. Guilt settles in like the persistent fog.

"He still call me his biggest disappointment?" My laugh is meant to cover how much it still hurts that he thinks of me that way.

"Oh, he doesn't either. Stop it." Linnie gamely plays her role, giving me a moment's relief from the reality that I let him down.

For an average student from a working-class family, my future was spelled out by my father and his father before him. Unless I had a really convincing reason to turn my back on a guaranteed decent wage, I was expected to stay local, work in the auto shop that had been in the family for four decades.

With two sisters he hoped to marry off, my dad turned to me to take over the business. "Your soccer chops don't mean you know how to fix an engine." He wanted me to give up on practicing and apprentice with him.

The day I told him no was the day he basically disowned me. Warned me I'd always be a disappointment, told me to move out of the house, even though I was a few months shy of eighteen. That was how I ended up in the States as a foreign exchange student senior year.

And now I hardly ever go back.

"I can't have this conversation over the phone, Timmy. Come for a visit and we'll talk it through." Mary bats her lashes hopefully.

The conversation goes on like that for a while, each of them taking loving digs at me while complaining I haven't visited, but I'm coming up woefully short on the advice I sought on how to keep my undeniable attraction to Jordan from derailing my soccer season.

"Either of you want to tell me how to thread this needle?" I ask, trying to get them back on track.

"You're worried you'll cave and let her put you on the injured list just because you want to bang her? Never been a problem with the soccer bunnies before," Linnie points out.

"Yes, but it's Danny. Or whatever she goes by now. Saying no to her once had him wallowing in the basement for months. I get that," Mary says.

"Great. So what do I do? Avoiding her was the initial hot take, but now that she's my fiancée, it's not an option, really." I scrub a hand over my face, still in disbelief that I'm basically right back where I was at eighteen.

"The option is you man up and stop acting like a twat. Full stop. You're a professional athlete, not a contestant on *Love Island*." Mary narrows her eyes at me like she might reach out and throat punch me through the phone line. So I nod and agree she's right.

They leave me with those words of wisdom and make me promise to visit.

"All depends on what I need to do in the off-season to rehab. But I'll make something work." I don't like that I haven't seen them for over two years. I should do better.

So I wrap up the call and make a promise I swear I'll keep this time.

TWO HOURS LATER, I stand in the exam room, trying not to notice that Jordan has ditched the lawyer-y skirt for a pair of black pants. Even though they still look a bit corporate, they highlight her ass in a way that has me acting again like a twat, thinking about how much I'd like to take a bite out of each ripe cheek.

I want our old sports medicine guy back.

"I'm here," I grumble, standing just outside the room.

"Good morning to you too," Jordan says without looking up from whatever she's reading. I lean on the doorjamb and watch her, marveling at the feisty tendrils of red that have already come loose from the pile of hair she's knotted on top of her head. The scent of gardenia wafts through the room, and I inhale it like a balm.

The loose strands dangle over her temples, and my fingers itch to tuck them behind her ears. Not because I crave order but because, despite my better instincts, I crave her.

Twat.

It's going to get me into far more trouble than a busted ligament.

When I get close enough for a glimpse at her reading material, I see that it's my medical chart on top of messy papers. "Don't bother with that." I try to swipe it but she holds it tight.

"Because everything in here is bullshit?"

If I flinch, it's not because she swears; it's because she wastes no time in getting to the point.

She directs me to the exam table. When I make no move to hop up on the grey cushion, she tilts her head, looks meaningfully at me, and crosses her arms. It's then that I notice the healthy tan on her arms, which are folded just beneath her ripe breasts, pushing them up.

"What do you do outside?" I ask because I'm game to talk about anything except my injuries.

"I'm sorry?" She closes the folder.

I flick a hand toward her. "You're not pale like you spend every waking hour in your office, so you must do something outside."

Her lips quirk up slightly in amusement. "I have a bike."

"A bike?"

"Yes."

I wait for her to explain as though I don't know what a bike is. When she doesn't, I search for some other way to talk about her. "Is that the only—"

She cuts me off. "Tim."

"Yes?"

"Were you told that a collateral ligament sprain normally heals in ten to fourteen days if it's managed the right way?"

"Ugh. You're so...persistent." I spit out the words. She smiles as though it's a compliment. "Yes, but that wasn't an option, so what difference does it make?"

"And now you're hurting worse. The weakness in your knee is

making you favor it, and now you have small muscle tears in your calf and a strain in your hip flexor."

Her assessment knocks the breath out of me momentarily. Because she's right. And she hasn't examined a damn thing. "How do you know that?"

"I've been watching you."

Even though I can't stand that she noticed things I thought I was hiding, I can't help the small uptick in my heartbeat at the thought of her watching me. Doesn't mean I trust her, though.

"I've been working hard during training, harder than I did before. That's probably why I look like I'm lagging," I lie. "No way Steiner deserves to start over me. He doesn't have the skills."

"You don't like him," she observes.

"He's not fast enough or versatile enough for my position."

"Your position."

"Yes. We have a clean sheet for the latter half of this season, no goals scored on us. That's not the sign of a player who should be on the injured list. With proper pain management, I'm fit to play."

"Ha."

I stare at her. I can't believe she had the nerve to dump a fake laugh on me. "What's that, now?"

She moves the chart aside, revealing a notebook which she consults. "How come your launch speed has decreased by a half a second over two months while you've managed your pain? How come your loss of sprint speed has resulted in seventeen losses of possession in games you played since your injury? In several cases, giving up the ball to the other team nearly resulted directly in a goal against. You're favoring your right side, and now your left side is out of alignment, so your kick has lost accuracy. Your teammates have covered because they have the speed to pivot, but they shouldn't have to wait for the ball to leave your foot to know where it's going. And you think Steiner is slow? Right now, you're slower."

She flips through the notebook, revealing pages and pages of stats she's compiled on my game, including photos where she's circled body parts and marked them with red arrows.

"May I?" I gesture to the notebook, and she hands it over. I glance through the sheets—dozens of pages. Thorough diagrams and assessments of me in game after game. She didn't just come in her spouting medical jargon. She did her homework, and it pains me to acknowledge it. Almost as much as it pains me to get out of bed in the morning because of my knee and the cascading list of other ailments.

"We had a deal, Tim—a full exam. Let me do my job. I'm good at it. The last guy may have pumped you full of pain meds, but I have a few better tricks up my sleeve. Please trust that I'm on your side here."

I know when I'm backed into a corner. Coach expects clearance from her before the next game if I'm going to play. Even if I can't fully trust her, I don't see too many other options.

"What kind of tricks?" I ask, willing to give only an inch of ground.

She points to the exam table. "Sit."

"Fine. I swing a leg over. Then the next. Haven't felt this defeated since our team lost the championship in penalty kicks seven years ago.

I flinch when her hands wrap around my knee. I wasn't expecting the warmth of her fingers. Or my reaction to her touch. I swallow hard, trying not to let my mind wander to other places I'd like her to touch me.

Her grip is firm, and she rubs the ligaments surrounding my knee with her thumbs. "See, there's swelling. Did you take anti-inflammatories this morning?"

"Yes. A thousand milligrams."

"Your body isn't responding. Right after an injury, the pain receptors tell your body to send what are basically healing agents to the injury. When you ignore it, and it becomes chronic pain, the receptors start to ignore the signals. So even with the meds, you may be getting some pain relief, but the inflammation won't budge."

"Not that much pain relief," I grumble, relaxing despite myself because her prodding has eased into more of a massage. The feel of her fingers kneading my flesh has my eyes drifting shut.

When she presses against the pouch of fluid surrounding the sprained ligament, I suck in a gasp. "Tender," she says.

"Just a bit."

Nodding, she reaches down to an instrument tray and extracts a metal object that looks like a shoehorn.

"Lean back," she instructs. When I do so, she uses the flat metal to knead into my quads. Initially, it feels great. "This is going to help you."

"I've had massage therapy before. Doesn't work. Not that I'm complaining at all if you want to keep doing it."

That's when the soft rubbing turns to an aching grind of metal against muscle. I nearly jump off the table. "Try to relax," she says, continuing to dig the metal into my muscles, fanning outward until she gets to my iliotibial band, which is ungodly tight. The sound I make is somewhere between a grunt and a blood-curdling yelp.

"Are you kidding me?" I bite out, trying not to writhe on the table like a half-slaughtered lamb.

"Breathe," she says.

Not like that's possible. I suck in ragged breaths as she rakes over the muscles with the hard metal. "It's hard to imagine you're not injuring me more," I rasp.

"Remember what I said about trusting me?"

"This isn't helping with that." I give up on dignity and throw an arm over my eyes. The pressure she's exerting is nearly unbearable. Maybe the point is to hurt my quad so badly that I forget all about my injured knee. "Fuuuck," I hiss out, wishing I was cursing for an entirely different reason—because she's underneath me and in the throes of an orgasm. That image is the only thing that's keeping me from launching myself off the table and away from this hell.

After another moment of brutal muscle beating, she stops. I feel like the survivor of a category six hurricane who lives to see another day of pleasant rain. Hesitantly, I remove my arm from over my eyes, glancing at her to make sure she isn't removing a chainsaw from its case.

I wouldn't be shocked.

"What the hell was that, love?" I'm still panting a bit.

Her eyes survey me from head to toe, observing me relaxing my shoulders. And my jaw. Then I see the hint of a smile.

The sadist.

"That," she says, "is how we get your body to start responding to the injury in the right way. I just woke it the hell up. And loosened up all the muscles and tendons that have been gripping, trying to correct the problem."

"I'll say you did. You also took a couple years off my life."

"Come on, footie player. It didn't hurt that much."

I realize I sound like a baby, but she's wrong. It absolutely hurt that much. I'm sweating, and my legs are shaking.

Without noticing she's doing it, I find that she's moved back to my knee, gently probing it again. I much prefer her gentle touch, though my mind can't let go of the image of her dominating me in bed. Probably won't ever leave my mind.

"Why don't you get up and see if you feel any looser."

For a moment, I'm not sure I can get up because she's just pulverized me. Not sure I want to get up if it means she'll stop massaging my knee.

Maybe she senses that because she stops. I move off the table, ready for the fresh hell that I'm about to feel.

But...I don't.

"Holy shit." I take a few tentative steps around the room like a colt testing its legs. I'm expecting my quads to give out after what she just put them through, but they hold up just fine. In fact, they feel more warmed up than after an hour of stretching.

Shock of all shocks, my knee feels…better.

"It feels—"

"Any better?"

"Yeah. Quite."

She nods, studying each step I take from several angles. Not smug like I'd expect after working real magic. "We're going to do this every day. Try to roll back the tension from everywhere else, so it stops pulling on your knee. I know it seems counterintuitive, but your body is trying to help itself, and instead, it's got you so locked up that you're doing more damage."

"My body doesn't know what the hell it's doing if it's supposed to be digging into my quads with a knife."

She laughs. "It's not a knife." She moves to the door and signals me to follow. "Come. Let's get some images of your knee, see how bad it is."

I follow willingly, still awed that each step feels better than I've been in a long time. And excited that she's just committed to putting her hands on me every day.

"Your sprain has progressed to a tear. A bad one."

My eyes close when I hear her voice behind me in the locker room. I'm the last one in here, as usual. I always wait for my teammates to leave so I can shower and change at my own pace, which is getting slower and slower, the more my leg aches from the grueling training days.

"Okay, well, the stuff you did earlier seemed to help, so we're good." I whip the shirt off over my head. Her eyes move to my chest, where they linger for a long moment.

She takes in every inch of visible skin, and I feel gratified that at least my appreciation of her form isn't one-sided.

Visibly shaking herself out of a trance, she forces herself to look at my face. "You could rupture the ligament. Then you'll need surgery and a six-to-nine-month recovery," she rasps, sounding a little choked.

Almost despite herself, she sneaks one more look downward, and I see her take in my abs, which clench under the heat of her stare.

"Um…" She stammers, and I can't help the smug smile that tugs at the corner of my mouth.

Proficient doctor unnerved by naked chest. Check.

"Yes?" I should grab a towel and head to the showers before she can wrack her brain for more syllables, but it makes me so damn happy to watch her jaw go slack.

She blinks and composes herself, and I make a move to drop my shorts.

Holding up a hand, she tries to control the quiver in her voice. "Hang on. Just…give me a second. Please." She swallows hard. "I'd just like to talk through some treatment options."

Crossing my arms across my chest, I shake my head. "We can talk tomorrow when I come for my rubdown."

"I'm not your massage therapist."

"That's what you say." I drop my pants.

Granted, I'm wearing tight boxer briefs underneath, but they don't leave much to the imagination.

Again, Jordan is left fumbling over her words. "Um… Stop. Doing. That."

"Doing what?" I ask innocently. Then I grab a towel, drop my briefs, and walk off toward the showers. I know her eyes are glued to my naked ass. I can feel it.

"Tim." The stern tone of her voice stops me. I wrap the towel around my waist and turn, knowing I'm going to regret it. Her eyes plead with me, and it loosens my resolve to act like an arse. Dammit.

"This is my job." There's something plaintive in her voice this time, not enough to make me change my mind about what I'm asking, but it does make me take a moment and think. I've been so caught up in gaming out the rest of my season and conjuring ways to get her to leave my game alone that I haven't really given much thought to her side of things.

This *is* her job. And she's new here. I get that she doesn't want to start things off by bending her ethics to suit my needs. But I don't have a choice.

"I get that. And this is *my* job. We both have a lot on the line here."

She nods. "I know."

"I want to help you, okay? But you have to stop doing the extra training. I'll clear you to play as long as you do exactly what I tell you to do, and nothing else. I'll be watching you like a hawk, monitoring that tear and the collateral damage to the rest of your body. If it starts to go downhill, I'll—"

"I get it," I snap. She closes her eyes and swallows hard, and I can see what it costs her to have me question her at every turn. She doesn't deserve that. I let out the air I've been holding captive in my lungs. "Sorry. Truly. I'll listen to you. Done."

"I know you don't want to, but…" It's her turn for a long exhale. Her frown pulls her entire face down.

"Jordan, really. Thank you."

She bites down on her lip, nodding. "Yeah. Okay." Her eyes turn a bit glassy, and she looks me over again from head to toe before swallowing hard and shaking herself out of it. "Anyhow, I'll see you tomorrow."

"Yup." I fucking can't wait.

ordan

A WEEK after Tim told the team about our engagement, he reported back that they were pretty much done giving him "a world of shit" for hiding his relationship, and he felt confident everyone believed the story. A few of the players congratulated me on our engagement when they came in for their medical evaluations, and even Reilly seems happy to know that "we're keeping it in the Strikers family."

Tim said he really played up the unrequited love from our high school days and the fire that ignited the moment we saw each other again.

It's not a bad story. I almost want to believe it.

Yeah, it's becoming a problem. Every day when Tim comes in for his physical therapy, I feel excited for all the wrong reasons. I like putting my hands on him. I like the grumbly sounds he makes in protest when it hurts, and the relieved exhales when he feels the tightness give way.

I like him.

Just the way I did when I was sixteen and ready to give him everything.

Then I remind myself of the mess I'm already in with the lies we're telling and the reality that I'm helping him hide a serious injury. That's when I question my sanity, and the lust goes skittering away.

It's evening, and I'm dying to go home, take off the navy platform heels Sofia had shipped from a designer I've never heard of, and climb into a tub full of suds. I want to forget I'm headed back here tomorrow to do it all over again.

But a bunch of lab work just landed on my desk, and I need to check the results. It's the full blood workup on each player, so I can look for electrolyte deficiencies that give clues to other things going on with their health. It's a goldmine for diagnosing issues before they become problems, and I've been waiting for these pages to land on my desk. It could be a late night.

I rummage through the executive kitchen because it has the best coffee. I heard Charlie sources it from a local company, and it's much better than the stuff the physical therapists drink, which smells like a burnt rubber tire and tastes worse.

And the bonus in drinking my coffee here is the healthy pour of real half and half from the mini-fridge. My cholesterol-watching grocery list never includes half and half, but if someone else buys it, I'm pretty sure it doesn't count.

When I return to the medical suite, I find it's not empty.

And Jordy Steiner isn't on my schedule.

I didn't lock the door when I went on my coffee errand, but I did pull my door closed out of habit. Evidently, he opened it and walked right in.

"Hey, Steiner." He doesn't move from where he's standing to the side of my desk, so I nearly rub against him to get to my chair. I catch a whiff of what smells like grain alcohol, which is strange an hour after training. I wonder if he started drinking a lot earlier.

He still doesn't move, and I take a quick look around my office to see what he sees.

The usual mess of files and papers litters my desk. For once, I'm grateful for my poor organization system because it's virtually impossible for someone snooping around to see what's what.

But from the way Steiner's eyes bore into the mess, I get the feeling he made sense of something. When he looks up at me, it's with a satisfied grin. He crosses his arms over his chest and leans against the wall next to my desk, still crowding my space with his large frame. He's taller than Tim but more wiry. More like a rubber band waiting to hurt someone with its snap.

I can't overthink it because Steiner pushes the door partly closed and starts talking. "So I hear congratulations are in order."

"You mean the engagement? Thanks." I sit at my desk and put my coffee down, noticing the ring on my finger. The stone suddenly looks very large and very fake. I wonder if he thinks so too.

"Yeah, that."

I roll my chair back as far as it will go to create some distance. The way he's hulking over my desk feels menacing, so I motion to the chair on the opposite side. "Have a seat, Steiner. Or are you just here to congratulate me?"

"Nope, I wanna talk."

When he moves toward the chairs, he lurches to the side. Yup, he's drunk. Plastered. It's alarming because he's a big guy, and he seems a little erratic in his movements. I need him to sit.

He glances from one chair to the other, then back toward me, as though one chair might have a strategic advantage. Choosing the one on the left, he drops into the seat and slumps forward, elbows on his knees.

"So…" he slurs. "You're engaged. To Chelty. You're engaged to

Chelty, and you're responsible for his medical clearance. That's a conflict of interest." For a drunk guy, he's making sense.

Of course, I've thought of this. "There are plenty of people on the medical staff who can evaluate Tim."

"So you're saying you don't sign off on his fitness to play?"

"I do. But we work as a team." An unwelcome sheen of sweat forms on my brow, but Steiner isn't really looking at me. He's right, though—a lot of doctors won't treat family members. How would they feel if they missed a crucial diagnosis? But there are just as many who will even perform surgery on relatives.

"So you're saying he should be in the starting lineup even with his bum leg, and that has nothing to do with you treating him special?"

"I can't comment on a team member's health, but my personal and professional life are completely separate."

"Not how it looks to me. I see blatant favoritism. Ethical violation. The guy should be on the injured list, and I should be starting."

"Now, who has a conflict of interest?"

"I want what's best for the team."

"Not your decision, obviously."

"Is it yours?"

He leans his elbows on the desk and cracks each knuckle on his left hand. Then his right. Like he's getting ready to crack my neck next. His eyes go flinty. I don't trust him, and yet a part of me feels self-righteous because I haven't done anything wrong. Yes, I'm giving Tim clearance, but I'm monitoring his every move. He's under my care, and he should still be playing.

Would you say that if he hadn't rescued you with the fake engagement? Would you say that if you didn't feel all the lust?

Not prepared to defend myself against Steiner *and* myself, I start gathering my papers and piles and moving them to the floor by my feet. Then I shut my laptop and start getting ready to leave. I can read the bloodwork results at home.

"Steiner, this is super fun, but I need to get home, and I think you ought to do the same."

He doesn't move until I get up, and then he stands directly in front of me. "Sure, *Doctor* Page. Just tell me to my face that you're not letting Tim fuck his way to medical clearance."

"I'm. Not." I overpronounce the T. Hopefully, I spit on him a little in the process.

"Says the team doctor without ethics."

Again with the ethics. I've worked my whole career to get this job, and no one has ever questioned my ethics. I know I'm just tired, and I shouldn't let him get to me. But dammit if anyone accuses me of not being ethical.

So I blurt, "It's fake. We're not a couple."

And I immediately regret it.

A slow smile spreads on Steiner's face. "Seriously?" He laughs. "I'm not even gonna ask what's in it for him because that's obvious, but is sex with Chelty really that good that you're willing to lie about his health and pretend to be his girlfriend?"

"It's not like that. It's nothing. Forget I said anything."

The words aren't out of my mouth before a pile of vomit comes flying out of Steiner's. He's close enough to my trash can that most of it lands, but if I didn't want him out of my office before, I really do now.

"Sorry. Coach worked us hard today."

"Uh-huh." Training to the point of throwing up is old news on soccer teams, but I know that's not what's happening here. And yet, I took an oath to do no harm. I twist off the top of my water bottle and hand it to him.

He reaches out a shaky hand for it and slurps some down. Then wipes his mouth with the back of his hand.

"You going to be okay?" I ask.

He nods again, slower this time. His eyes are bleary, and a part of me wants to help him since he's clearly in a bad way. I debate calling Tim, but I decide against it when Reggie, my lab tech, leans through my office door. "Doctor Page, did you get all the results?"

My eyes light up with relief. I nod at him meaningfully and shift my eyes toward Steiner. "I did, Reggie. Thank you. Are you heading home now?"

He looks from Steiner to me. From where he stands, he can only see the back of Steiner's head, but my office smells like a bar bathroom. He looks around for the source and sees the trash can. "Yeah. You still need me?"

"No, but I think Steiner could use a ride home. What do you say, Steiner? You need a trip to the bathroom first?"

He grunts something unintelligible and looks at his lap. I gesture to Reggie with my thumb and pinky that Steiner has done some drinking, and he nods.

"Sure. Steiner, can I drive you someplace? Call you an Uber?"

Without a word, Steiner pushes himself up from the chair, wobbles to the side, and moves toward the doorway. Reggie catches him before he falls over and escorts him out the door, picking up the trash can and handing it to Steiner. "Here, you carry this."

"Thanks, Reg. I owe you big," I call after him, vowing to buy him a dozen donuts in the morning.

And then I need to tell Tim that I just screwed everything up. Steiner may be drunk, but I've just handed him a grenade.

Tomorrow. I'll tell Tim tomorrow.

And maybe he can help me figure out how to deal with Steiner before the team event. Which is in one week.

ordan

I DON'T END up telling Tim about Jordy Steiner's visit to the clinic and my regrettable mistake. I intend to do it, but Tim texts that he's in a meeting with Coach Jaynes and will need to skip our session.

I'm distracted, worrying that he could get hurt if he doesn't loosen his muscles enough, when Steiner comes by my office. "Hey."

"Hi. You doing okay today?"

He nods. "I'm sorry about all that. It wasn't my best look."

"Yeah, no."

"I understand if you need to say something to Coach, but if you don't feel you must…I'd really love it if we could just forget it happened. All of it." He seems contrite, and I actually feel a little bit bad for him. I'm sure it's stressful trying to work his way to a starting spot. Maybe it just got to him.

I'm still new, and I don't need enemies, so I figure I can let it go. This time. "Yeah, okay."

"Appreciate it. So…we're good?"

"Sure, Jordy. We're good."

He gives me a salute on his way out the door.

I should still tell Tim. And I will. But I don't want to rattle him more than he already is about Jordy.

Besides, Tim has nothing to lose if the truth comes out about our fake engagement. The only one at risk is me.

With that in mind, and with no players scheduled for physicals for the rest of the day, I decide to work on the other issue plaguing my mind—what the heck I'm going to wear to the team event on Friday night.

I text Sofia frantically on my way to my car.

Me: Fashion emergency. Are you home?

Sofia: Just got home. What's the emergency?

Me: Need something to wear to a work party.

Sofia: [laughing emoji] Work party? Wow, living on the edge.

My thumbs go into hyperdrive, madly typing before I lose bars, which only seems to happen when I'm in dire straits. I don't have time for her to make fun of my lack of a social life. I need to know if she can help me find something to wear.

Me: Forget that. Can you help? Can I come over?

I watch for bouncing dots. My eyes bore into the screen, willing a speech bubble to appear, telling me Sofia will come to my rescue. The memo from the team's social director was specific. "Festive dress."

At the same time, completely unspecific.

I have no idea what festive dress looks like, and the last thing I need is to show up wearing Strikers gear when everyone else comes in cocktail attire.

Tim, ever unhelpful, told me to "wear a little black dress," which I don't own. "Oh, and wear your hair down," he said as an afterthought. I can vaguely picture myself in said dress with too-high heels, tottering around until I face plant. Hence the panic, hence the emergency run to whichever chic San Francisco shop will help me.

Finally, bouncing dots. But before a message comes through, my phone battery chooses that moment to drain its last bit of juice.

By the time it springs back to life on the charger, I have a dozen messages from Sofia.

Sofia: Sure. Now?

Sofia: Jordan???

Sofia: Oh, come on. Don't be offended because I made fun of your social life.

Sofia: Okay, fine. Don't answer.

Sofia: Where'd you go?

Sofia: Are you on your way? Not texting while driving? Yay!

She instructs me to come straight to her house.

Sofia: I have snacks.

Her final text heartens me slightly. Maybe this errand requires snacks. Or Xanax. I feel sweaty and it's a breezy sixty-degree day. It's not just the idea of a black dress I don't own that has me worked up. It's the idea of wearing it with Tim and acting like a couple in a room full of people. Work people. And athletes.

Face-planting might be a blessing.

There's also the small part of me who's still the sixteen-year-old girl who Tim hurt when he turned her away. She wants to look amazing. She wants Tim to see her differently, even if it's just for one night.

"I need a dress!" I reiterate when I get to Sofia's apartment in the Marina. I've barely tumbled through her front door when she calmly hands me a glass and an open bottle of pinot grigio and ushers me over to a purple velvet window seat that overlooks the water.

Like a game show host, she gestures to the view. As I said, Buckingham Pals is a thriving business, and her gorgeous two-bedroom apartment with a sweeping view of the Bay Bridge and the water is her reward. Normally, I can sit in this perch for hours and let the lofty view carry me away.

Today, even the sun-dappled blue can't pull me from my frantic mood.

"Drink," she instructs. I take a sip. "Finish it."

It takes me a few longer-than-normal sips, but I manage to swig the entire glass in under a minute. "I need a dress," I say weakly, already feeling the effects of the alcohol and a wave of exhaustion from my mental anguish. Again, I'm vaguely aware that my job has upped my drinking by a thousand percent, and I can't even worry about it. Sofia refills my glass halfway.

"I know, honey. Why are you so worked up? You wear skirts every day to work."

"Because…because I want the guy who turned me down in high school to find me irresistible. I know it's dumb. I know I'm—"

"A freakin' goddess. A gorgeous, amazing, smart woman who should definitely be seen that way." She pours herself a glass of wine and raises it toward mine for a toast. "Ooh, we're doing a makeover. This is going to be so fun."

Grabbing her phone, she's snapping pictures before I can form the words, "Stop. No pictures!"

"Come on. We need a before and after."

"Why?"

"For evidence. No one would believe a butterfly was once a caterpillar without photo proof."

"That makes no sense. They'd believe it because they'd watch it build a cocoon and hatch."

"Whatever. I already got the picture. Stop arguing."

"Just please don't post them anywhere."

"Fine. These are just for us."

She swigs more of her wine and looks me up and down. Then her eyes grow large and round, her dark irises looking like chocolate donuts as she taps her lip with a finger. "How bold are you feeling?"

"Not bold at all. I just need to fly under the radar, so I don't embarrass myself by wearing the wrong thing. Preferably something that isn't see-through if drinks spill on me."

She shrugs and walks across the pale parquet floor, signaling for me to follow toward her bedroom. "Come along, Cinderella. Let's find you a dress your fiancé won't be able to resist."

"I thought we were shopping. And he's not my fiancé."

Her voice echoes down the hall. "I know, but it's hard not to give you shit for this tangent of crazy when you're so practical all the time."

"Great," I mutter to myself. Tottering in my brown leather wedge heels, I inhale a fortifying breath. There's no way I'm going to make it for an entire night in higher heels without a guard rail, but dammit, I'm determined to try.

She only walked into the room a minute ahead of me, but somehow she's already managed to retrieve seven dresses, which she has lined up on the fluffy white comforter on her king-sized bed.

Sunlight blasts through the paned windows, coloring the dresses in a shiny, fairy godmother glow. Sofia points to a peach-colored settee at the end of her bed, so I sit.

After rustling around for another minute in her closet, which would be a third bedroom or office for anyone who didn't love clothes as much as her, she pulls out several shoeboxes.

"I can't believe you keep your shoes in boxes. How do you remember what's in them?" My question is answered when Sofia points the end of one box in my direction, showing me a taped-on Polaroid photo of the shoes inside. "Of course."

"Anything else is amateur hour."

Sofia may be miles ahead of me when it comes to fashion

savvy, and she may be the first one to knock my orthopedic shoes, but she's exactly the kind of stellar best friend who I trust with my life. Especially the fashion-related part.

Placing a shoebox next to each dress, Sofia signals for me to get up from the settee, where she perches like Anna Wintour getting ready to watch Chanel models on a runway. Only I'm no model.

Clumsily, I pull my jeans off, leaving on the comfy sports bra and my granny panties until Sofia shakes her head. "No. Nope."

She leans toward a distressed white dresser and pulls open a drawer, withdrawing some sort of strapless Spanx thing with bra cups and handing it to me.

Rolling my eyes, I take off the bra, feeling self-conscious when my breasts bounce free. I pull on the stretchy contouring garment and warn her, "Not taking off the underwear."

She puts a hand over her eyes. "I'm going to pretend I don't see those. Just…get yourself a thong before the night of the event, please. And a bra that matches."

"Seriously? No one will know."

"Stop it. I will know." Her smile turns wicked. "And if we do it right, so will Tim."

"Fine. I'll pick something up." I lift the first black dress from the bed, noting its light weight, before I slip it over my head. The slinky silk feels comfy, and it hugs my curves. The full-length mirror on a stand in the corner tilts backward slightly, making me look about a foot taller. "This one's good. I can even wear flat shoes with it since it's pretty long. No one will—"

She stops me with a shake of her head. "Tim is tall. You need tall shoes."

I feel the blood drain as she gestures to the row of boxes which might as well contain stilts for as well as I'll be able to walk in them.

Sofia puts her wineglass on a coaster sitting on the bedside table—I swear, the woman thinks of everything. Before I know what's happened, Sofia lifts the black dress over my head and tosses it on the bed.

"Not this one. Nope. I hate that for you."

I pull the next one off the hanger and struggle into it. It's shorter and tighter, and I find myself pulling on the hem as I look in the mirror. My legs look miles long at this angle, but between the short length and the sleeveless top, I feel too exposed. "I don't think so."

Sofia *tsks*. "Not if you're going to pull on it all night like that. No, no. I want you in a 'put it on and forget about it' dress. I want it to be fabulous and make you feel confident and great."

"Is it a magic dress, this garment of which you speak?"

"Why are you like this? Clothes are fun. This should be fun."

"Ugh, I don't know. I guess it feels like I'm trying to be someone I'm not."

She holds up a finger. "No. You're still you. You're just wearing something that makes you feel better about being you. Something glamorous and sultry and eye-popping. You're awesome. Quit trying to hide it behind boring clothes. It's like you're apologizing for being smart and beautiful by dressing down, so other people don't feel bad by comparison. Stop it. Wear an awesome dress. Be your awesome self."

Put that way, I have to admit she's not wrong. I started wearing my go-to safe wardrobe right around the time my mother started pestering me about finding a husband—in other words, the day I graduated from med school.

She beckons to the dress. "Take that off. I don't like it."

While I wrestle out of the tight little thing, she dives into her closet. She emerges a moment later holding a short red dress with a skirt that swishes when she shakes the hanger. My eyes go to the plunging neckline, and I shake my head. "Are you kidding me with that?"

"You're a redhead. Redheads look amazing in red. It's a missed opportunity if you don't wear this."

"I was told to wear a little black dress. This isn't black."

"Nope. It's not."

"It's red."

"Yup. Little and black is just a metaphor for a sexy dress."

I huff a laugh. "Um, no. I just need a black dress that's passable. I don't want to go overboard."

"Why not?"

I sigh and look away. I know exactly why not, and I have a feeling she does too. "Because if I make this big effort and Tim ignores me, I think I'll feel worse."

She picks up my wineglass, places it in my hands, and talks to me like I'm in preschool and don't understand the bathroom rules. "Tim told you to wear a little black dress. He wants you to wear a sexy dress," she says slowly.

"He—"

"Shut it. Just trust me. This man is hotter than sin, he's your fake fiancé, and you are going to walk into this party with him looking like you belong together. Not in a dumpy black dress that's passable." She unzips the dress, carefully takes it off the hanger, and hands it to me.

I pull the dress over my head, bracing for what I'm certain will be a good portion of my C-cup breasts hanging out, but somehow the halter top of the dress not only keeps the ladies where they belong but the undergarment creates some sexy cleavage.

The length is pretty perfect, too—a couple inches above my knees, but not so short that I feel overly exposed. And the light fabric skirt swirls around me when I move.

This is a good dress. It might even be a magic dress.

For a moment, I imagine myself walking in and catching Tim's eye from across the room. I see Tim pausing with a drink halfway to his lips, his jaw dropping because he can't believe the nerdy doctor has transformed into a real date.

Then, like a record scratch, I bring myself back to reality. Tim is never going to look at me that way. He told me so when I embarrassed myself fifteen years ago. The idea that he'd see me as anything more than a way to stay off the injured list is ludicrous.

It pains me how easily I slip right back into my sixteen-year-old persona, wanting to get the attention of Tim Cheltenham. Only now, she's thirty-one and she wants him just as much.

Get over it.

But I do like the dress. And Sofia is right. I'm wearing it for me—if Tim likes it, that's just a bonus.

"Okay," I tell Sofia. "This is the one."

She smiles and takes a pair of shoes from the box. I gape at the four-inch stiletto heels.

"We'll practice on the carpet," she says. Because she knows I'm not getting my goddess cred with the wave of a wand. But she also wants the best for me, and that includes wearing the right shoes with a badass red dress. And I kind of love her for that.

im

JORDAN'S EXCUSE for why we need to meet at the Strikers event is that she's coming from Oakland, and I live close to the stadium.

She's right, but I kind of wanted to pick her up, open doors for her. Treat it like a real date.

I'm getting tired of gritting my teeth through physical therapy sessions where Jordan has her hands all over me, then going to practice with blue balls. And every night, I'm fucking my hand in the shower thinking of her and wishing, for once, she'd put her hands where I want them.

"That's ridiculous, love. We're engaged. I would drive to Oakland and back for you," I tell her when I come by her office.

She can't stop the blush from feathering across her cheeks, and I'd say a million more cheeky, sweet things to see it over and over again. I hate that she can touch me the way she does and feel nothing.

Or, if she does feel something, as suggested by the way she

gets glassy-eyed when I take off my shirt, she's hell-bent on keeping everything professional. And feeling attraction is different from wanting to act on it. I should remember that.

But my resolve is wearing thinner by the day.

"Tim, you don't need to spend an hour-plus in traffic for show."

I almost tell her that it's not for show, that I'd make the drive because I want to be with her. But that's not part of the fake fiancé arrangement.

"We'll have all that time in the car to talk about my injuries and how idiotic I am for continuing to play. You can reprimand me all you want. I'll have nowhere to run."

"Ha. That does sound like fun, but no. It's just not practical for you to do all that driving."

This woman and her practical ideas. My filthy mind goes right to a long list of ways to wipe that practical look off her face, none of them fit for a team gathering. None of them fit for a fake relationship.

I intended to call my sisters for advice about how to do some good quality wooing, but with the eight-hour time difference, they were at work when I had a break during training, and now they're likely asleep.

So I head to the bar, where Steiner turns and smacks right into me. He's already pretty drunk, as per usual. Weston guides me away from him before it becomes a confrontation. He knows how much that guy grates on me. Everyone knows.

"Where's your woman?" Weston asks, signaling the bartender so I can order.

"On her way. She lives in Oakland. Insisted on driving herself."

"Nice of her to save you the trip."

"I never mind time in the car with her," I say, feeling guilty for letting my best mate think I'm engaged. But I'm not even sure I know what's going on myself. We're still playing our roles, obviously, but there's no question what I feel. And it's not fake.

Weston stares over my shoulder, and I see the exact moment when his expression shifts. He grins and gestures for me to look. "Enjoy, man."

I see the long, auburn hair first. She's wearing it down, and it hangs in loose waves over her shoulders. My fingers twitch like they always do because I want to touch it. I won't. At least, not in the way I need to, wrapping it around my fist while I guide her lips to mine and devour that pretty mouth.

Can't do that.

I know my role tonight—doting fake fiancé, appropriate date, displaying just enough affection to sell the lie but not over-doing it. But that's not what I want my role to be. Not even close.

Then I see the fire engine red dress. It hits every curve, offsets the golden tan of her skin, and reveals cleavage I haven't dared imagine.

Fuuuck.

Every high school fantasy wrapped around every adult fantasy of this woman comes alive at the sight of her.

I was going to behave myself, give her a peck on the cheek, and stand by her side, but she's not playing fair. Which makes me wonder if maybe she does feel a glimmer of what I do when I'm around her.

Match.

Strike.

Boom.

Without thinking, I'm like a bull charging at the waving field of red, only one thought in my head. I want my mouth on hers, and I've never been so grateful for a concocted excuse to take exactly what I want.

What I've wanted since I was eighteen and afraid of screwing up everything in my life by even imagining it.

What I've wanted since she walked into the room two months ago and turned my world upside down.

There's no denying it now, and I'm only partially aware of other people's eyes on her because it doesn't matter. They don't matter. Side characters.

She doesn't see me weaving through the crowd until I'm right in front of her. I walk past Reilly to make sure he sees.

From the dip in sound around us, I'm pretty certain everyone sees.

But I really have no fucking idea because all I see is her.

"Hello, love." The words scrape my throat like gravel. Pretty sure I've forgotten how to breathe, but I know exactly how I can be resuscitated.

Jordan's large eyes light up when she sees me. Her ruby lips part, and she levels me with a smile that seals the deal on every impulse I tried to keep at bay.

She extends her hand awkwardly, and I shake my head. No. Shaking hands is the last thing I'll accept from her.

But I grasp her hand anyway, letting her warmth radiate over my palm, making sure I give myself a moment to feel every shock wave over my skin. It's just like each one of those little touches during physical therapy—only now, we're not working, and I'll be damned if she looks at me as a patient.

Pulling her toward me, I encircle her waist with my arm and sink my fingers into her hip. The silk material of her dress is so light I can feel the heat of her flesh. I can feel the lace of her thong panties beneath my hand, and I have to stop myself from lifting the hem of her dress to feel her skin.

Her eyes go wide, questioning. She looks concerned, a little bit frightened…then a boldness sets in. The flecks of gold in her irises spark and dance. Game on.

She licks her lips, watching me, waiting to see what I plan to do, but the glassy haze that takes over her features tells me she knows, and she's ready.

"I guess…let's make this look like the real thing," she whispers.

Right.

This is no seduction as far as she's concerned. She's playing a part like we agreed to do.

Ridiculous for me to think a red dress and wearing her hair the way I like it would signify anything different. Reality is a rock on my chest, daring me to ignore it.

But I'm not one to squander an opportunity that's standing in front of me, moist lips parted, chest swelling beneath the fabric of her dress. Even if it's just for show.

Tugging her even closer, so her full breasts press lightly against my chest, I swallow back every primal urge—the need to gather her to me and carry her from the room. The need to let every animal instinct drive me forward.

I keep it sweet, kissing her lips softly in greeting, brushing them over hers once—then again and lingering to drink in her tiny sigh. She tastes like spun honey. Stifling a groan, I linger, wanting so much more than an appropriate kiss.

But I can't have it. When I pull back and see the cautious, curious way Jordan is looking at me, I know I need to shove the feelings down. Play the part. Be aloof. Chill.

I've played soccer on a world stage, taken game-winning shots on goal under pressure. I've outrun the fastest men in the sport. But releasing my hold on her is a bigger challenge.

I let my fingers graze her hip as I take one step backward, giving her some space. My chest feels ice cold as soon as I do.

I don't surrender my grip on her hand, though. A man falling ass-over-face in love wouldn't let go of this woman. We're engaged. I have full license to keep her close to me tonight.

"That was…convincing," she breathes, her eyes dilated and dreamy. Her words may tell me she's putting on an act, but her body says otherwise. Her body says she wants to be kissed again, harder this time. With abandon.

Good.

"Yeah? I've got some fiancé moves?"

"Um, yeah. You've got moves. I don't think anyone ever doubted that." Hearing her say it makes me hate that she thinks of me as a player. "People will believe we're a couple now. Nice work," she says, wiping her mouth delicately with one finger and straightening her hair.

I drape an arm over her shoulder and pull her in tight, escorting her along with me toward the bar. "I think a newly engaged couple would have a hard time keeping their hands off each other."

She barks a laugh. "You do, do you? What makes me think you're using our little lie as a chance for some action?"

Guilty. As. Charged.

"Right, you caught me." I continue guiding her through the crowd. When we reach the bar, it's almost the same spot where we stood that first night when I bristled at the idea of a know-it-all woman who stood to keep me away from the game I love.

Now I see her for what she is, someone with drive and a level of caring about our health. The searing feeling I have tearing at my insides has nothing to do with hatred, but when she squirms and pulls away to pick up a paper cocktail menu from the bar, I reel myself back in.

You're playing a role. For the sake of her job security.

"What are you drinking?" she asks, the sparkle in her eyes no different from what she displays at work when she's fired up about knees and ligaments.

You're not special. You're a prop, an actor.

"I ordered a pint earlier," I say, looking at the table where I put it down. The high-top tables near us are empty. "Probably been cleared by an overzealous waiter."

"You want another? Newcastle brown?"

My head swivels to look at her, but she doesn't move her eyes from the menu. "How'd you know that?"

Her face pinks and she flinches. Caught. "Oh. Um, I noticed it was what you had in your hand the last time we were here."

Over a month ago. When her shirt was wet, and she had bigger things to think about than what I was drinking. I tuck away that fact.

"It's my standard. Love a good dark ale." Maybe she's just detail-oriented, and I'm the sucker who wants it to mean something. "What'll you have, love?"

"How about a gin and tonic with a lime?" I notice she doesn't flinch when I call her love. First time she hasn't told me to stop calling her that. Of course, it's appropriate tonight when we're selling her bosses on her stable, engaged status, which I still think is bullshit. But that's a fight for another time.

I order our drinks and take a look around the place. A few people glance our way, probably getting used to the idea of seeing us like a couple. Or trying to reconcile the two warring images—brute strength boy toy athlete with brainy, beautiful doctor.

"I wouldn't believe it either," I mutter to myself.

"What's that?" she asks. It's far too loud in here for her to have heard me, so I clear my throat and shake my head.

"Your dress. I like it."

She blushes again, her cheeks creeping closer to the color of the dress. "Thank you. Not too much, the red?"

"Never too much on you, love."

Leaning in, she gives me a peck on the cheek. "Thank you, footie player." I feel my neck get hot, and I'm glad my telltale signs of embarrassment are where she can't see them. "And thank you, again, for doing this. I know it's ridiculous to be pretending we're engaged. I don't even know how we got ourselves into it, but I really appreciate you faking…"

"No." I put a finger on her lips, and she goes silent. "No more talking about our fake relationship."

And no more pecks on the cheek.

I want the full, hot kiss I've been thinking about since she walked in the door. My willpower is worn down to a nub. I don't want to hear any more about how much she appreciates my acting abilities. And I'm not pretending how interested I am in having my lips on her.

I wouldn't be much of a player if I didn't know how to make the most of a clean shot.

Tracing her jaw with my finger, I watch her body shudder at the contact. My finger follows a long tendril of her hair, which I twirl and tuck away over her shoulder. I slide my hand from her shoulder to the column of her neck, then cup her cheek in my palm.

Her eyes search mine for signs of what I plan to do. It's pretty damn simple. I want that mouth.

Just barely brushing my lips against hers may be the most painful thing I've ever done when what I want to do is dive in. But I take it slow and feel her shudder again under my palm.

Tilting her face to a different angle, I kiss her again.

Just a brush. A promise. The barest details of what I'll give her if she wants it.

A moan so soft leaves her throat, too quiet for me to hear, but I feel the vibration against my hand.

Then I go in for a deeper kiss, sucking lightly on her bottom lip and giving her a hint of what I'd like to do with my tongue, given enough time and an empty room. Swirling it against hers once—twice—is barely enough to satisfy my need.

It's still a kiss appropriate for a bar full of onlookers. But just barely.

It's also a punishing kiss, in that I'm punishing myself, denying what I want in favor of making her want it more.

I need to rock her world, just a little bit. I've tried with this woman the normal way, and she just won't budge. She's so damn set on her charade that she can't think outside the box. So I'm forcing the issue.

I need to throw this fucking fake relationship onto the funeral pyre, and if there's one talent I possess outside of soccer, it's the ability to make a woman want more.

When I draw back, it takes a moment before she opens her eyes. When she does, they're unfocused and hazy. She doesn't move a muscle. I'm not even sure she's breathing.

Well, that makes two of us.

"Just thought we needed one more to drive the point home. New love and all." My voice sounds like sandpaper, but my point is made. She's unsteady and confused.

I reach for our drinks and hand her the gin and tonic with a kind smile. Then I drink down half the pint of ale because this whole courtship dance is fucking dehydrating.

"Tim!" The voice doesn't sound familiar, just female. And since I don't really have female friends, I'm putting money on either a soccer fan…or someone I dated. Really hoping it's the former.

I turn to see a woman I vaguely remember, mainly because she shows up from time to time at team events, the guest of someone or other. Pretty sure the team pays a guy to gather jersey chasers and make sure they attend our various parties. It makes for a more festive evening, and the single guys on the team sure appreciate it.

"Charlotte." She extends her hand to Jordan, who introduces herself calmly. I can't imagine what she's thinking, except the obvious, that Charlotte is one of my many conquests. And from the way Charlotte bats her lashes and smiles coyly, she'd hardly be wrong in assuming it.

I fumble over some perfunctory greetings and try to steer us away before it becomes blatantly obvious that I have a type.

Yes, Charlotte is a redhead. She's also petite. But that's where the similarities end. Charlotte doesn't captivate me, never did. She's sweet enough and pretty enough, but there was never going to be more than the one night for us. I was honest about it when we met.

With Jordan, I look at her and I can't stop. Can't stop staring at her face, noticing new little things like the constellation of freckles across the bridge of her nose and over the apples of her cheeks, losing myself daily in the deep sea of her eyes and watching them dance when she smiles at me.

"Heard you got engaged, Chelty. Congrats," Charlotte says, turning to Jordan. "And lucky you, you get to go out on that beautiful boat."

Just like that, the air is sucked out of the room. Charlotte's never been on my boat. Our one date took place mostly at her apartment.

Jordan looks like she wants to drop-kick Charlotte across the road. I can't help feeling gratified at the little streak of jealousy.

She has no idea what Charlotte is talking about because not only have I not taken her on my boat, I haven't told her I own one. Going to have to remedy that now before we look like the fake couple we are. Or I look like an asshole.

"We're going out next weekend, actually." I lock eyes with Jordan, trying to communicate that I'm not just trying to get her to substantiate a lie—I'm promising her a nice day on the boat. She nods.

"Right. I almost forgot. Been working too hard, I guess. My brain's scrambled." Her voice is wooden. Charlotte wouldn't notice, but I do.

I put an arm around Jordan and tug her closer, but her frame is stiff against my shoulder. I can't tell if it's discomfort with Charlotte, the boat, our continued charade, or something else. Shit just keeps piling up.

"You'll let go of all that when we get onto the water," I tell Jordan, willing her to let all of it go right now.

She nods, and I feel a slight give in her body. I've been so worried about my knee and my career and the lies we've been telling, I haven't been paying attention to her like a real fiancé. Or a real person.

I should at least be aware that she's been working her ass off since she started her job with the team, and she's been doing everything she can to keep me on the playing field. She could probably use a day off. Some time outside of the physical therapy room or the Strikers building where everything is built on a lie. Some time on the water.

And lucky me, I've got a boat.

CHAPTER 16

 ordan

No question, this is a magic dress.

And maybe I'm not ready for its effects. They're confusing. They probably don't mean what I want them to mean, and that's a problem.

Yes, Tim agreed to put on a convincing show to prove to Reilly that I didn't lie about being in a relationship, but there's a difference between standing next to me like a date and kissing me like…that.

The problem is that I really liked *that*.

Sign me up for more of *that*, please and thank you.

I shouldn't be surprised that Tim takes his performance seriously. He takes everything seriously. If I've learned anything about him over the weeks I've spent assessing his injuries and trying to help him, it's that he works himself hard.

Like right now, when he stands with his arm casually draped over my shoulder while we chat with Coach Jaynes and Bo

Taylor, the strength and conditioning coach. The way he slides his hand across my back and positions it over my shoulder feels like he's done it a hundred times. I'm certain it looks that way to Coach Jaynes.

I'm vaguely aware of photographers snapping shots around us, but I can only focus on Tim. Practically frozen still, I'm acutely aware of the warmth of his hand on my bare shoulder. Telepathically, I'm urging him not to let go. My skin craves his touch in a way I never imagined, even if it's only for show.

It'll probably turn out to be a problem for me later when the charade is finished, but right now, I'm letting myself buy into it. It feels too good to be near him.

Holding Sofia's tiny black clutch under my arm between us, I feel it buzz…and buzz again with an incoming call. I ignore it, but Tim can clearly feel the vibrations because he leans in close and whispers, "Need to attend to that, love?" His nose grazes my earlobe and I shiver.

I shake my head, words stuck in my throat, and nuzzle into him. He folds me in closer. It feels natural.

I'm sure we look like a real couple, especially given the story Tim sells so easily—that we reconnected and were so besotted after more than a decade of longing that we fell hard. Like if Romeo and Juliet had lived to fall in love a second time.

He's good. And I find myself buying into the story. Even as I tell myself it's merely a story.

"My wife will accuse me of being unromantic if she hears that tale, so I'd appreciate it if you keep it to yourself," Taylor says, looking over our heads as though his wife might be lurking.

"Rightly so. You are unromantic," Coach says, turning to me. "He was the first guy to warn me against using a courtship analogy with a roomful of surly players."

Tim laughs. "Probably won't be the last. I figured someone tried to talk you out of it, but it was a good analogy, Coach. Resonated with me."

"Glad to hear it," Coach Jaynes says.

Tim explains, "Soccer is like a dance, each player taking cues from the others, moving separately but in unison. When it plays out properly on the field, it looks choreographed, but that's because each of us knows the rules."

"Who's the girl in this analogy?" I ask, picturing the players moving in a ballroom.

"Whoever has the ball." Tim's cheeky grin is magnetic as he removes his arm and demonstrates a waltz in the small space where we stand between high-top tables. His dance takes him around the backside of Taylor, and for a second, I think he's going to pull me into his arms for a dip.

Instead, he returns to my side and reaches for my hand, interlacing our fingers and warming me from the inside out. It feels natural to be with him like this, maybe because we've gotten to know each other better with each of our physical therapy sessions.

I like this side of Tim, the non-work side. Liking it is dangerous, as I find myself drifting away from the conversation to think about how I can spend more time with Tim outside of work. He mentioned going on his boat, but that whole conversation was just plain awkward, so I'm not putting much stock in that. But I can't deny that I'd like to see what we're like together without all the noise of sports and medicine and people. Like a real date.

Two fake kisses and I'm sixteen again, pining for the player I'll never have. Risking making impulsive decisions. I need to keep reminding myself this isn't real. I will. After I enjoy it for one night.

My phone buzzes again. Persistent. Tim meets my eyes. I shake my head again. I should turn it off, but I don't want to let go of his hand.

"I really need to spend some time listening to your team pep talks. Feels like I could learn a lot about how to approach the players with some of my ideas," I suggest, tipping my chin up at him.

"Yeah, no," Tim says, planting a gentle kiss on my lips. "Your ways are working. And I'm too possessive to let anyone else dance with you."

I feel every kiss, every touch rippling over my skin. I'd be embarrassed for the inescapable sigh when his lips touch mine, except that it's so loud in here that he probably doesn't hear it. "You keep making those little noises, I'm going to get ideas, love," he whispers in my ear.

Well, crap.

If I thought I was ready for Tim Cheltenham at age sixteen, it's a good thing he left when he did. No way was the teenage me built to withstand the kind of reaction he evokes and walk away unscathed. The thirty-one-year-old me is career-focused and unflappable, and she can barely take it.

I urge myself to stay grounded in reality—Tim is here because he needs my medical clearance, and he's never been attracted to me. Things like that don't change. It's basic physical chemistry, and if it doesn't exist, it doesn't exist.

Unfortunately, my body has not gotten the memo. Not at all.

My face is flushed, my lips are begging for more attention, and my skin feels so hot under my dress I'm praying Tim doesn't run a hand down my back because it'll probably catch fire. Not to mention that every nerve ending seems to dead-end between my thighs, where the aching need for release has me shifting from foot to foot.

And there's Tim, standing next to me, casually rubbing his thumb over the back of my hand like he does it every day, and having a conversation about…high school?

"Yeah, she didn't think much of me back then. Just a sweaty bloke with a funny accent who loved footie more than he loved girls. And that's saying something for an eighteen-year-old kid full of hormones at a new school full of cute girls."

Tim laughs, and my brain tries to play catch-up with his story, which bears no resemblance to the truth.

I thought a *lot* of him. And right before he high-tailed it back to England, I'd come out and told him so.

But Tim contradicts all this. "Jordan was busy with her own life, so it was a bit like being an only child at times. And I come from a family of three, so you can imagine. There were some lonely days."

"Haha." I play along, but I remember the string of women lined up for him.

Taylor gives me a playful punch on the shoulder. "Wow, doc. Sounds like you were a tough crowd."

He has no idea what he's asking of me. I have to lie and say I barely noticed Tim when I spent nearly every waking hour wishing he'd notice me. All the pretend annoyances were flirtatious banter. At least that's how I'd interpreted it. And then…I'd been wrong. "It wasn't exactly like that. It's not as though Tim was dying to hang out with me. Once the girls at my high school caught sight of him, I was pretty much invisible."

Tim gives my shoulder a squeeze and pulls me in. "You gentlemen really believe that? She was never invisible to me. My problem was that she just didn't fancy me. Not at all."

"Why not?" Jaynes asks.

Three pairs of eyes turn toward me to corroborate the story. I choke over my words before coming up with my own version of the fairy tale. "Well, *at first*, I didn't like him because he came to live with us right after my parents basically kicked my brother out. I felt like they were trying to replace him with the son they wanted. I'd have resented anyone who came in that situation."

"Hmph," Tim says quietly. I give him a side-eye, and he leans close to me and whispers, "I never knew that, love. I'm sorry."

I shake my head and whisper in his ear, "I'm just making up a story, same as you."

His eyes stay locked on mine. I know he's trying to discern

whether there's any truth to my story. I school my expression, telling him nothing. He leans in again. "I'm still sorry." Ribbons of chills roll down my skin, a reaction to his breath against my ear when he speaks.

All I want is to shoo everyone from the room, lay back on one of the pub tables, and see what else Tim's mouth is capable of.

Tim shakes his head skeptically. "Jordan was fierce and brainy and as gorgeous as she is now. She had plenty of friends, probably why she ignored me."

"Oh, I hardly ignored you." I turn to Jaynes and Taylor and tell them how it was. "The day Tim arrived, you could tell he was more than a pretty face who could kick a soccer ball. He had presence. People were drawn to him."

"Just not you," Tim confides, too quiet for anyone to hear but me. I want to tell him how wrong he is, but...he knows. How could he not?

Tim lets go of my hand and wraps it around my waist, pulling me in front of him and holding me tight against his body. I'm acutely aware of his hand on my stomach. If he moves it a few inches lower, he can give me the relief I desperately need from the way my body responds to every touch.

But...no. This isn't real.

My phone again. Jesus, why is it ringing off the hook on a Friday evening? That never happens. Which makes me concerned it could be something urgent. Maybe I should check.

But that would mean moving, and I'm addicted to the feel of Tim's hard body against my back. The phone can wait.

"Didn't those legendary soccer moves impress you at all?" Taylor asks, still fishing.

Tim laughs. "I was more of a legend in my own mind."

"Oh, don't be modest," Coach Jaynes says, taking a sip of something brown like scotch and setting down his glass. "I remember back when you were at the Man City academy, every team in England was hoping for a shot at you. Most thought you'd stay in Manchester." He leans against a table and crosses his arms over his chest. "Strikers got lucky you came to the States, that's for damn sure."

I feel Tim flinch at the words but looking over my shoulder, I can only see part of his face. A tiny muscle pulses in his cheek, and I know from working with him these past weeks that it's a sign of stress.

He covers by taking a sip of his beer, but I wonder why the conversation bothers him.

"I'll say," Taylor agrees.

Tim swallows and nods. "Happy to be here." He clears his throat and changes the subject. "Glad I gave it a second go, at any rate."

"Maybe not such a coincidence you settled back here? Did you ever try to look Jordan up?" Taylor asks, winking at me. I had no idea the man was such a sucker for romance.

Tim laughs again, but it sounds hollow. The muscle ticks in his cheek. "Thought about it. Many times. But I heard she was a pretty renowned doctor, not surprising, given her brilliance. What's a sporty bloke got to offer someone like that? It's what I figured, anyway."

His words, even if just part of a fabricated story, knock me sideways. The idea of Tim being intimidated by me is ludicrous.

I think back to all the months Tim either ignored me or seemed to be annoyed unless it was to talk about school—the one area where I excelled, the one area where I could be useful. I knew how the guys in my class thought of me—the brainy one who could help them through a chemistry lab assignment. I was not the one they asked out on a Friday night. Tim saw me the same way.

It never bothered me back then because I soaked up the approval of my parents and teachers. Some people peak in high school, and I decided that my peak would come later. I'd go to medical school, find a guy who respected my brain instead of trying to use it for his own purposes and ignore me the rest of the time.

Isn't that how Tim saw me? How he still sees me now?

My persistent phone jars me out of my messy thoughts. "I should answer this," I say apologetically, vowing to hurt the person wresting me from Tim's grasp. I excuse myself and go out to the hallway to check my messages.

A few minutes later, Tim comes looking and finds me there, stiletto sandals hanging off one finger, pacing in a circle. I'm locked in a heated debate with my mom on speakerphone, and she won't back down.

"I'm not asking. I'm telling you," she says, her sing-song voice betraying her seriousness.

"Mom, this is a toddler's birthday party, not the debutante ball. Quit trying to line up dating prospects for me."

"Chet won't care."

"I care," I growl, ready to let loose on her, but Tim reaches for my hand again, squeezing it reassuringly. I glance around to see there's no one out here to witness his act of coupledom, and the idea that he's doing it anyway steals the venom from my argument with my mom.

"I need to go. I'm at a work thing, but I'll see you tomorrow." I hold the phone away like a smelly diaper while my mom continues talking.

"This is your problem. You use work as an excuse for avoiding your life—"

"Bye, Mom." I hang up before she can finish her rant and look up at Tim. "Sorry about that. Family drama."

"What's wrong?" He hands me my drink, and it's then it strikes me how much he's acting like a real date. His drink is gone. He smiles and I try not to melt.

Something about the way he's looking at me—open, genuine —doesn't feel fake. And it sends my brain into a lap around crazytown.

"What are you doing tomorrow?" I ask, still unsure exactly how roping him into a party at my parents' house could possibly end well.

Tim shrugs and takes out his phone. "Unlike you, I don't have my calendar 'in my head'," he mocks with air quotes. He scrolls a moment, concluding, "I'm free. Why?"

"Can I drag you to a party?"

"Sounds lovely. Will you wear this dress?" His wolfish wink makes me blush.

"Nope. Jeans. Casual."

He shrugs. "Where are we going?"

I let out a long exhale, giving my rogue brain one more chance to come to its senses and decide to call off this whole ridiculous proposal. Then I launch headlong down the rabbit hole.

"My parents' house. It's a birthday party for my nephew, but my mother's planning some sort of coming out party coup."

"Your mom is a lesbian?"

"No, not that kind of coming out. You're English, you should know about coming out parties, cotillions, debutante balls."

He lifts his hand in a mock attempt to drink tea with his pinky pointed outward. "Oh yes, that was my world. You've caught me."

I don't know much about Tim's home life in England at all, except that he has sisters. In high school, I was either too tongue-tied to talk to him or annoyed by his brotherly ribbing. I certainly wasn't sitting around on the porch swing asking for stories about his family, though I vaguely remember that his mom passed away when he was young.

"Where's your hometown again?"

"Saltney. It's a little area near Manchester, where I trained for the academy team."

"Sounds charming."

His sharp bark of laughter surprises me. "Spoken like a person who's never ventured to Saltney. It's a small village near the border of Wales. Think blue-collar workers, a couple of dingy pubs, and a lot of cows."

"I like cows. And the rest sounds nice too." The idea of a small English town appeals to me in a fundamental way. Maybe I've been living and working in a city for too long, but I often find myself exhausted by all of it—the traffic, the people, the…effort. But I don't tell Tim any of this.

He lets out a quiet chuckle. "It is nice in a way. But hard in other aspects. Family can be…a lot sometimes."

"Which is why I need a buffer at the party." I must be crazy to think about bringing him to a family event, but I need to do something to keep the matchmakers at arms' length, and he's just distracting enough to do the trick. "My mom hates that I'm single, and she's made it her mission to rectify the error of my ways. I think she's up to three now."

"Three what?"

"Three sons of her friends who she's invited to the party to meet me 'in an informal, low-pressure setting.' Ha! How can it possibly be low pressure when she lines up three strangers to meet me and bid for my affections?"

"You sound like you belong in a Jane Austen novel."

"If my mother had her way, I'd have been promised to a gentleman suitor years ago. Which is the last thing I need."

"Got it. No suitors. How can I help?"

I perk up at his willingness. "Oh. Well, just being there will be a distraction. She'll have to ask about how you've been since you lived with us, and that will divert her from her relentless match-making. You'll keep her talking, keep her busy. And then there's the whole soccer player thing."

"What thing?"

"Just that you can interface with whichever guys she trots out to meet me and talk sports. They'll be far more interested in you than in me. And after that and a little happy birthday song, we'll bolt."

He cocks his head and smiles. "Sure, love. Sounds simple enough."

And just like that, I've got myself a date. A date with my parents and a yard full of random bachelors, but it's a date.

CHAPTER 17

*J*ordan

By the light of day, Tim and I return to work mode. At least, that's what I think is happening when he proposes that we meet at Café Strada near the Berkeley campus for a quick jolt of caffeine before heading to my parents' house in Oakland.

Tim pays for both of our to-go cups of café au lait, carries them out, and puts them on the roof of my car. "Thanks for treating," I say, popping the locks on the little blue Toyota hybrid SUV that's been my reliable companion for seven years. "I can drive, then we can come back here for your car."

"Sure, but let me grab something first."

He jogs down the block to where he parked and opens the passenger door. Leaning in, he seems to be wrestling with something before emerging with a large driftwood bowl filled with… plants? As he gets closer, I can see they are, in fact, an assortment of green, dusty plum, and gray succulent plants of different sizes.

"For you," he says, holding it out.

"Wow. These are really cool." My heart swells at the gesture. "Tim, thank you so much." My eyes roam over the various species, which I can't identify because I know nothing about plants. But there are some taller gray ones as soft as lambs' ears, a green variety that trails out of the bowl, rounded bunches of pale green and deep purple spiny shapes that look like sea anemones…

"These are my favorite. Aeonium rosette." He points to some dark purple petals that fan out like roses. "They're hard to find, but I got lucky at Trader Joe's."

I squint in confusion. "Trader Joe's? The grocery store?"

"Yeah. They have succulents sometimes."

I look at the large, perfectly arranged bowl of living things in my hands and know for a fact this is no grocery store purchase. Even a non-plant person can tell as much. "You didn't get these there."

"Sure I did. Not the bowl, though. That I bought at a craft store."

I take a step backward to make sure I'm with the person I thought I was meeting today. Yup, it's still Tim. Hot soccer star. Fake fiancé. And also…florist? "You…arranged these?"

He nods. "Hobby. I like to pick and choose what looks good together, rather than—"

"Buying a random thing, forgetting to water it, and letting it die?" I put up my hand. "Guilty."

His smile melts the lace off my panties and sends my heart skittering through my chest. "That's the beauty of these. They're hardy. Tough to kill. I'll prove it by leaving them in the car all day while we're with your family."

"Wow. I kinda feel seen, Tim. Thank you."

"I'm glad you like them. Just a gesture to say thanks for dealing with my shenanigans last night." He points to my car as my heart rate slows. Right. The fake date. "Shall we?"

We hop in, and he positions our coffee cups in the center

console holder. No handing me the cup, no fingers delicately brushing fingers, no electric zings of attraction to knock me sideways. The lace reaffixes itself to my panties.

"Ready to see my parents?" I ask on a shaky breath.

His smile crinkles the corners of his eyes, and his eyebrows bounce. "I'm good. But I'm a little worried about you drinking this coffee. You already seem a little…jittery."

"Yeah, well, that's because my mom will be there."

"At her house," he deadpans.

"Yes."

"Where she lives."

Now I'm getting annoyed. With the situation, not with him. "Yes."

I put the car in gear just as he chuckles quietly. "I am really looking forward to this. After the torture you've put me through with that carving knife, it almost feels like payback."

"It wasn't a knife." But I smile a little. Even if this isn't really a date, being with him is lightening me up.

I really need it now that I've somehow managed to combine a reunion between Tim and my parents, our fake dating that I wish was real, the eligible sons of my mother's friends, and whatever drama transpires between Chet and my parents. Never a dull moment.

My mother has arranged for cake and a petting zoo for a dozen toddlers, and knowing Chet, he'll adopt half the animals and take them on a road trip. My family is bonkers, but my nephew is adorable, so my back seat contains the biggest yellow Tonka truck I could find, wrapped with an even bigger bow.

Chet has been "off the grid" at Burning Man for the past week, but he left me a message saying he's grateful I'll be there to diffuse some of our mother's nuttiness. And for the same reasons, I'm grateful for Tim.

He looks out the window as we drive through an industrial part of Oakland near the harbor, where the large dinosaur-like loaders move the containers on and off of the ships that carry them.

"You remember it here?" I ask.

He shrugs. "Some of it's coming back."

As a kid, I liked to come down here and watch the machines in action, always moving, day or night. It was a fascinating universe, so different from my suburban world just a few miles away. My dad took me whenever I asked, and I never questioned whether he found it odd to have a kid who was so fascinated by harbor machinery.

To me, it was more interesting than the dollhouse collectibles, the ballet classes my mother insisted on, or earning another Girl Scout badge.

"Hey, was that always there?" He points out the side window to a postage-stamp-sized park shrouded by the kind of live oaks I loved to climb as a kid.

"Um, not sure. I don't remember it *not* being there."

The park is barely large enough to qualify as a dot on the landscape, and a second later, we're already past it, and the taller buildings in the area have taken over again.

"Let's stop. Can we? Do we have time?"

I try to see Tim's face, but he's still fixated on the scenery outside the passenger window. "Really? You want to go to the park?"

He turns toward me and shrugs. "Just thought it might be fun."

"More fun than seeing my parents again, you mean?"

He holds up a finger. "I didn't say that. I'm game. I brought wine and everything."

"You brought wine to a two-year-old's birthday party?" I look toward the bag at his feet, which I assumed contained a toy or some other gift.

"The wine is for your mom. Maybe she'll drink it all and leave you alone." He grins, and I want to launch myself into his lap because he gets me.

"You are brilliant. Welcome to the family."

I turn off the engine and open my door. Tim is already outside the car and moving toward the small city park, which has two wooden benches flanking a square of grass with an empty fountain in the middle. At the far end, I see a small playground, which is where Tim is headed. I grab a sunhat and trail after him, barely able to keep up with his long strides.

Tim doesn't stop until he reaches the ladder of the climbing structure, which he mounts in two easy steps. By the time I get there, he's sitting on a platform at the top of the structure with his legs dangling over the side. He beckons me to join him.

It takes me a small effort to climb the ladder without stepping on the hem of my navy blue maxi-dress, but Tim extends his hand when I mount the last step and guides me to a spot next to him. And he doesn't let go of my hand.

Oh, I could sit here all day.

"Nice, right?" Tim looks out over the playground, which is surprisingly empty for a weekend. Then again, it's a tiny park in the middle of an otherwise industrial area. Not a lot of homes around here, which makes me wonder who had the idea to build a park in the first place.

My phone buzzes. Reluctantly, I let go of Tim's hand to check it. A text from my mom. "My God, my mother must have me under radar surveillance. She knows the second we veered off course."

Tim chuckles. "She really rattles you."

I put the phone down without reading her text. "Um, yeah. Just a bit."

Tim doesn't respond right away, and I wonder if my words drifted off on the light breeze I feel kissing my face. "Tim... Is this... Do you even want to go? You really don't have to." I suddenly feel like a wimp for making him act as a human shield.

Though, at this point, I've driven him to the middle of Oakland, so I can't exactly abandon him here.

I nudge him with my elbow, and he turns to face me. He's so beautiful that it hurts a little to look at him.

"I'm game to go. It's not that. I just liked the looks of this place."

"It's kind of awesome that it exists in the middle of the dead zone. I wonder who uses it."

"Kids, I imagine. Haven't you ever driven by and seen people here?"

"Honestly, I've never noticed it until today."

"Well, now I'm even more glad we stopped."

I let out a long exhale and take in our surroundings. A metal teeter-totter sits in a corner of the sand next to a newer-looking swing set with two green bucket swings and two straight regular swings. They barely sway in the calm breeze. In front of the platform where we're sitting, a winding slide ends in the sand.

The large oaks that punctuate the postage stamp of grass have probably been here longer than some of the buildings. "I have no idea why this place is here, but I'm glad it is."

"Yeah, you seemed like you needed the detour."

"Really? I thought we stopped for you."

"No, love. This was for you."

I turn to look at him and he shrugs, still staring off toward the trees. I'm kind of bowled over that he wanted to stop for my benefit. And he's right. "It's dumb. I'm full of nerves about seeing my family, which makes no sense since they're supposed to have my back more than anyone."

"Oh, yeah? What kind of fairy tale idea of family do you believe in?"

I laugh. "Right. Guess it's silly. So, two sisters, eh?"

He nods. I let my eyes trace the line of his jaw, strong and sharp. It takes effort to restrain myself from reaching out and running a hand over his stubble. My mind wanders to how it would feel between my thighs, and I draw in such a sharp breath Tim turns his head.

I look away, hoping he doesn't notice my hungry expression. My cheeks heat anyway, and I don't dare look back at him.

"Hey." He nudges me with his elbow.

Keeping my focus on the swing set, I nod. "Yeah?"

He nudges me again and tucks two fingers under my chin, turning my face to look at him. "Why are you so wound up?"

"I'm not," I say a little too quickly, not wanting to admit that sitting this close to him has my brains scrambling. Being near him has been messing with me since I started my job, but last night pushed me over the edge.

"You're like a hummingbird who ate a wad of cotton candy soaked in speed."

The image makes me laugh. "Must be the coffee."

"Nope, not buying it. Why do you let your mum get to you? I mean, I'm happy to come along, but come on, Jordan. You're tough and independent. You made it through med school. You command respect. I can't believe you care one way or the other about a bunch of blokes she wants you to meet. So I'm guessing it's something else."

Damn him.

It's bad enough I'm working overtime to keep my hormones from hosting a parade in his honor—now he's a mind reader too. Or just really damn intuitive. So much worse.

My phone continues buzzing with more texts from my mom, which I ignore.

"Come on, at least tell me something. I promise I'll counter with some awful detail about my family that will make yours seem bloody genteel."

"I didn't know you had issues with your family."

"My father, specifically, if we're going to get into it."

"Everything okay?"

He stretches his back and cracks his neck like he's preparing for battle. "Yeah. Mostly. Not sure we ever talked about this back then, but he basically disowned me. My mum passed when I was young, so what he said was the law."

"Tim, what? How did I not know this?"

He shrugs. "I didn't exactly broadcast it. We've repaired things since, but I'm still a disappointment to him for pursuing soccer instead of taking over the family auto body business."

I turn to him, agog. "He's disappointed that you're a soccer star?" Pressing his lips together, he seems embarrassed. The edges of his ears turn pink. "Oh, come on. You know you're a soccer star."

"Just strange hearing you say it, love." And there it is again. The nickname I've grown to like. A lot. "Anyhow, yeah. It's just him. I don't take it personally. Not anymore." He turns slightly away from me, and I can tell he's closing the window on this glimpse at his family life.

"Wow. I'm really sorry. You don't deserve that."

"Thanks. Anyhow, tell me about your mum."

"It's nothing like what you just said. Gosh, I feel terrible even complaining now when you'd probably really love to have a mom to complain about."

"It's okay. It's completely different. And your issues don't need to be huge to be valid." Oh, be still, my galloping little heart. If he keeps saying insightful things and arranging succulents, I'm a goner. I *like* him.

But I'm not sure he feels the same way, so I do the equivalent of taking a cold shower. I start talking about my mother.

"I guess. She'd be the first to tell you she's bored. Tons of hobbies—French club, tennis, two bridge clubs, and the woman reads like she's on a mission to finish every book on the planet. She's really, really smart, and my dad would be sunk without her bookkeeping, and yet she's never had a career. Then, every second she gets, she's criticizing how hard I work and asking if I shouldn't be refocusing my priorities."

"You ever just come out and ask her?"

"Well, that's overly logical. You mean *talk* with my mother?"

He laughs. "Yes, it's amazing what can be learned about humans that way."

"Yeah, sure. Go and be all evolved right before I dive into the lion's den."

But he's right. And on that note, I should talk to *him*. Ask him about all the kissing last night. Ask him if it meant anything. Act like a grown-up.

The problem is that I don't know if I want to hear the answer to my question. Not if he tells me that he was just playing a role. Maybe I'd rather live in my fantasy world of possibility. Why open myself up to a hard no?

I suddenly feel exhausted by the whole charade. It's too much to want him and have to pretend I don't, all the while pretending we're a couple. My brain hurts and my heart hurts more.

"So, three months seems about right," I mutter.

"You're having a conversation in your head that I'm not part of. Stop that."

"Sorry. Yeah, I was thinking three months would be a good amount of time for me to prove myself at work before we can break off the engagement."

He doesn't respond.

"Tim?"

"Yeah?"

"Did you hear me? Three months seems—"

He cuts me off. "Yeah, I heard you. Why are you so keen to break it off?"

"Well, we're going to end it eventually, so why not do it after the post-season?"

"Right," he grumbles.

I watch him rake a hand through his hair, sending it off in all directions, and that tousled look *does* things to me. I feel my breath hitch, and a flicker of heat darts down the center of my body, ending between my thighs.

This is why we need to end it. Because he brings out that reaction in me just by messing up his hair. I sit mesmerized by how his long fingers move between the strands like a symphony conductor. I can't fathom what I'd feel if he ran his hands through mine. Thinking about how much I want it, a thrill of anticipation rolls down my spine, and I shiver.

I'm fighting an uphill battle against my emotions, and I know which of us will lose. No wonder I'm exhausted. I'm also comfortable here with him in the silence. Right now, the faint trace of breeze between us feels like communication.

There's so much to look at here in a tiny park in the middle of an industrial zone—the gray tops of buildings contrasting with the green tops of trees, the sounds of birds calling to each other and answering after a pregnant beat, the faint murmur of traffic on the road behind us because there's always traffic in Oakland. It almost sounds like ocean waves, and I allow myself to hear it that way.

This is what I remember from when we were teenagers. It wasn't only the shy girl looking lustfully at the hot athlete. Well, it was a lot of that. He was hot then, and he's hotter now. I can't lie and pretend the teenage me didn't see a good thing when it landed in front of me, fresh from the English countryside.

But even though we either annoyed or ignored each other, I always knew there was more to Tim. Soccer demanded most of his free hours, and he quickly became a celebrity at our school. The player with the English accent. The guy whose smile I mistook for more.

Until that one night…

"Jordan…" Tim's voice is quiet, a husky growl that gets my attention. Resting a hand on the platform beside him, he's turned to face me, and I'm struck by flecks of yellow in his eyes that I haven't noticed before. They make the green more vivid, more intense.

Everything about Tim is intense right now.

He leans toward me, eyes roaming over my face, and I feel my skin heat as his gaze crawls along like it's leaving a mark. It's different than the way we've been together. For the first time, I don't feel weighed down by the baggage of the lie we created. It's just us, and as his face draws near, I feel it in my bones—the impending brush of his lips against mine, the burn of his stubble across my jaw…

I want it so badly that I can feel the whisper of his lips before he draws near, and I feel my eyes drift shut, but only partway. I still need to see him, and it's a good thing I do…

Because…his focus shifts to a spot just beyond me, and when he gently raises his hand, it's not to stroke my cheek like I'm expecting. My skin aches as his hand moves gingerly past me and returns with a monarch butterfly on his index finger.

"Easy…don't be scared." His voice drops low as he talks to it and guides the beautiful orange-winged creature toward my hand. "Want to hold her?"

"Her?" My voice sounds gravelly and awkward since I'm still in an aborted kiss stupor.

He shrugs and smiles. "I think she's a her. She's pretty."

"She is pretty." I let him guide the calm butterfly to my hand. As he transfers her delicately to my palm, the brush of his fingers against my skin burns, affirming everything I'd have felt if he'd kissed me.

My face feels hot, and I stay focused on the pretty delicate wings that are barely moving as she sits trustingly on my hand. Then…as though she caught a whiff of dinner just over the tree line, she lifts off and flutters away.

"We should probably head to the party, get it over with," I say, holding up my phone with its string of unread texts.

When Tim looks at me now, the gentle expression is gone. The normal set to his jaw returns, and he looks almost irritable.

"So, three months, huh?"

"Um, I was just—"

"No, sure. Whatever you want, love."

He pushes himself up and extends a hand to me to do the same. I'm about to climb down the ladder, but Tim hasn't let go of my hand. When I look to him for explanation, he shakes his head.

"No, not that way." He gestures toward the twisting slide. "This way."

"Fine. You're a child, you know that?"

Situating myself at the top of the slide, I'm about to push off when I feel Tim sit down behind me, his legs coming up and over the sides of the skinny slide, so he'll fit. When he pushes us off, we slip and clunk down the thing until my feet stop us at the bottom.

I turn around. "Happy now?"

"I am," he says. "Quite." He gives me that big smile again, and once again, I have no idea how to stop myself from falling for him.

CHAPTER 18

*J*ordan

We make it to my parents' house halfway through the party. As we're heading up the front walk, Tim stops. I'm a few steps ahead before I realize he's no longer beside me.

When I turn, I see Tim looking around the front yard, turning slowly in a circle to take it all in. I hadn't put much thought into how strange it might feel for him to come back here. It's been so many years since he lived with us, it feels like a different lifetime.

And yet, not much has changed around here. Same boxwood hedges, same white mailbox shaped like a miniature craftsman house. The trees are taller than they used to be but just as untidy. My dad never would agree to pay for tree trimming, insisting on doing it himself, which got harder and harder the higher the trees grew.

Now in his sixties, he grudgingly lets my mom hire a guy every couple years, but he still prunes the lower branches in between, which means the trees look like half-eaten lollypops most of the time.

Tim points to the fuzzy blue cover on the porch swing, where

I finally kissed a few guys in my later days of high school. "Crazy. I remember sitting on this porch the day I arrived while your mum told me the house rules. I still always scan rooms before I enter, looking for breakables."

"She hasn't changed."

I get caught in my own wave of nostalgia, remembering times when he and I used to reach for the same snacks in the kitchen. Still, every memory ends with the mortification of him saying no to me and leaving.

When I feel his hand on my shoulder, I turn to see something new in his eyes—desire? His gaze, which is as soft as his eyes, caresses me from head to toe in a way he's never done before.

My eyes flit around, but there's not a butterfly in sight.

I take in a rough breath, suddenly unsteady on my feet. I'm so confused by what we are to each other, and I'm not sure how much more of it I can take. These gestures may be meaningless to him, but they're slowly killing me, one by one.

Needing some way to deflect his gaze, I fumble for my phone as if to read the texts from my mother.

That's when some of her exclamation points and shouty caps come into focus for the first time. "Oh, no."

Tim gives my shoulder a squeeze. "What?"

"Oh, no, no, no." I can't verbalize anything else, and Tim moves to peer over my shoulder at the screen.

Leave it to my news junkie mother—or whichever of her equally meddlesome friends alerted her to a tiny social media item about Tim Cheltenham getting engaged to "a girlfriend he's kept under wraps for some time."

She has included the article and used her phone's drawing tool to circle it in red with arrows pointing at me. Even though I wasn't named in the article, and the picture of me is mostly-obscured by the people at the Strikers event last night, there's nothing like a mother's ability to sixth sense her own daughter, even if only four pixels are visible.

"It'll be okay," he says confidently.

"How? She thinks we're engaged. I'm throwing you to the vultures, you realize that, don't you? It will be very not okay."

"I can handle it. It'll be fun. Don't let her get to you."

"You really don't remember my mother, do you?" I'm visibly shaking, and Tim interlacing our fingers does nothing to change that.

"Come on. We're pros. We've got this."

His lips quirk into a smile, and I find the same warm affection in his eyes. His smile comes so easily that I almost believe him.

"You're really on board?" I feel like I might be sick, so it's hard to fathom how he can seem so normal.

"Sure, love." *Love.* The endearment sounds a little sweeter now.

"Really?"

"Yes. Why not?"

I can think of a hundred reasons why not, but I don't have time to articulate them. "You're sure."

Tim nods almost imperceptibly. When he fixes his gaze on me, the humor is gone, replaced by a stare I think I've seen before —in those first few days when he only looked at me with stony distrust.

But no, this stare is different. This time, he's drinking me in like the world just fell away and he only wants me. No, like he *needs* me. Like I might be the difference between suffocation and a breath of clean air.

He pulls me closer, sandwiching our clasped hands between us and holding mine against his chest. With the other hand, he grazes a finger down my cheek and tucks two fingers under my chin, but this time he doesn't tell me I seem wound up. This time, he sweeps his mouth over mine and drinks me in, kissing me the way he did before I left last night, fusing our mouths together in an endless, soul-melting kiss. And this time, I don't stop to question what it means. This time, I think I know.

His tongue delves between my lips, dancing, swirling, tasting. It's a tiny speck of whipped cream on a decadent sundae, and he stops before I've even had a satisfying bite. He presses his lips to my forehead and kisses me twice before taking a step back so we can walk inside the house. "I told you," he says. "We're pros."

"O-okay." I'm a trembling, confounded mess of desire, but I manage to fish the ring from my pocket and slip it on my finger without dropping it.

Instead of the look of fear I'm sure I have plastered all over my face, Tim's expression looks almost pleased. "All in," he says, giving my hand a squeeze while I drag us through the house and into the yard, where I see my mother under our big elderberry tree.

All in.

im

IT IS the yelp heard around the world, I have no doubt.

There is no louder sound than that of a mother who's been waiting ten years to hear her only daughter say the words, "I'm engaged."

Those weren't Jordan's exact words—there was a lot of throat clearing and explaining and awkwardness while her mother half glared at me for not asking permission and alternately squeezed the living breath out of me in delight.

I don't have brothers, and over the years, my dad viewed my sisters in a very different light than what was happening here. The main concern was that they hadn't gotten pregnant.

What can I say? I grew up in a poor neighborhood with two sisters and a dad who worked a second job at night to put food on the table. Having another mouth to feed was the overriding concern.

"Why didn't you tell me?" Jordan's mother, Melinda, demands.

"We were keeping it quiet. We had to. For Tim's career," Jordan says. I have no idea if anyone would accept such a banal excuse, but Melinda seems somewhat satisfied.

"I'm your mother."

"Yes."

"You tell your mother things like this. I could be sworn to secrecy."

Jordan rolls her eyes. "Um, no, you can't."

To her credit, Melinda does more hugging than glaring, but as Jordan recounts our made-up story of running into each other and keeping our budding romance under wraps, she also does quite a bit of inquisitive staring at me, like I might be a unicorn bound to fly off at any minute.

It's hard to fathom Melinda's skepticism when her daughter is as smart, gorgeous, and funny as she is, but I guess that's her flaw. Jordan wraps a hand around my bicep and squeezes, looking up at me adoringly while she tells her mother everything.

She almost has me believing that my nonexistent proposal made her heart beat so loudly she was nervous I could hear it.

"I love this story. I'm going to be telling this story for a long, long time," Melinda gushes, pulling two of her friends over and recounting the tale verbatim while Jordan and I stand idly by, grinning like hand puppets.

Then there's Bruce. I'm more than a little bit wary of the reaction of a protective father when Melinda flits off like a prima ballerina to find him and tell him the "news." All fathers want the best for their daughters, and if I'm a disappointment to my own dad, I don't feel too confident about one who only wants the best for his daughter.

"Jesus, she's practically skipping," Jordan says, looking up at me with a smile so wide it puts my other concerns aside. Even if I'm just here to play a role, I'd rather be with her than anywhere else.

We follow Melinda's progress as she dances between guests, sharing her glee like a spritely fairy.

"Guess all moms are excited when they think their kids are getting married." I wouldn't know. My mum died before she could weigh in on my sisters' dating prospects. Still, somehow I doubt it would look like this.

Jordan takes a sip from a glass bottle of iced tea and shakes her head. "She's no ordinary mom. She's been waiting for this day since I was born. This is the finish line after a marathon of waiting and wishing. And somewhere along the way, I hit a wall and pushed it all away indefinitely."

I grab her hand. She looks down at where I've intertwined our fingers and tilts her head against my shoulder. Leaning down to kiss her temple feels natural, and I'm starting to get confused about how fake our fake relationship is.

This feels good. The outdoor party, the meddling family. I wouldn't trade it for anything. The canopy of large elderberry trees makes the yard feel like we're in a green snow globe, protected from the outside world.

"This is nice." Jordan sighs against my chest, and I inhale the faint plumeria scent of her shampoo. It is nice.

A minute later, Melinda comes back with her husband, who basically looks the same, which is to say formidable, a little gray around the temples, and fierce when he stares me down.

He's a doctor, so I know he's as smart as Jordan, which intimidates a guy like me who barely cracked a book in school. Of course, he'll think I'm unworthy of his daughter. And even though we're faking this engagement, a part of me wants to believe I'm good enough for Jordan.

A big part.

"I thought we were done with this one," he growls after he saunters over. He looks physically fit enough to kick my ass back across the pond if he wants to.

I consider bolting right then and there.

My running speed may be up for debate at the club, but I'd wager good money that I can outrun Bruce. Every fiber of my being is telling me to get the hell out of this man's yard before he can throw me out. I know how it feels to be a disappointment to a dad.

When he reaches his large hands toward me, I flinch, thinking he's going to wrap them around my throat. Instead, they pass my neck and keep going until he has me in a tight bear hug. "Been a long time, Tim. I'm glad to see you again."

The shock must show on my face when he releases me because he lets out a loud laugh from deep in his gut. "Don't look so scared. I'm glad to hear you make my daughter happy. All that matters to me in the world is that my girl found love."

He studies me for a moment longer before punching my shoulder and walking toward the house. "Come on. I've had enough of this fruit punch. Let's a get a real drink. Okay, if I borrow him for a bit, Danny?" I like hearing him call her that.

Jordan nods at her dad and lets go of my hand, which I realize has started to sweat. I wipe it on my pants as her mom puts an arm around Jordan and steers her toward her friends. I feel a bit guilty because I'm getting the far better end of the deal here—being led away from the unseasonable heat while her mother trots her around and shows off the ring I bought.

It was an impulsive purchase, not meant to be seen by the masses, and suddenly I worry that it's not good enough. She deserves the biggest diamond any man can afford.

And with that thought, I know I'm in way over my head.

I don't have time to dwell on it because Bruce has pulled me through the sliding patio doors and into the den. It still has the same wood paneled walls I remember from when I lived here, only they've been painted white. The carpet is newer, and I'm pretty sure the couch has been replaced, but being here feels eerily the same as it did all those years ago. It feels like...home.

"Can I get you a beer? Or d'you want something stronger?"

Bruce lines up a couple bottles of craft beer that he's pulled from an under-counter fridge and turns to where a couple shelves display high-end liquor.

"Water's fine. Thanks."

He nods, searching a drawer for a bottle opener. "You're a Brit. Isn't beer like water to you all?" He laughs at his joke, and I start to feel uncomfortable. What am I going to talk about with this man? My sweat glands are working so hard that I end up slugging down the entire bottle of water to keep up.

Toasting my empty bottle with his beer, he says, "I couldn't be prouder to have you as a son-in-law, Tim. Always liked you back when you stayed with us, but today takes it to a whole new level. The way Jordan looks at you fills me up with joy I didn't know existed."

I'm almost too speechless to reply, but I manage, "She's spectacular. I only hope I can make her as happy as she makes me."

"Already doing it. I can see it on her face. My girl is in love and it looks great on her."

I nod and smile, but my insides are buzzing like I'm on a sugar high. Could there possibly be any truth to what he thinks he sees in his daughter?

I catch a glimpse of her sitting outside on a lounge chair by herself. Her mother has left her alone and stands in a corner chatting with her friends. All Melinda needed was the idea that her daughter was in a relationship to let up on her.

Jordan does look happy. She looks calmer and more serene than I've seen her since she started her job with the Strikers.

A part of me hopes it has something to do with me. And if it does, I really hope I don't let her down.

ordan

"I SHOULD'VE THOUGHT of this years ago." I give Tim a playful punch in the arm and lean into him. My mother is watching us leave the party with a mammoth smile plastered across her face.

Tim has reached celebrity fiancé status, giving my mother the show of shows with little affections here and there. And she's been eating up every kernel of fake-buttered popcorn we throw her way.

"Dude, you really saved my hide today." Chet's long, brown hair tickles my face as he hugs me goodbye. "With all the hoopla about you two, Mom didn't say a word about Burning Man. You sure you don't want to stay another few hours? Because I'm sure my errant ways are at the top of her playlist."

Tim laughs. "I'd love to help you, mate, but I'm worn out."

I have no doubt he is. Two hours of lying to people will do that. "I'm so glad you guys got to meet each other." After I toss out the platitude, I realize how much I mean it.

We say our goodbyes, and Chet promises to send me pictures from his Arizona trip. Then we hit the road.

"Was that terrible?" I give Tim a side-eye while staying focused on the streets. Saturday late afternoon traffic is out in full force, turning the drive down Claremont Avenue into a slog.

He doesn't answer immediately, and at the next stop sign, I turn to look at him more fully. He stares out the window, and I'm not even sure he heard my question. "Tim?"

His head turns slowly toward me, revealing his furrowed brow and the firm set of his jaw. Even those signs of distress manage to look good on him. Truly. "Yeah?"

Since traffic is terrible anyhow, I figure we're not getting home anytime soon, so I take the next right and pull into a super-market parking lot. His expression remains complicated, but he doesn't ask why we've stopped.

"Was it okay today? I'm sorry I dragged you into it, I just—"

I don't finish my thought before Tim reaches a hand toward me and slides it up my cheek until it's buried in my hair. Then his mouth is on mine.

Firm, demanding, insistent.

Delectable.

His lips are soft despite the intensity of his kiss. And holy moly, it's intense—fiery like a molten stream of lava. His lips meld with mine as though it's their only purpose in life.

I sink into those lips, letting them absorb the pent-up desire I've been fighting all afternoon.

Plain and simple, I was in denial. Complete denial about how much I wanted Tim until the delicious feeling washes over me. And now I want him more.

It's every fantasy I've had about him, every thought I've pushed away because I was sure it wouldn't happen.

Not like this.

This.

This is a kiss.

The thrust of his tongue demands more, and I feel myself respond while the rest of me goes slack against the seat. I hear a soft whimper—I think it's mine because the sound coming from Tim is a deep groan that tells me he's feeling everything I am.

There's no time to think. I can't be in my head asking what we're doing or why because this is all instinct and lust and sensation. I just go with it and let Tim take me where he wants.

Wrapping both hands around his neck, I shift in my seat, so I can get a better angle, and he turns my cheek to rest in his hand while his mouth continues to take me prisoner.

The car feels hot and awkward as we fumble past seat belts and bucket seats to connect, but it's working for me. The lack of planning or finesse fuels my need for more of him. I love that he's impulsive. I love that it's messy.

His tongue rakes against mine, tasting every corner of my mouth and asking for more. I want to give it to him.

I haven't taken a breath, but I don't care. I don't need air when I have this.

And then, I don't.

Just as abruptly, he pulls away, pinching his forehead between his fingers as he leans an elbow on the dashboard. I can see the regret on his face, but he hasn't turned away, which feels like progress for him. "I'm sorry," he says, blinking hard.

"Why are you sorry?"

"I didn't intend… I shouldn't have done that."

"Why not?" I don't mean to sound like Chet's toddler, but I can't think in long sentences. I'm at a loss as to why he thinks kissing me was a bad idea.

"I wasn't thinking. I just took what I wanted."

"I didn't stop you." I want him to be clear on that. "And I'm not sorry."

His eyes search my face, maybe for signs I'm not being honest.

But it would be dishonest to pretend a part of me hasn't wanted this since the night I first saw him at the Strikers party. Hell, I've wanted him since the day he walked into our house when I was a teenager.

A small bubble of hope rears up through the chaos in my brain and tells me this could be the beginning of something long overdue.

He throws an arm over his forehead. "I don't know what the fuck I'm doing."

And the bubble pops like the weak little excuse for soap fluff it is. I roll down the window. It feels suffocating in here. The air outside is so still and warm that I still can't get the breath I need, so I push open the door and get out of the car.

"Well, you better figure it out," I call behind me as I walk away. The parking lot is full, so I weave between cars looking for some space. I need to put some distance between myself and the awkwardness. Then Tim and I can go back to annoying each other.

That was so much easier.

I don't expect Tim to chase after me. This isn't a ploy. I just need air.

"Jordan." His hand is on my shoulder, but I don't move. I don't need to see any more regret on his face or hear more apologies. This day has been draining enough already.

"It's fine. Just…go back to the car."

He doesn't move. His hand stays where it is, and I wriggle out from under it.

"Love…"

"Don't call me that. Not right now."

I don't have to look at him to know that he's raking a hand through his hair. And most likely making it look so much sexier in the process. Even more reason that I should stay focused on the upside-down shopping cart in the corner of the lot and continue wondering how it got that way.

"I need to talk to you. Will you look at me?"

"You can talk."

He exhales a long, frustrated breath. I'm right there with him. Frustrated. Exhausted. And deeply tired of this whole charade.

"Let's call it off," I say.

"Sorry?"

"The fake dating, the engagement, the whole thing. It's not worth it. Let's just forget all of it."

"Jordan, that's what I wanted to talk to you about."

Against my better judgment, I turn to look at him. Damn. His hair looks amazing, and his gaze bears down on me with an apologetic yet somehow sexy smirk which makes me want to wrap myself around his body and climb him.

Which I will not do.

Instead, I bite down hard on my bottom lip. And again, against my better judgment, I don't flinch when his hand reaches out gently and frees my lip from between my teeth, and he smooths his thumb over it, sending a lick of fire through my veins.

"Stop."

"What?"

"If you touch me…like that." I point to his hand and my lips. "I'm going to want to do that." I point to the car.

He nods. Crosses his arms and fixes his olive eyes on me. It's hard not to get lost in them, and I hate that I'm so easily rocked from my steady foundation.

"Good. I just don't want to disappoint you, of all people," he says softly. I'm about to ask what he means by that when he reaches for my cheek the way he did in the car. Only this time, his motion is slow, as though he doesn't want to scare me off. I'm skittish in his presence now, so it's the right decision.

His fingers brush the side of my face and light up every nerve ending in their wake. I shudder with this gentle touch, willing him to continue while bracing myself for the moment he stops. Again.

But he doesn't. His hand finds its way into my hair once more and continues on its path until his fingers curl around the back of my neck. He pulls my face closer but not so close that he's out of focus.

"What I want to do…is this," he says, grazing my lips with his own. I'm unsteady on my feet from the contact, swaying so much he has to hold me up.

I nod like a zombie. I want him to keep going. What else do I need to do to convince him?

He closes his eyes again. Anguished. "But that's not smart. It confuses things. And we're already got ourselves into a bit of a mess." He's so close, staring into my eyes until he melts me with that laser field he seems to possess.

"I don't care."

He flinches at my words, an unsure cloud falling over his eyes. They're so beautiful, I can't look away. I don't want to, even if he plans to keep telling me how wrong we are.

"Fine, then."

I could close the gap between us and sink into his lips again. I want to, but I also want to know what he plans to do. So I wait.

Tim shakes his head and tilts it so our foreheads meet. "I'm an idiot, and I'm sorry."

"Why are you an idiot?" My voice sounds breathy and calmer than I feel. He's knocked nearly all the air from my lungs with his proximity, and I don't want to lean away, but I need to see his face.

I pull back just enough so I can see him better. His eyes are unfocused and dreamy, exactly the way I feel. But I can't give into dreamy. I need to understand what he's telling me. "What happened back there?" I ask.

"Same thing that's happening now. I can't…I can't say no when it comes to you. I should. If I had any amount of self-control. But the eighteen-year-old with willpower is long gone, and the man I am now can't resist you. Not at all."

I do my best to inhale, but it doesn't work very well. I still feel short of breath, and he's confusing me with words that taunt me to swoon into his arms and push back against whatever resistance holds him back. I want to tear it down. Obliterate it.

"Why do you need to resist?"

He shakes his head. "I have a habit of letting people down."

"Tim," I say quietly, venturing a hand to the side of his face and fighting to ignore the whole-body reaction I have to touching him. He shudders at the contact. "I'm not worried about that."

He shakes his head. "If I kiss you again the way I want to, I'm not going to be able to stop."

My heart thunders in my chest, vibrating the earth around us. I'm sure he can feel it. Shoppers in Safeway are probably crawling under paper towel displays and going through earthquake drills because of me.

My brain is shuffling through these deep thoughts while we stand here frozen between a Prius and some ridiculous giant SUV that no one needs to run to the market for canned goods.

He takes a deep breath, and when he exhales, I feel the resolve harden even more. "We work together and I respect that. I respect you. So like I said, I'm trying to be a better guy than I want to be."

I've been with guys who give lip service, trying not to seem too horny, but this is absurd. Does he really not get it? I can't believe he's standing this close to me, and he can't feel how much my entire body hums under the touch of one hand on my neck.

I can't take it anymore. "Tim. Thank you. You are a good guy —*believe* that. I appreciate your respect and your consideration for my vulnerability, I do. But if you don't fucking kiss me right now, I'm going to lose my mind."

That does it.

Tim's eyes flash with the heat he's had bridled under white knuckles. They go a deeper green than I've ever seen, and his eyelids drop right before I lose the ability to focus. His lips crash into mine, and his hand tightens around my neck, urging me closer to him, but I'm already there.

He has both hands in my hair now, and our tongues are an insatiable tangle, going deeper, searching for more. I have no idea whether we're in the path of shopping carts or cars, and I don't give a damn. They can just avoid us because this needs to happen right now.

We're a tornado.

My hands push up over his pecs and shoulders, gripping the taut muscles and appreciating every inch of him.

Tim's hands roam down my back, and I hear him groan when they reach my ass. He gathers the skirt of my dress and lifts me. My legs encircle his waist like I do this every day of the week, and now I know how I'll program my calendar.

We're moving, and I don't bother to worry about where he's taking me, though I do wonder how he can see. But regardless, I don't open my eyes or worry too much because I'm busy taking in the sensation of his lips—the kissing.

The kissing.

Holy mother of all Belgian chocolate and salted caramel ice cream in the world—food porn's got nothing on his mouth. It saps me of all ability to care about much else. We can play human bumper pool amid the cars, and I'll be down with it.

Instead, I feel my back hit something metal and cold. A truck? A dumpster? I don't care because it allows me purchase to wrap my legs more tightly around him and get some friction where I need it.

His hands come back to my face, his touch gentle, and everything slows down. His kisses grow more deliberate, more liquid and molten. I loosen my grip around his neck and let my hands roam down his back. But then I start to slip.

"I've got you, love." One arm loops beneath me and holds me up like I weigh no more than a powder puff. He kisses the underside of my chin and marks the skin with a tiny nip that sends another river of chills down my spine.

My hands drift into his hair as his lips glide against mine, still gentle, finding the right angle before our tongues take over.

It's possible we spend an hour kissing in the Safeway parking lot. It may not be a first for Safeway, but it's a first for me. Impulsive actions don't end well for me, and this is definitely impulsive. Public displays are not my thing.

Until now. Now, when the way I normally behave seems silly when the alternative is this.

Tim sucks hard on my bottom lip, and I feel a new thread of sensations pulse through me, ending between my legs. So I swivel my hips a tiny bit and grind into what I can feel is a fierce erection.

"Jordan…" Tim pants, tipping his forehead against mine. "I don't know where we go from here."

I have thoughts.

Most of them involve the nearest horizontal surface, and honestly, I'm not even that picky. But I know what he means. I wait for him to freak out again.

He trails a finger gently down my temple and winds a strand of my hair around his finger. Then another one, because let's face it, my hair is a freaking mess.

As I come out of the kissing haze, I start to notice my surroundings again and discover that I am, in fact, pressed up against a large yellow recycling bin. I unwrap my legs from around Tim's waist and slide down to my feet. He allows this, but he keeps his hands on me, and my hands slide down to rest against the hard planes of his chest. My breath catches, and I play it off by clearing my throat.

"Maybe we don't need to know," I say.

His laugh is low and deep. The sound of it is addicting. "I like the non-work Jordan," he says, surveying me. My hands go to my hair, which I smooth down, even though I know it's futile.

"Non-work Jordan likes you too," I say because she's done lying to herself. Or to him.

im

I HAVE no idea what it says about me that spending the afternoon with Jordan's parents has my dick so hard that I've barely made it out of her parking garage before pushing her up against the wall of the elevator.

She's had me in a trance from the moment I drove here this morning. Watching her flit around the party, saying hello to relatives and playing with toddlers, made me like her so much more than I ever thought possible. It made me see her in a way that opened possibilities for me—a future I could never visualize because all the versions I wanted had her in them. And that seemed impossible.

But now I feel myself edging down the near-vertical slope of falling in love with her. Not like it's a new feeling. I'm just allowing myself to believe in it for the first time. And allowing myself to want her.

To be clear, the way I want her currently has nothing to do with her parents.

"C'mere, love," I say against her mouth. As though she could be any closer when I have my body pressed flush against hers.

"Wait," she breathes. "The succulents, they're in the car."

"Beauty of cactus. They can stay there all night because I'm not taking my hands off you."

Her mouth tastes like honey drizzled over berries, and I feel like a man possessed. I want to find my way through every corner of it. Wrapping her tongue with mine, I draw her in further and hear a tiny moan that makes me even harder than I've ever been in my life.

Makes sense because I've never wanted anyone as much as I want her. Everywhere. All the time. It's relentless, the way I think about her when I'm awake and in my dreams when I'm not.

All the time.

I have my hands in her hair, and hers have looped around my neck. Her fingers brush against the skin at the nape.

When she scrapes her nails over my scalp, I nearly fall to the ground.

The elevator stops at her floor, and she indicates our direction without coming up for air. I move us as one from the small compartment and down the short hallway without letting our mouths separate. I can't.

I won't.

Fumbling in her pocket for keys, she has to look down. Then we're inside, and I press her against the front door. "This mouth," I gasp. "I can't get enough."

She moans her agreement and succumbs to the kiss that lasts for a month.

"This is my place," she breathes, which makes me laugh because it's dark, and I can't see a damn thing in here.

"Not asking for a tour now, love." I'm only focused on navigating around furniture, so we make it to her couch in the living room without bumping into things. "Unless there's a dog or cat I'm about to step on."

"Nope, just a goldfish. You're safe."

My hands trail down her back until I can grab both delicious cheeks in my hands and lift her up. Placing her gently on the couch, I climb over her, holding myself up on my forearms, my eyes never leaving hers.

Her hair splays across a white throw pillow in the way I've always imagined it would look, long russet tendrils in every direction, picking up the moonlight that streams through the tall panes overlooking some trees.

"Beautiful." My voice sounds like a growl, which feels fitting because I want her with an animalistic need I've never felt before.

She tips her head in the direction of the windows. "I can't see outside right now."

This woman. She still doesn't get it.

"Wasn't talking about the view, love."

I see the realization on her face, and I love the way her fierce denial of the effect she has on me melts away as my words sink in. "Not just beautiful. Extraordinary. Fucking amazing."

"Tim…" Her chest rises beneath me, and her breath shudders. "Thank you."

I shake my head slowly because I don't deserve thanks when I'm the beneficiary of everything, and I still can't fathom how I've finally gotten this lucky.

Having her here makes me whole.

And there's still so much in front of us. Bending to kiss her, I take it slower, brushing my lips over hers and absorbing the quiet sigh each time I find a different angle and increase the friction.

I haven't lowered myself onto her, and every inch of my body is screaming at me in protest, but I'm living for the sounds she makes when I kiss her, so I won't let my eager, swollen dick get in the way of what she wants.

For now.

But I sure as hell am lifting that ridiculous long dress out of the way. "I'm fucking burning this dress. It swallows this gorgeous body." I push it up over her hips and drag my knuckles over her white lace panties. Up and down. And again. "Tell me, love, were you picturing this when you put these on this morning? Did you wear them for me?"

"Yes," she pants.

"Good girl."

Her hands twine in my hair and she pulls me closer. "Tim, I—" Her eyes close, and she sighs.

"Show me, love. Show me how you want me."

The words seem to fuel her, and her tongue finds mine. Our kisses grow deeper, more searching and hungry. Dropping myself down, I let our bodies meld with each other. Her hips buck up to meet mine, and her legs wrap around my waist.

With both hands on my face, she kisses my lips, my chin, the line of my jaw. When her head falls back, her eyes glassy, I run my tongue along her jaw and let my breath feather against her ear. I hear a tiny gasp and it fuels me.

"Are you wet for me, love? What am I going to find underneath these panties?"

"Take them off and find out," she pants.

First, I push the voluminous blue waves of fabric over her head, revealing a lacy bra like the one I recall desperately trying not to gawk at beneath her damp shirt that first night. It feels like ages ago, and yet I can't deny that some part of my brain dared me to believe I'd end up here.

Desperate wishing.

"Fuuuck," I groan, taking in her petite form, perfect breasts cupped by irrelevant lace. I'm so overtaken by the need to touch every inch of her skin that I don't know where to begin.

She helps by peeling down the straps of her bra and unsnapping the clasp in front. The lace cups fall to the sides, and I drop my mouth to the soft pale skin of one breast, then the other. My tongue circles her nipple, coaxing it to a hard peak in an instant.

This isn't me going through the motions of getting myself off by touching a woman. This is me finally feeling like I've come home to a place I didn't know existed for me. I didn't think it could.

Every inch of her skin feels sacred, and running my hands over her abdomen and feeling her breath heave from her chest lifts me higher. When I feel her delicate skin just above the elastic of her panties pebble under my fingers, I'm pounded by the sensation of wanting every touch to linger, to ripple on and on.

This is where I belong.

She reaches for the hem of my Henley and pushes it up over my abs, higher until I rip the thing over my head. I watch her eyes grow hazy as she takes in the hard planes of my chest. I know she saw them that day in the locker room, but I feel more naked with her now.

And when she licks her lips, my eyelids drop in anticipation of her hands on my skin. But only for a moment. I want to watch her.

She reaches both hands for my abs and runs her fingers up and down, tracing her fingernails over my pecs and back down toward my aching dick.

"Take them off," I growl. Jordan doesn't hesitate, quickly slipping the belt through its buckle and unbuttoning my jeans. I help her push them down my legs and feel a more intense throbbing when we're finally skin on skin.

All my life, I've known purpose in the game of football or soccer or whatever the hell a person wants to call the game that's been my home. But this—this is a different kind of purpose. It makes everything else seem trivial.

Somehow I had the wherewithal to know at eighteen that being with Jordan would be the endpoint, and it would derail me from everything else if I didn't leave. Now, I have no such fear.

I'm not going anywhere. Couldn't if I wanted to. That's how bad I have it for this woman.

Walking away again isn't an option.

Lust and love and gratitude spill forth in a punishing kiss that goes on and on until we're both left gasping for breath.

"This is what you do to me," I grit out, pressing into her soft flesh so there's no mistaking how hard I am and how much I need to be inside her.

She moans against my neck, and her hips circle against my erection. Over and over again.

"Tim…oh my God. I'm already…"

No.

I mean, yes. But no.

The frantic feeling of needing every part of her winds down to a languid pace. Now that I finally have her here, underneath me, I want to draw out every second into slow motion.

I want to push her over the edge again and again, but not yet. "I want your first orgasm on my tongue," I growl, coaxing the whisp of fabric down her legs.

I'm certain she can feel my heart, which is beating hard against my ribs. Her eyes watch me watching her, and I'm hit with the full weight of a moment I've been anticipating for half my life. I slide down her legs, letting my tongue roam over her sensitized flesh until she's trembling underneath.

Coaxing her legs apart, I tease her entrance with light brushes of my fingers, watching her eyes drift shut. She licks her lips again, and her hands grapple with the couch cushions, looking for purchase. Finding none, she grabs my shoulders and holds on.

"Tim, oh God…"

"I'm just getting started, love."

Then I stop talking and let my tongue have what it wants, licking her lightly before drinking her in like I've been dying to do for days. Among her gasps, I bury my own, drawn in by her sweet flesh like a drug I'll never get over.

I find her sweet clit and circle my tongue over the tender bud, feeling her body coil beneath my hands.

Over and over, I tease and lick and suck until I can feel her orgasm build. Then I back away, giving her a chance to recover before starting again. Sweet, sweet torture.

"That's right, love."

She's past the point of responding with words. Her teeth sink into her bottom lip, and all I get is a moan. Hands fisting in my hair.

Then I start to feel her clench on my tongue. I can feel her orgasm unspool as she loses her ability to hold back. One more second, and she shatters around me.

My name on her lips. Only mine. A few curses thrown in for good measure. And complete surrender.

The moment is better than a shutout against the number one football club in the Champions League. Even if you don't give a fig about the sport, you get the idea.

My boxer briefs are around my ankles before she's recovered enough to utter a word. I can't wait a second longer.

She's nodding as I ransack my wallet for a condom and practically tear the packet in two with my teeth. I'm set to roll it on when her hand wraps around mine.

"Wait." Her voice is soft but definitive. I meet her eyes.

Wait?

No. Can't.

She takes the condom from me and slowly, torturously, rolls it on before taking my length in her fist and stroking hard. Then delicately. Then...okay, she actually might kill me.

Holy. Fuck.

Her mouth turns up at the corner, and I see that every bit of delicious torture I unleashed on her with my tongue is about to be repaid. And then some.

She pulls me toward her and I sink into her kiss. Our mouths mold to each other like missing puzzle pieces. It's almost enough just to kiss her.

Almost.

With the stroke of her hand, she has me climbing to a place I can't fathom. "Love, if I don't—"

The words die on my lips as she guides me inside her. I can't hold back anything, and I don't. I thrust. One push and I fill her, press her to her limits. She moans into my mouth and takes it.

Then I start to move. She circles against me, and our rhythm builds. Higher. Better.

"Tim…I'm already…" The words get lost in a sigh.

Faster. Can't stop this.

Want her.

Need, need her.

And really, don't need a bloody lot of anything else. Ever.

When I crest and come hard inside her, I feel her clench and ride me harder. Her cries match my own. My shudders reverberate in hers.

Every last bit of us in sync.

CHAPTER 22

im

Sleeping doesn't happen.

It's a good thing, actually, because if Jordan hears me moan and groan as my knee seizes up at night like it does, she'll probably change her mind about letting me play.

So, sex it is.

Not exactly a hardship to keep her up all night trying to outdo ourselves.

By morning, I slip out of her bed after she falls asleep and walk down the hill to Claremont for smoothies and some coffee. And I stretch the hell out of my damn quads and calves, trying to loosen up my torn ligament before she sees me limping around. A couple Advil, and I'm feeling pretty good by the time I head back to the bedroom and kiss her swollen lips awake.

Sleepy eyes blink open, and I watch her pull me into fuzzy morning focus. I'm wearing boxers and nothing else. I ditched the rest when I walked in the door.

The slow smile spreading across her face might as well be a fishhook for the effect it has on me. I'm caught. Captive. Hers.

I put the tray with the breakfast drinks on the wicker bedside table, which is otherwise empty. The one on the other side of the bed has a water pitcher, empty glass, and a stack of books I want to look through, but not right now.

Reaching a lazy hand for me, Jordan beckons me to climb back in beside her. When I do, she curls her legs around me and tucks her head into my chest.

It's a version of heaven I didn't think existed on earth. "G'morning, love."

"Did you sleep?" she asks, stroking my cheek with her hand.

"Little bit. I'll need a nap for sure."

My thoughts return to my knee as I feel my leg cramp up a little. I haven't spent enough time stretching, but I'm not about to leave her behind in this bed.

"Jordan."

"Yes?"

"Can we talk a minute?"

Her brow furrows. "Uh-oh." She untangles herself from me and sits up higher. Her hair spills around her shoulders like a goddess. But her mouth is quickly drawing down into a frown, and I realize what she's thinking.

I move closer and cup her cheek in my hand. Then I kiss her softly, hoping to convince her this isn't about her. "No, this isn't me saying last night was a mistake, if that's what you're thinking."

She doesn't look convinced. "O-kay…"

"It's a knee question."

Her features relax. "Oh. Okay, sure. What's up?"

I inhale a fortifying breath and let it out slowly. "I know I arm-twisted you into letting me finish the season, but now there's post. What does it look like if I stop playing and let it heal? Would I miss a game? Two?"

Her face falls and she shakes her head. "It's past that point now that it's torn. You're risking a complete rupture of the ligament every time you play."

"And if that happens, I'll need surgery to replace the ligament."

"Yes. This isn't new information. What's going on?"

I'm basically stalling. I want to tell her the real reason I need to finish out the season, but I've already put her in a clear conflict of interest position, and I don't want to exploit it. "But so far, you still think I look okay to play if I follow all the protocols, do the physical therapy, take all the precautions?"

"Yes. So far. We've talked about this."

"And you still believe it. Not as someone who just had a dozen amazing orgasms, but as my doctor?"

"I'm offended that you don't think she and I are the same person." She's smiling, so I don't think she's overly bothered.

"Yeah? How offended?" I reach down and let the tip of my finger roll down her stomach, hinting at where I'd like to take it next.

Her smile twists into a naughty smirk. "If I tell you I'm very offended, will it lead to orgasm number thirteen?"

I want to give it to her so badly. I want to give her everything. "You only need to ask, love. I'd prefer not to offend you at all."

My finger continues its path downward, and she stretches her neck and lays her head on the pillow with a sigh. Her eyes drift shut. We don't have much chance at a long discussion if I keep touching her, and she keeps making those seductive noises, so I pull my hand back.

"So there's no way to let a torn ligament just heal?

She opens her eyes, and I watch the hazy lover give way to the grounded thinker. I can't decide which I prefer. "You really want to talk about this now?"

I nod.

She sits up and pulls the sheet up over her bare chest, tucking it under her arms. I yank it down, the playful urge unencumbered by thought. It earns me a growl, and she pulls it back up.

"If you're making me have a serious conversation right now, this sheet stays."

"Your loss." I waggle my eyebrows.

Her face grows serious. "It can heal, but it will take months to get to where you can start training at full strength. Or there's the other option."

Surgery.

I exhale a long breath. I hate this, but I'm starting to love her. And I trust her.

"Tell me more."

She reaches for me, cups my cheeks in her hands, and kisses me lightly on the lips. "You'd be okay, I promise. It's minimally invasive, and the recovery is much shorter than ACL surgery. That's the good news."

I nod, not wanting to shift so much that it causes her to remove her hands. "It's the bad news I'm worried about."

"I know. There are always unknowns. But I've had great results with PRP, reducing the healing time."

"What's PRP?"

"Platelet-rich plasma. We draw blood from you pre-surgery, spin it to isolate the platelets, and inject it into the joint. It's amazing. Not FDA approved yet, which is why insurance doesn't cover it."

"I'm not worried about the insurance. Team covers that." Just thinking about this exhausts me. Maybe she had the right idea— talking about this when I'm in bed with a naked woman I can't keep my hands off of makes zero sense.

"That wasn't my point. I mean, it's still considered experimental, but the evidence is there. I really think it's your best chance at getting back to full strength and getting back in the game. You just need to be smart in the short run so you can play in the long run."

I grimace at that. Not my strong suit.

"I know." She pats my cheek. "I get it. You wouldn't be the

player you are if you waited your turn. But for this, it's crucial to think big picture. A couple months is nothing in a career."

But I don't have a couple months.

I have my chance. I should tell her why it matters so much. I want to, but spending the afternoon with her family reminded me of the differences between us. She comes from a line of doctors, and I'm still that upstart kid from a small English town, son of a mechanic who still owes something to his family. Playing through the season is my only option.

She plunks her head against the pillow behind her and gestures for me to get everything off my chest. "Talk to me, footie player. What are you worried about?"

But I chicken out. "Nothing. Just asking. Am I seeing you tomorrow for my evaluation?"

"Do you really need to ask me that?" she laughs.

I shake my head and yank the sheet down. Before she can protest, I press my lips against hers. Conversation over.

ordan

THERE'S nothing like the smell of sweaty athletes running through physical therapy drills to erase the fatigue and sharpen my focus on a Monday morning.

Sitting in my office, I outline my lips with a fingertip, recalling how Tim did the same on Saturday night and well into Sunday. Every nerve ending fires, even as my skin feels the withdrawal from his touch. Jesus. I've never, ever experienced anything like that.

I give my sixteen-year-old self a pat on the back. "Good job, younger me. You were right all along." But if I'm being honest, sixteen-year-old Jordan was *not* ready for Tim Cheltenham. No way, no how.

But she's sure ready now.

My coffee has gotten cold while I've sat at my desk replaying the weekend in my mind. I didn't get much sleep, even once I went home yesterday, so I need the liquid gold more than ever. I'm willing to drink the swill that passes for coffee in the physical therapy room, and I head that way with my lukewarm cup.

"Hey." The voice sends a delicious zing of heat over my skin, and I feel my cheeks edge up into a smile.

Turning, I spot Tim coming down the hallway, a hand casually stuffed in the pocket of his training jacket, which is zipped to his neck. His hair still wet from the shower, he looks even better than my memory of him from twenty-four hours earlier. I lift my face to his for a kiss when he catches up to me.

"Good morning. I thought maybe you were going to be a no-show." I try to sound casual, but it's impossible to keep the smile from my face.

"Never." His lips quirk to the side as he looks me up and down. "No lawyer clothes today?"

Looking down at my hip-hugging jeans and long-sleeved Strikers tee under my white coat, I nod. "I'm trying out a little business very casual."

"More like business very sexy."

We stand there grinning at each other like lovesick loons until I somehow shake myself back to sensibility. "Thanks to our fake engagement, I've had the pleasure of talking to my mother six times in one day."

He grimaces. "That's pretty bad for a Sunday."

"That was today. Yesterday, I lost track after a dozen calls and texts."

"Oh, no. That's bad." Smiling, he nudges my hand with his, but even that minute contact thrills my senses. I look up and down the hallway and don't see anyone, so I wrap my fingers around his and give them a squeeze before taking a step back.

"I was coming to see you. We have an appointment, Doctor Page, do we not?" He gives me a salute to go along with my title.

Holding up my empty cup, I explain, "Needed a quick cup of sustenance."

Holding up a cardboard tray I didn't notice, he points to the two cups of coffee and a paper bag. "Problem solved. Let's go."

He turns around, and I follow him back to my office, sneaking a look at how his broad shoulders taper down to the rest of his athletic build. As my eyes roam over his tight ass, he throws a smirk over his shoulder. "You checking me out, Doctor Page?"

Blushing, I pray no one can hear him. "Hardly. Just wondering why an athletic guy like you walks so slowly."

We reach my office. As soon as I cross the threshold, he closes the door behind me and presses me against it. "It's because I'm carrying hot coffee," he says before kissing me. He puts the tray on my desk behind him and kisses me again, this time lingering for a deep sweep of his tongue, which has me weak in the knees. I feel him holding me up and hate that he knows how limp and willing he makes me, but I love that he's here for it.

Within a minute, his hands have pushed into my hair, and he's torn away the hairband tying it into a neat bun. The strands fall over my shoulders, and he groans, pressing his erection into me. This could get very hot very fast.

We're already there.

I have very little hesitancy in letting Tim's mouth take the place of my morning coffee. None. At. All.

But after a few more breathless kisses, I feel his hands roam down my back and over my ass. His appreciative moan tells me exactly where this is headed, and I have enough self-awareness to know that my door isn't locked. And this job is still new.

Pulling back with a whimper, I draw in a breath. "Good morning, footie player."

"Morning, love. That greeting sounded much better the other day when I was in your bed." His hands move up my back, and he drapes them over my shoulders, leaning in to kiss me again.

I fall into the kiss and momentarily allow its current to take me before I once again come to my senses. Reluctantly, I pull away, gratified when I hear Tim's wistful sigh.

"Ah, I kinda like that I can see you at work. And I kinda hate that we can't do this all day."

"Same," he says. "And then there's the part of your job where any day, you tell me I'm too injured to play. I hate that too."

Defeat visible in the sag of his features, he shoves his hands back into his pockets. We walk down the hall to the treatment rooms. He swings a leg onto the exam table and sits on it, facing me.

We run through a battery of tests. The MRI results go to the radiologist, and while we wait for them to be read, I do a series of manipulations to test Tim's reflexes, his mobility, and his launch speed, which is key when he goes from zero to sprinting on the field.

Pointing to the treadmill in the corner, I check to make sure he's wearing running shoes. Check. "Hop on there, and get yourself going at a ten-minute pace. Warm up for a minute."

He does as told, and I back away to watch his stride from the back. "You checking out my ass again?"

"I'm evaluating your stride," I say through the grin I can't push away.

"Ha. Okay, doc. Evaluate away." He cranks up the speed.

"Did I say to run faster?"

"No, but a ten-minute pace is practically a stroll for a bloke with legs this long. Come on, give me something."

"Just keep it at a jog, please." I'm glad he's facing away, so he doesn't see the hot flush on my cheeks. I'm not gonna lie—this is probably the best moment on the best day in a job I already love. Watching Tim's calves flex and his quads rip as he speeds up his pace to just over eight minutes per mile gives me a full body chill. Mixed with heat. Ending at my core.

I shift a bit and press my legs together, needing to relieve some tension. Then I talk myself down.

You are a physician. You are at work.

Tim is really goddamn hot.

"How am I doing?" He snaps me out of my inappropriate thoughts. But, oh, they're so much more fun than taking everything so seriously all the time.

"You look great." It comes out breathless. He hops onto the side rails and turns to look at me, an obvious smirk on his face.

"I do, do I? Have you been looking at my stride at all, or just undressing me with your eyes?"

Caught, I give up on trying to pass it off. "I've been doing both."

Without stopping the belt on the treadmill, he hops off, and his hands trail down my back and grip my ass—hard. His mouth is hot, claiming what he wants.

He's so good at this. At the first press of his lips, my whole body flames with anticipation. I'm hot and bothered and so, so into this.

Anyone could walk into the treatment room, but my over-worked brain is busy doing calculations as to the odds. It seems like the chances are good we'll be left alone, at least long enough for me to get good and kissed. I need this like I need my morning coffee—it's a vital requirement for feeling alive. Without it, I'm barely human.

My heart flutters unevenly in my chest—thank God we're in a medical facility because I might code. Moaning into his kiss, I press against the hard planes of his chest.

I grip his shoulders, feeling the swell of muscle under the soft jersey knit of his shirt. My nails rake over his flesh, and I hear him groan.

We've gone from zero to a thousand in seconds, and I'll be naked on the floor in another minute if I don't put the brakes on, so slowly…regrettably…I pull away and lay my cheek against his chest. "I think…"

I don't know what I think.

Tim laughs quietly, stroking my hair and trailing his hand down my back. "What do you think?"

"I think…you make it hard to think."

"Ha. Thinking's overrated. I'll take it as a compliment." He kisses my forehead, my nose, my chin. I melt a little bit more.

He looks back at the treadmill, which is still rolling along swiftly in the corner. Hitching a thumb over his shoulder, he asks, "Are you going to make me do more of that, or would you like to not think some more?"

"I'd like to do both. But since I also don't want to lose my job, get your ass on the treadmill."

He obeys, hopping onto the side rails, holding himself over the belt and dropping down onto it. His feet start flying again, hitting close to an eight-minute pace.

Still a little dazed from the kiss, I try to focus on his form. Which distracts me again. "Focus, Jordan," I mutter to myself.

"What's that, love?" he asks, not even out of breath.

"Nothing. I'm good!" I call.

Liar.

I've completely flipped for him, and I've never felt so unsteady before. Never felt so happy either.

By the time I'm done evaluating everything from his speed to his reflexes, I've formed a more complete picture of what I'm dealing with. The MRI confirms it—Tim needs surgery to repair his ligament and a tear in the meniscus if he wants to get back to full strength. Even if he nurses the sprain back to health, the tear is the bigger limiting factor. He probably won't be able to post the kind of stats he needs without it.

"Tim, I need you to trust me."

He waggles his eyebrows. "Does that mean I should lock the door? Because I'd like to have you examine me *everywhere*, Doctor Page."

My panties get wet at the thought. Yes, we are definitely doing that.

I put a hand lightly on his bicep and dig my fingers into the hard muscle. Then I lean toward his ear. "Talk first, then I'll do anything you want," I whisper, letting my breath fan over his neck until I hear him groan.

Dropping onto my rolling stool as if under a spell, he nods. "Start talking."

I've spent enough nights with Tim by now to have heard him whimper or outright scream in pain while he sleeps. It guts me. However hard he tries to grit through the pain when he's awake, the nights tell me everything he won't.

I keep my voice calm, not too worried about hitting him with bad news because he's seen this coming for months. He has to know what I'm about to say. I'm hoping it will land softer coming from me. If he trusts me. "I think you need surgery."

He visibly startles. "Sure. Right. Not doing that, at least not during the season. We have a month break coming up. We can talk about it then." His mouth settles into a hard line. His eyes look flinty and suspicious suddenly. I don't like it.

I shake my head. And we're back where we started.

CHAPTER 24

Tim

We're done training for the day, and I look up after our cool down stretches to see Jordan sitting in the low bleachers just above the field. I have no idea how long she's been there, and I wonder if she's cataloging every twist and turn of my knee for her records.

Probably.

I felt better today than I have in a while, so I have to give credit where it's due. She's changed my physical therapy protocol, changed everything, changed me. It's brutal, but it's helping. I finally feel like my muscles are rebounding, rather than limping along under duress. The underlying injury is still there, but I've managed to correct the areas where overcompensating was hurting me more.

Bigger question is whether she'll decide I'm fit enough to play in this weekend's game, now that she's hell bent on me having surgery instead of finishing out the season. We're going day by day, and I'm basically holding my breath.

So far, every scan and test has shown that my ligament is still intact. But I hate the feeling that I'm disappointing Jordan by not listening to her advice.

I can see Steiner licking his lips every time I take a prescribed break from training to ice down my knee and stretch. He has no idea these remedies are making me stronger, and I feel no need to satisfy his curiosity with an explanation.

Every day, he's a little more ruthless in his pursuit, coming at me a little harder in training than is necessary, trying to knock me off my game. He's done everything short of outright tackling me.

Everyone notices, and everyone knows why he's doing it. He's not the only second-stringer who resorts to underhanded methods to earn some playing time. The good news is that Coach doesn't seem to be falling for it.

I can be accused of being daring. It's how I make some of my best plays on the field. I go by instinct, seeing an opportunity, an opening, and taking a shot. More times than not, taking a risk pays off. Either my team gets a shot on goal, or we catch our opponents flat footed and give ourselves an advantage.

But Jordan and I...lying to everyone about my fitness to play...we're on a whole other level of risk-taking, and I'm not sure anyone can win at this game.

I also can't convince myself to stop. Even if I wanted to follow her recommendation, it feels too good to be out there playing, even injured.

And it feels too good off the field as well, but it's so intertwined. I'm starting to lose sight of where my gratitude for letting me keep playing ends, and the feeling that I might be in love with her begins.

If I'm honest, somewhere in the back of my mind, I've never let go of her.

At sixteen, she had a confidence about her, a brilliance that had nothing to do with being a good student. She shined brighter than anyone else in the room, and the beautiful thing was that she didn't act that way. It was almost as if she couldn't see it herself, didn't know her worth—which is impossible, right?

My attraction to her back then was purely accidental. More than that, it was unwelcome and inconvenient. The last thing I needed to do at eighteen was throw away my chance to live in the States.

It's no secret that by the time players reach academy level in England, we're playing quite high-level soccer. Take any one of those players and plunk him down in a regular US high school, and it's a game changer. I wasn't anything special as far as English academy players go, but in the US, I was a star.

I made a decision right then and there that after I finished university or played for a semi-pro team in England, I'd take the first opportunity to come back to the States for good. I liked the idea of being a key player on a well-run American team rather than busting my hump to ride the bench on an English Premier League team like Arsenal, where our keeper, Holden Sanders, is spending the year.

And with my dad kicking me out of the house, I just needed to get through that final year of high school in my new US high school, become a legal adult, and hopefully get recruited to play on scholarship at university. It was a good plan.

But Jordan crept into my world and turned it upside down without even understanding her power over me. I defy any eighteen-year-old, even one with an eye on an elusive career prize, to resist that kind of temptation. I knew I didn't have the wherewithal.

I tried ignoring her, got up even earlier because I noticed she was getting up a bit earlier too. But I'd manage to leave the house before we had to cross paths in the kitchen or in the hallway.

So I had to leave. I had to get away from the beautiful temptation to wade into her waters before I drowned. But make no mistake, she remained as a fixture in my rearview, an image that urged me to turn around at my peril.

Leaving felt like the only way to preserve any hope of the future I wanted. My future was soccer. It still is. It has to be.

And now, I see the rearview image front and center in my present, and instead of scaring the crap out of me, it thrills me. I shouldn't want this woman as much as I do. That's the problem with pushing something away. Maybe it makes a person want it that much more, and that's when careless mistakes are made. I hope I can avoid making them this time.

Jordan looks up from her paperwork, and her smile calls to me like a lighthouse beacon on rough seas. That image sets in motion a plan I didn't know I had until that very moment, but now that it's taking root, it's there for good. I owe her some time on my boat.

I jog into the stands and squat on the bleacher seat directly in front of Jordan.

"Hey, footie player." Her mile-wide smile warms me more than two hours of drills.

"Hey, gorgeous." I wait for the blush I know is coming. There are no two ways about it—I'm falling in love with this woman.

Fallen. Felled. Done.

Leaning closer, I inhale the scent of her plumeria shampoo and let my eyes drift shut at the confluence of sensations—the smell, sight, and feel of her. I whisper in her ear, "I want to take you on the boat."

Drawing back, I lock eyes with hers, searching them to make sure she knows my meaning.

"You said that a while back." Her voice is quiet, a little raspy. I shake my head slowly, then run my tongue across my lips even more slowly. She swallows hard.

I lean in again. "No. I want to take you. On the boat."

Her sharp intake of breath assures me she understands this time. "Oh."

"Yeah."

"Um…" I exhale a breath against her ear and feel my dick grow hard when she lets out a tiny moan.

"Tonight, love," I rasp against her ear before running my lips down the curve of her jaw and leaving a searing kiss on the column of her throat.

I can't leave without one more look at her, so I cast a glance over my shoulder on my way down the bleachers. Eyes hazy. Lips plump and pink. Cheeks flushed. I can only imagine how much better she'll look beneath me on my boat.

And I can't fucking wait.

CHAPTER 25

ordan

AT A TIME of year when it's reliably foggy, I look up at a night sky blacker than I've ever seen. "There are stars," I murmur without shifting my eyes away from the pinpoints of dancing light on black velvet.

Tim's quiet chuckle is what finally makes me look away. "What?" I ask.

"There are stars." His amused expression makes me realize this is nothing new for him, but it doesn't blunt the revelation that getting out of the city, even a short distance on the water, feels like another world.

I've gotten myself so accustomed to the grind, convinced myself I'm not missing anything, that I haven't considered what I've been missing.

I've definitely been missing time on a boat under a romantic evening sky with the Bay Bridge lights shining from the north-facing side. My eyes shift from the stars to the brilliant strings of light reflecting in the water. Coupled with the city lights that fade as we head toward Angel Island, the setting feels like it's part of a movie set.

Perfect.

Once we get out past the breakwater and take a few speed runs under the Golden Gate Bridge, Tim cuts the engine and slows the boat to a stop in the middle of the bay.

The anchor's loud chain rolls out of the hull until it hits bottom. Nothing around us but an easy current lapping the sides of the boat. And without the motor, it's virtually silent out here.

In the distance, I hear some gulls and maybe other boat noise, but there's no question we're alone. "It's so peaceful," I say, leaning my back against Tim's side on one of the bench seats behind the captain's chair.

His arm wraps around me, and Tim dips his nose into my hair. I snuggle in closer and bring my knees in tight. There's a light breeze, but he's keeping me warm under a red plaid blanket.

"When did you get interested in soccer?" he asks.

I hope he can't see the blush spread across my cheeks. "When a cute soccer player from England came to live with my family."

"Seriously?"

"Yup."

"But he left without an explanation and hurt you."

I shrug. "I was really hung up on the guy." Then I admit, "Still am."

He pulls me in tight. "Then how lucky that the Strikers was the first team to offer me a contract." His voice is a growl against my neck, and it sends delicious ripples along my skin.

"And lucky for me, the team had an opening when I started looking for jobs as a team medical director. I just happened to know a lot about the players. One in particular." He nuzzles my ear, and my head falls back against his.

Under the blanket, one hand snakes down the front of my

body until he reaches my inner thigh. He leaves it there, promising. Taunting. Possessive.

"So you started watching soccer after I left?"

I nod. "First just US teams, whatever I could find on ESPN. Then I talked my dad into adding a few channels to our satellite lineup. Soccer's a pretty cool sport, turns out."

"It is a pretty cool sport," he agrees. "But it's called football."

"Not here, it isn't," I purr as he rubs circles with his hand.

A gust of wind blows my hair into my eyes, and I shove it away, but it's a futile effort. The wind sends more rogue flyaways flitting around my face. Tim reaches over with his other hand, snags the strands, and twists them around. Then he tucks them away like I just did, leaving his hand a beat longer than he needs to for a simple gesture. I love that nothing he does is simple.

My eyes dart to where his hand lingers. He removes it slowly, letting one finger trail down my cheek. My back arches at the contact, and he continues to draw a line along my neck, ending at the oversized Strikers hoodie I borrowed from him.

"You're wearing too much clothing for the boat."

"Really? Does the boat object?" My voice is a rasp carried on the breeze.

"I object. I really fucking object." He stands me up in front of him and wraps his arms around me, walking us forward. "You have no right to be this goddamn sexy a giant hoodie, Jordan Page," he rasps in my ear, sending ribbons of heat to my core.

"Is that making you mad?" I tease as we move along the deck.

"Furious," he groans. "And oh, the ways I will punish you for it."

He tips his head toward the stairs leading down to the captain's suite, otherwise known as a tiny room with a wall-to-wall bed and a soft down comforter. Otherwise known as paradise. He unwraps his arms and offers me his hand. I follow him downstairs.

Inside the stateroom, he spins me around and lays me back on the bed. Leaning back on my elbows, I watch him take off his shirt, his gorgeous, chiseled torso filling my vision. Okay, *this* is paradise.

He lets me enjoy the view for a few more seconds before pulling me toward him by the legs with a whoosh against the sheets. I hear a squeal and it takes me a moment to realize it came from me.

"C'mere, love."

"Aye, aye, captain."

He laughs, then peels my leggings from my body like he's deftly skinning a grape. I have no doubt my thong beneath is soaked for him, and he proves it by dipping a finger beneath the lace in one sweep through the folds of my flesh.

I feel dizzy with desire as he slips it inside me, curling it and finding friction, teasing against the perfect spot.

Inhaling a jagged breath, I watch him watching me. So I wrap my hand around his wrist and slide his hand away, my body crying out in protest at the loss of him.

He looks unsure about why I'm stopping him until I bring his hand to my lips and suck every bit of my taste from his fingers. One by one, ending with a pop.

His eyelids grow heavy, and the olive of his eyes turns into a furious storm of lust.

"I was going to take this slow, but that's not fucking happening," he says, yanking the hoodie and my shirt over my head in one motion.

In the next second, his pants are on the ground, and he's unrolling a condom he's produced from nowhere. "You're like a sex magician."

"I'm going to remember you said that, love." With one finger, he sweeps my thong away like a meddlesome gnat.

He picks me up easily and takes my place on the edge of the bed. Then he lowers me gently onto his lap. His breath against my neck and over my ear feels like a toe-curling breeze. His lips nip at the skin along my neck as my head falls back against his chest.

"Yes…" Even the one word sounds garbled through my sigh.

And that's the end of gentle. His first thrust inside hits me hard and deep. He owns me with every grind of his hips. I love it, and I love the power he has over me to make me feel untamed. Wanted. Sexy.

Palming my breasts with both hands, he shoves down the cups of my bra so he can massage my flesh, kneading and pinching until my nipples are hard and tender.

I reach down and grab his thighs, nearly choking on air when I feel the hard, rugged flex of pure muscle. So, so hot.

Every part of me is achingly sensitive to his touch, and it only takes me minutes before I'm crying out as his sexy-as-hell forearms hold me tight against his chest and his hips buck against me over and over again.

"Oh my God. I'm… I might…" So much for that coherent thought.

He renders me speechless, and all I can do is let it happen. Stars ignite and explode. A building of gorgeous heat takes me over, and I feel Tim pulsing inside me, matching me with every thrust of his hips.

"Love…" he growls. "So fucking good."

So. Fucking. Good.

Magic.

THE BOAT ROCKS GENTLY, its hull lightly slapping the water outside. Tim has the skylight propped open, and I swear there are twice as many stars as I saw earlier.

It's also possible that I'm still seeing stars from another orgasm trifecta. Very, very possible.

Tim lays on his side with me curled against him. He runs a

finger lazily through my hair, twirling it between the strands. It's perfection, floating here like this.

"I've been wanting to explain what happened back when I lived with your family…" Tim begins.

The bliss I'm feeling starts to ebb. "We don't need to talk about this. Not right now. I don't want to hear—"

"It's not what you think."

I stop protesting, frozen. Because he's watching me, I try to force a smile. "What do I think?"

"You think I left because I didn't want to be around you." He shakes his head at the ludicrous falsehood of that idea. "It was the exact opposite. I wanted to be with you from the moment I got off that plane, and your family came to meet me at baggage claim. Do you remember that day?"

I nod. "I was super shy, and I didn't know what to say to you. You seemed so confident. And so cocky about everything."

"Because I was an eighteen-year-old arse." That makes me laugh. "Anyhow, they made us sign something." He looks up through the skylight as though he can see the people he's talking about.

"What? Who made you sign something?"

"The soccer federation. The one that arranged the study abroad experience back in high school."

"Oh?"

"If we were selected, we had to sign a waiver committing to a certain number of hours of training per week, no extra-curricular activities, no drinking, and no 'excessive socializing or dating.'" He air-quotes the last part. And suddenly, I'm interested.

"It really said that?"

"Word for word. 'Course, we broke most of them." Laying on his back, Tim puts his hands behind his head.

I turn and sit cross-legged next to him so I can see his face. "Because you were eighteen."

"True. But I can see now what they were worried about. You

can't very well have students represent England and go off getting drunk, making them look bad, getting arrested, having sex with a minor… Or the thing I almost did—fall for a girl, give up soccer to chase her off to college in the US. Whatever the scenario, it couldn't happen. By signing, we committed to being soccer players before, during, and after. Coming back to England, playing for two more years for the Motherland."

I nod, waiting to hear the rest of his story, eagerly soaking up whatever droplets of information he tells me about himself. I realize I barely knew him then, even though he lived with us. "Who was the girl?"

"Cute."

"What's that mean?"

He watches me. When he seems to conclude that I'm not joking around and I don't have anything else to say, his shoulders drop. "*You* were the girl. You've always been the girl. You know this, yes?"

The whoosh of my beating heart floods my ears. "Um…"

"Jordan…"

I stare at him, unsure. My brain is normally quick off the mark when it comes to compiling medical data or making a decision about an injury protocol, but right now, I feel like the neurons are stuck in quicksand. What he's saying doesn't make sense.

"No. You turned me down and left."

He shakes his head. "No."

Now I'm getting worked up. He can't rewrite history even if he likes me now. "Yes. You left."

"Yes. I did."

"So why are you trying to tell me I was the girl you fell for and gave up soccer for? We both know what happened."

He reaches for my hand, but I pull it away, not ready to have him touch me.

"I don't think you do," he says quietly. "I didn't leave because I was trying to get away from you. I left because I knew I couldn't have you. Not in the way I wanted."

"But..." He's right. I'm not understanding. I remember what happened like it was yesterday. I went to his room. I offered myself to him. And he...said he didn't want me. That he couldn't. Then, he left.

"Love, you gave me no choice. I couldn't stay living in a house with you, see you every day, dream about you every night, and not do anything about it."

My brain is tripping over his words. He didn't dream about me. He didn't want me anywhere near him. "But I gave you the chance to do something about it. I would've given you everything."

How can the pain of rejection still hurt so much all these years later? How can I still feel it so acutely?

"I know I hurt you. And I'm so...so sorry for that. But it was the right thing to do."

"How was it the right thing?" I still don't understand. Yes, I went to school for advanced degrees and studied lots of science, but in matters concerning my own heart, I've never been a savant. Far from it.

He wraps a hand around the back of my neck and massages muscles I didn't even know were sore. He tips his forehead against mine. "Because you were sixteen, and I was visiting from another country and leaving again."

"So what? I just wanted to have fun."

"So...everything. It was never going to be just fun with you. It was always going to be more. It was going to be everything."

"Define everything."

He presses his eyes closed. When they open, I see determination, focus. And fire. "I was already half in love with you. And that was without ever touching you, ever kissing you. If I'd said yes when you walked into my room that night, there would have been no going back."

"But that-that's a good thing, right?"

He shakes his head slowly. "I'd already disappointed my dad by choosing soccer over the family business. He'd already disowned me. So at that point, it had to be soccer. I couldn't mess that up too, because it was all I had left. I'd ruined my family relationships for it. So I couldn't risk getting distracted by you. So I bolted." He pushes a hand through his hair, mussing it perfectly. The conflict doesn't leave his olive eyes. "I was…a complete mess when I went home. Took me a while to get my head on straight. Then I focused on my game, got myself moving again. It's always been that for me—soccer, football, whatever you want to call it— it's always been a way forward. But make no mistake, I'd have given it up for you. I knew it in my bones. I knew it that first day I met you. It would have been such an easy decision. So I left before I had to make it."

The revelation forces the air from my lungs.

All these years, while I worked hard to be smarter than the person next to me because I thought relying on my brain was my only option, I never understood anything at all.

I start to explain, but I'm left with my jaw hanging open and no words to do justice to what he's told me. I have no excuse for being so blind—to him, to myself, to everything.

"I'm the one who should be sorry," I finally choke out. "I'm so bad at this. At all of this." This time when he pulls me in, I let him. I curl into him like the safe haven he is. "You made the right decision. If signing that paper made sure you put soccer first, it was the right thing to do. It would have been wrong to derail your future over a girl."

"She wasn't just a girl to me," he says quietly. Words that burrow deep into my soul. "Problem was that I wanted more. It's always been my downfall, wanting more."

"That isn't a bad thing. Goals are important."

His eyes close, and when they open, there's a fire there I haven't seen before. "You're not getting it." The way his gaze fixes on my eyes feels magnetic. I can't fight its force. "*You* were the goal. You've always been the goal. It's why I came back to the Bay Area, an incorrigible part of me hoping to get back in touch. But then I learned you'd gone to medical school…and somehow the image of you as a doctor—stubbornly brilliant like I remembered you—brought me back to the look on your face when I turned you away. And I lost my nerve and didn't contact you. But make no mistake, you're the one I love."

"Tim, I—"

He presses his thumb against my lips, halting words I want to tell him, but I worry that he'll think I'm only saying them because he did.

"Just sit with it." I can see the smile in his eyes, and I nod.

"Okay."

But I love hearing his words. I love the confirmation of what I felt for him then, but something about how definitive he sounds shifts everything in me.

For all the years I've spent pursuing my own goals, I now wonder how much of my drive was born of running from what I couldn't have. I never thought I could have a real relationship with a man. Some of that was born of being rejected by Tim years ago, but I can't pin everything on that. Somewhere along the way, I gave up on wanting more.

And now I see it laid out in front of me. Maybe I can have it all. Maybe I can have him. Suddenly my steadfast insistence that I have to do everything by the book starts to crumble. I want to help him. Because I'm falling for him, and I can't see anything else outside the blinding light it casts over everything.

It doesn't feel impulsive. It feels right.

CHAPTER 26

*J*ordan

LOVE MAKES A PERSON DO CRAZY, stupid things. That's the only explanation I have for what I'm considering.

I want to let Tim him play even though my medical opinion is that he needs surgery, not another five games on the field. Ninety minutes per game. Plus stoppage. Five times. He could make it through without more damage to his knee.

Or, one wrong move, one twist or cut to the side, and the ligament could rupture. He'd be out for almost an entire season. Career-ending.

It's reckless and a potential insurance liability. It puts both our careers at risk. And it calls into question the oath I took where I promised to do no harm.

But what If I care about Tim more than I care about all those things?

We've spent almost every night together—casual nights on the couch with takeout and TV, short walks to the Ferry Building to watch the Bay Bridge lights turn on, long nights in the bedroom, and longer days at work after very little sleep.

He's everything I never believed I could have.

But before I consider letting Tim keep playing when I know he shouldn't, I need to understand a few things. It can't just be about the game. It can't.

It can't just be fear of losing his starting spot. If he's healthy, he can win it back, so it doesn't make sense that he's willing to risk further injury to finish this one season on the field. Even for a person who loves the sport and plays it for a living.

So before I make the mistake of agreeing to help him—which I really want to do because that's the kind of stupid shit a person does when she's in love—I need to know what's really going on.

I decide to use steak as my weapon of choice. Cooked with butter in a cast-iron skillet and finished in the oven with a pan of applewood smoked chips to flavor it. I learned the technique from my medical school roommate who loved to cook.

"Oh my God, this is amazing," Tim says, still chewing. I consider it a good sign when a person can't even finish a bite before singing the praises of my cooking.

I smile and slice off a piece of my own steak. He's right—it's perfect. "Glad you like it."

And because he already knows me pretty well, he questions my motives. But not before taking another bite, moaning, and finishing it. "What's up?"

"What do you mean? I wanted to cook for you. I told you that."

"I know, but I can see the wheels turning in that head of yours, and you have something else in mind. Is this where you try to bribe me with steak to have the surgery tomorrow? Because it might actually work."

"Seriously?"

He nods. "No. But if any food could do it, it would be this. And if any woman could do it, it would be you." He leans closer so he can kiss me, hand cupping my cheek. Every time, it's like this. His kisses never feel like accidental half-thoughts.

I'm almost ready to give up on my questions because we can end the whole night right here. I don't even remember what we were talking about.

But…I need to know. "Tim…" I sigh when I feel the vacuum when his lips leave mine. He pops another bite of steak into his mouth. It doesn't even need steak sauce. I swear, it's that good.

He levels me with his piercing eyes, and I'm gone. "Talk to me, Danny. What's up?" My heart melts when he uses the old nickname.

"Explain it to me. Why is it such a big deal to get through this season? It can't just be because of Steiner."

His expression sobers, and he puts down his fork. Slowly, deliberately, he brings his napkin to his lips and wipes them. I can't tell if he's stalling or just exceedingly polite.

I love him either way. I *love* him.

That's what makes all of this so hard. I want to go with my heart and do whatever makes Tim happy. But I care enough about him to want him to be healthy, so if he's taking risks, I need to know why.

So I wait. I wait for Tim to nod and think and come around to deciding to talk to me. I sit patiently and I wait.

"There's a bonus clause. You know about those, yes?" he says, finally.

I know a little. "Like when players get a bonus for scoring a certain number of goals?"

He nods. "Those are for strikers, but we get those offers too. For a season without any goals against. A clean sheet."

Which he told me he has in the second half of the season. Which is great. "But…" I don't want to say it out loud.

He fills in the blanks. "A clean sheet in the playoffs. It's a separate bonus clause that kicks in if we advance, which we obviously have."

"So it's a money thing."

"Yes and no."

"What's that mean?"

"It means that if it were just money for me, I wouldn't give a shit. I'd have the surgery, end of discussion."

My stomach drops. "Do you owe money to someone? Are you being threatened?"

His laugh startles me out of the dire scenario already unfolding in my head. "No, nothing like that. It's…my dad. I told you a little bit."

Sliding down into one of my kitchen chairs, I remember everything he told me. Very clearly. "He wanted you to take over the family business." I don't say the rest. It still shocks me that a man could disown his son—a kid—and think it was okay.

Tim nods soberly, the guilt still raw after this many years. "He's kept it going all this time, getting older, life taking its toll on him."

"Couldn't one of your sisters help out? Don't they still live nearby?"

"Dad wouldn't hear of it. Has to be a Cheltenham man, carry on the legacy. He's stubborn like that. Stuck in old thinking."

What is with these men of the previous generation? How have they not evolved in their ways when the world abounds with capable women? Maybe they don't want to evolve. Maybe it's threatening.

Then I realize, "That's why you wanted to help me. When I told you what Reilly said."

Tim says nothing, but his cheeks pull up as he fights a smile. "It's hardly the same. But Reilly reminds me of my dad in some ways, I guess."

"So what's happening now? How is getting a bonus for a clean sheet such a big deal?" Players make good money. I'm not seeing the issue.

"It's a…substantial bonus, and this year, it's acutely relevant."

He looks away. I reach for his hand, drawing him back to the conversation, back to me.

"Why?"

"My dad's health is failing. My sisters don't know how bad it is because he refuses to see a doctor..." His words hang, and I don't bother to point out the irony. "I know. Like father, like son."

I tighten my grip on his hand.

"I should go see him, but that's a separate issue. The thing with the bonus is that it will allow me to buy the place outright. Land, business, all of it. It's not a small amount of money, and I definitely wasn't saving for it. But the bonus will get me there, and I want to do it. It'll keep it in the family in some form for as long as we want it, and I need my dad to know I did this for him in case he—"

His voice breaks on the last word. I don't need him to say it.

Tim is silent, working the emotion back from his throat, a muscle ticking in his cheek as he swallows it down. "I just need to keep playing." He barely chokes out the words, and my heart breaks for this man who would rather be seen as a stubborn rebel than a grown-up kid still trying for a shred of approval from his dad.

I nod and drop my forehead against his shoulder, the fight in me gone. "Okay," I say softly.

He tries to shift, but I don't let my grip up. He has to peel my arms away to turn and look at me, and when he does, his eyes are moist. But he chokes it back, firming his expression. It's the same fighter I see on the field every day, only now it pains me in a new way because I know what's behind it.

"Okay, what?" he asks, finally.

"Finish the season. I'll help you play through the injuries for now, even though it's the wrong thing medically. I don't need to explain why."

"If I tear the ligament, I'll need surgery. Six-to-nine-month recovery. I know." He clenches his teeth.

"Tim, I'm doing this because I love you."

I can see it in his face—how much it means that I'm giving him this time. And I'm glad he understands because I'm making another impulsive decision that may turn out to bite me in the ass.

Like they all do.

"I know." His face relaxes, and he kisses me. It's sweet and hot, and I don't know how he manages to put so much feeling into a kiss.

"Please be careful."

I know he knows. It's no small risk, but I understand now why he doesn't think he has a choice. I don't even have to ask how much money he'll get from the bonus to know it's more than I have saved. If I want to help him, this is how I can.

I just hope it doesn't sink him. Or me.

CHAPTER 27

Tim

Every player has superstitious rituals on game day. Some have lucky underwear. Some refuse to get a haircut too close to a game. Ritual breakfasts, warm-ups, calls to mum—the rituals are as varied as they are often ridiculous.

But ask any player, and there's a ritual.

Mine has always been to eat a half a peanut butter and strawberry jam sandwich. On training days, the jelly flavor doesn't make a difference. On game day—strawberry jam, crunchy salted peanut butter, wheat bread.

It's so important that the ingredients be consistent that I keep several jars of the correct peanut butter and jelly in my cupboard at all times. Common sense.

Also logical is not to have conversations with other players about anything other than the game itself.

So I shouldn't even respond when Steiner shows up in the locker room before any of the starting players. It doesn't make sense for him to be here this early, but it doesn't register because I'm busy with the ritual Jordan has me following to the letter before each game.

Anti-inflammatories, stretching, ice, ultrasound, heat, more stretching. It takes an extra hour, but with the specific weight training to strengthen my quads and protect my knee, I feel strong.

"So… you been faking it, eh?"

I'm not sure Steiner is even talking to me until I take a look around and confirm we're the only two in the room.

"What's that again?"

"Heard you and the good doctor aren't actually engaged. Don't know why you're lying about it, but I assume the sex is off the charts."

My fists get twitchy the second he starts talking about Jordan, and I feel the heat prickle the back of my neck.

"Shut the fuck up, Steiner. You're out of line."

"Am I?"

"Yes."

"Not what she told me."

I know he's trying to get my goat. I shouldn't indulge this rubbish for a single second. But some dumb part of me keeps talking.

"Who is 'she'?"

"Jordan Page, your fake girlfriend?"

My jaw ticks, and I try to school my expression, but I can feel my cheeks go slack. Steiner notices, and I've lost any edge I may have had.

He wags a finger at me like he's scolding a child. "What are you two playing at? I've been wracking my brain, but I can't figure it out. Which takes me back to the sex, but even though she's a hot piece of ass, I still don't get it. Why fake an engagement? Did you knock her up?"

My fists flinch. It's all I can do to hold myself back from taking a swing at him.

I want to tell him to go fuck himself, but my brain is caught in a blender of warring thoughts. Why would Jordan tell Steiner anything? If she told him, has she told other people? Am I the patsy with real feelings for her when this is all a big joke?

Would be fitting. I'm exactly the same kid who flew off on a plane trying to escape the disappointment of his dad and ended up disappointing the one girl he cared about instead. And I'm about to do it again.

Steiner laughs at my stupor. "Or is it about the surgery she told Coach you need? I'll admit to being excited about that since I've been training to take your place for months. Suppose I should thank her for pushing it."

No.

Right?

After everything I've told her—after everything she promised me when I opened up and told her about my dad—she wouldn't tell Coach I need surgery. She knows he'd put me on the injured list. She knows even mentioning surgery is a guaranteed risk to everything I want. She knows why I need to finish out the season. She loves me.

Right?

Stop it. Stop listening to Steiner. She wants the best for you.

Or, she wants what's best for her. Because all I'll ever be is a guy who plays a game for a living, a guy too stubborn to take medical advice from someone smarter than him. I don't know why I thought that all these years later, I could fool anyone into thinking I'm something better than I am—a fake fiancé, a player too dumb to listen to medical advice, a disappointment.

The alarm on my watch dings, and I realize I've already missed the whole heating pad session I was supposed to be finished with by now. All I can think of is finding Jordan in the medical suite and letting her know she can stop worrying about my medical care. I can handle things from here.

I grab my bag and a water bottle.

"Go fuck yourself, Steiner," I tell him as I head out the door, hoping like mad that I'm not the one about to get fucked.

ordan

It's quiet in the treatment room, a white-walled space with a few anatomy posters on the walls and tidy drawers with instruments inside. The complete opposite of the inside of my brain, which is messy, worried, and upset.

There's a flatscreen TV in the hallway, and I can hear the pregame announcers bantering about the game that will start in under an hour, but I can't watch. I can only hope that Tim gets through the ninety minutes in one piece. I've never had an ulcer, but I'm pretty sure I know what one feels like—it's this, jittery nerves and so much acid in my stomach that I might keel over.

The last time I felt like this was before my oral exams to get my medical degree. That was my future at stake. Today is merely Tim's knee, my career, and once again, my future at stake. Considering that, I'm surprised I don't feel worse.

Watching the team warming up on the field earlier, I could see every instance when Tim babied his knee, every hesitation before starting to run. In a game that will cost him. He knows it, so he's saving everything for game time.

So far, so good.

So why is he standing in the medical suite scowling at me? Why is he in here at all when he should be with the team?

"Hey." My serves settle at the sight of him. I also want to close the door and climb him like a tree. "Have I mentioned how sexy you look in the new home jersey?"

He presses his lips together and studies me.

"Tim? You okay? What's wrong?" I ask, immediately worried about his knee. On auto-pilot, I walk to the freezer for extra ice packs.

But they're not necessary, not when Tim's stare is colder than ice.

He crosses his arms over his chest and leans against the wall, something I've seen him do so many times in so many different circumstances—all related to not trusting that my medical advice had his best interests at heart. We've gotten past all of them.

Until now.

Something is different, and it's not just that he hasn't said a word since he walked in the door.

"Tim, what's wrong?"

"I just had a very interesting conversation with Jordy Steiner."

I gulp a breath, but it's not nearly enough air. Panic sets in. And regret. So many chances I had to be honest about Steiner, and I blew each and every one. I feel the blood drain from my face.

Tim clocks my reaction and nods. "So it's true. You told him— the one person on this team desperate to see me fail—you told him our relationship is fake. You confided in Steiner. Of all people."

The room starts to spin. White walls blur with pale wood floors and medical equipment I know better than I know myself.

Through it all, I'm aware of a pain tearing through my gut like a lava stone.

"It-it's not what you think," I stutter.

The hard look in his eyes was painful before, but what I see now—disappointment mixed with hurt—is devastating.

My brain scrambles to catch up. All this time, Steiner said nothing, pretending he'd keep the conversation to himself, when really, he was waiting for the right time to drop a bomb. I should have anticipated it. No, I should have been honest with the man I love so much I've put my job on the line. It seems so clear, and yet I convinced myself I could get away with a lie of omission. Stupid.

"It was weeks ago that I told him that. Before—"

He shakes his head, interrupting. "Weeks ago. *Weeks* ago? Before or after I told you I was in love with you?"

"Before," I say numbly.

"And we've spent nearly every night together, and you said nothing to me. Didn't tell me you confided in a guy I hate, the one who's been riding my ass, hoping to replace me."

"That was…we hadn't…I didn't know you like I do now. You have to believe I'd never betray you to Steiner or anyone else."

"But you did."

"I was trying to convince him I wasn't doing you favors. He was threatening to go to management and say I was letting you keep playing because we have a relationship. Which would have—"

"Affected your job," he finishes.

It hits me like a wrecking ball. The decimated pieces fall to the floor around me, and I know there's no putting them back together. I made the mistake, I told Steiner, and I need to own it.

"You're right. I blurted it out and immediately regretted it." I look around the room as though I'll find some object amid the organized metal instruments and therapy bands that will fix this.

That's always my go-to—science, medicine. I still don't know how to deal with the stuff that matters.

"Why didn't you tell me?" His voice sounds so stiff and tight that I feel like I'm talking to a stranger.

"When it happened, we were still fake. Still, I intended to tell you. Then…I didn't want to create more tension between the two of you when you already had so much at stake on the field. Tim, I'm so, so sorry. You have every right to be angry I told him, but please believe I would never betray what we have now." I reach for his hand, but he pulls it away. His face is a stone mask.

He closes his eyes for a long blink, but when he opens them, I see pain, sadness. "Except that you told Coach I need the surgery. You told him to bench me." Now I see betrayal.

"What? No."

He shakes his head.

"Tim, *no*. I didn't do that."

"You have to put your career first. I get it. I shouldn't have asked you to sacrifice your ethics for me. And you shouldn't have offered." His body is rigid, muscles tense and flexed.

I feel blindsided by a conversation I don't seem to be a part of. "Hang on. Back up and tell me what you're talking about. I didn't say anything to Coach about surgery, at least not recently."

He pounds a fist on the wall. In the quiet room, it sounds like a truck hitting concrete. "Wow. Not recently? Is that supposed to make it better?"

"Tim, you and I talked about surgery at the outset. I told Coach Jaynes the same thing I told you. I haven't said anything to him about it since then. Did Jaynes say he's benching you, or did that come from Steiner?"

Tim doesn't answer, but I see it in the way his face falls. He's letting Steiner get in his head, same as always.

"Dammit, Tim. Coach knows I'm monitoring you closely, and I've cleared you to play even though it's extremely dangerous. I told you that. You can trust me."

"I'm sorry, but I don't." He holds up a hand. "Well, that's not entirely true. I trust that you have your own self-interests at heart. Your job comes first. I trust that."

My mouth opens, but no words come out. I stare at him, dumbfounded, processing what he's saying and why. He doesn't trust me. It sticks in my throat. He doesn't trust me.

Maybe the Steiner thing gives him reason to feel that way, but I've given him so many bigger reasons to know I have his back. But he doesn't believe it, and maybe that's our permanent roadblock.

"That's about the worst thing you could say to me." My voice scratches out the words, hurling them over the strangling tension in my throat that's holding back tears.

His face goes slack, but the hardness doesn't leave his eyes. Then he composes himself, his voice even. "The fake engagement was fun and all, but I think it's time to end the charade. Like you said. Like we agreed in the first place."

It's a gut punch. For a second, I wonder if he did actually punch me because I feel the air leave my lungs. I can't make them take in oxygen, and I feel faint.

Dropping onto a stool, I slump forward with my elbows on my knees until I'm able to draw breath. But I don't feel any better.

"What…that's what you want?" I need to ask better questions. Actually, I need to tell him he's wrong. Nothing about us is fake. But I can't, not when his words hit me like daggers. "I thought we—"

"We were having fun. Sure." He shrugs, but when I look at his eyes, they're missing conviction. He's saying hurtful words, but he's the one who looks hurt. "But let's be honest about what it was. Maybe we both were curious after all these years, but it's time to live in the real world."

"Tim, what are you saying?" I know what I felt when we were together. I feel it even now when he's trying to push me away.

And I know what he said to me on the boat. Those weren't just words.

But the ones he's using now are tearing everything down that I thought I believed.

He shrugs. "We're not real. That's what you told Steiner. At least you were being honest, even if it wasn't with me." He practically spits out his teammate's name. Hot, flushed.

Finally, my fight or flight instinct kicks in, and I harness some anger. He doesn't get to decide everything about us based on misinformation.

I stand from the stool so quickly it spins and slides away, creaking noisily. "Look, I am really sorry I told Steiner. I regretted it the second it happened. But I did not tell Coach to bench you. I wouldn't do that."

He picks up a blue stress ball and palms it from hand to hand, studying me. "Just seems like Steiner has an awful lot of information."

"He doesn't. And you don't even like the guy, so why would you trust him over me? Come on, Tim, think about it."

He waves his hands in front of me. "I don't have time to think about it. I have to go out there and play for ninety brutal minutes and hope I don't fuck up my knee beyond repair."

"I know, and you shouldn't play when you're this wound up. You're not clear-headed. I don't want you to push too hard."

"What you want and what I want aren't the same thing. I know how important your job is to you. And mine's important too. So let's just walk away from each other before it gets more complicated and do our jobs."

This is the Tim I remember from high school—gone at the first sign of conflict. On a plane before we can have a conversation. Why did I think he'd have grown up just because he got older?

"Tim, my job isn't more important than you." I need him to understand that.

"You asked me to trust you. That was the first thing you said when you came to the team." He's less wound up, but I see the hurt return to his eyes. "Problem is, I don't know if I can do that now."

"You know how I feel about you. You should know when someone is telling you lies. And you should know me well enough to believe I'm not that person. But you've got your head so far up your ass you can't see the truth."

His eyes stay with me, challenging. I stare him down with equal ferocity. If he doesn't believe me, if he doesn't understand that I wouldn't intentionally hurt him, we were finished before we ever started.

"Have a good game. Stay safe."

I walk out of the treatment room and leave Tim standing there. It's the only chance I have to get away from him before he sees the tears.

CHAPTER 29

*J*ordan

IT'S ALMOST like the succulents are mocking me. Day after day for a week now, I've starved them of water, willing them to dry out or wilt or whatever miserable succulents do. I thought they were on my side. I thought they'd somehow know that the guy who lovingly arranged them is gone. I thought they'd wither in solidarity.

But here they are, perky as all hell, healthy and reaching toward the daylight flooding my apartment through the big windows. I should pull down the shades, but I don't have the energy.

The Strikers won their game on Saturday, and Tim got through the ninety minutes without taking the kind of blow to the knee that will tear the ligament beyond repair.

At least, that's what my medical team tells me. I didn't do his exam.

Nor did I see him in my office all week.

With four more potential playoff games, there's a chance Tim can get by in one piece, but I'm worried. And because I love him, I don't want him hurt.

When my phone buzzes, I pad from the living room to the kitchen in white slippers with bunny ears. It's the first personal day I've taken since I joined the Strikers. It's also the first personal day I've taken ever.

I never needed them before. I never had a personal life that broke me into pieces. Maybe it was better that way. There's a reason why I've always chosen career over relationships. At least I have some control where my job is concerned. It just feels emptier now.

Retrieving the phone, I go back to the couch.

Sofia. It's probably the millionth text since I called to tell her about the crash and burn fallout from my worst impulsive decision yet.

Sofia: Stop being so hard on yourself.

Me: Not being hard on myself.

Sofia: You weren't impulsive. You were in love.

Me: Same difference.

I drop the phone on the couch next to me and slump into a pillow. Maybe it's not the same, but it got me the same result, so I don't really care.

"You can go ahead and die now," I tell the succulents, flicking the bowl with my foot. The trailing plants bob like they're nodding. They're still the most perfect arrangement I've ever seen.

My phone buzzes again. Probably Sofia.

Nope. My mom.

Mom: Is it true?

Me: Is what true?

Mom: You and Tim broke up?

Me: How do you know these things?

Mom: Social media.

I roll my eyes at the phone. Before I can reply, she texts again.

Mom: Come over. I promise I won't ask you to cook or bake.

I huff a laugh. Then, because I don't have anything better to do, I peel myself off the couch and get in the car. I drive to my parents' house, bypass the breakables, and hunker down in a chair in the kitchen.

When I decided not to change out of my grungy clothes or stop for lemon cake, I knew my mom would probably comment, and I prepared to fight back. I did it with Tim. I'll do it with her.

But my mom ignores my messy bun, says nothing about my worn shapeless gray sweatpants, and actually smiles at the bunny slippers.

Then, she puts a plate of Girl Scout Thin Mints cookies on plate with a blue rim and goes to the stove to boil water for tea.

"Can I make you a cup of coffee?" My mother startles me with the question. She never offers to make me coffee. In fact, I'm fairly certain she doesn't own a coffee maker.

"You have coffee? Here, in the house?"

She rolls her eyes and smooths her auburn bob, which makes me notice that it's shorter than the last time I saw her. "Your hair looks good, by the way."

Nodding at the compliment, she stares me down. "Of course I have coffee."

"Um, okay. Sure, coffee would be great. I can make it if you want." My offer lacks conviction.

"I've got it."

I watch her move to the pantry, where she retrieves a ceramic cannister that indeed says "coffee" in gold letters on the side. She makes a point of showing it to me as though to prove she'll make good on her offer.

"Looks great." I watch her place the cannister on the counter with a flourish and start opening cupboards.

She heats water in the kettle and rigs up a pour-over setup on top of a coffee mug. When the whistle sounds a minute later, she wordlessly pours the water into the funnel and waits for it to drip into the cup.

Presenting it to me with a spoon and a carton of cream, she sits back in her seat and begins stirring her tea.

"Thanks, Mom." I pour in the cream and give it a swirl with the spoon. For the first time, I understand the appeal of her rhythmic stirring. There's something soothing about watching the liquid circle in the cup. Weirdly, being in this house, I start to feel a little better.

"Hey, Mom? How come you never change anything around here? Is it some kind of museum thing where we're supposed to tiptoe around the set pieces?"

Her brow furrows, and she turns her ear toward me like she didn't hear me correctly. "Museum? Hardly. I don't change things because I don't really care how they look, and I don't want to bother trying to make new stuff match."

Not what I was expecting. "Really? So basically, you're kind of lazy?" It's never how I've thought of my mother, and she may very well smack me for the temerity. Instead, she nods.

"Basically."

She looks around the kitchen at all the sameness and shrugs.

"I love that," I say.

Then, I open up and tell her everything—the fake parts, the real parts, the love, the pain that feels worse than anything I've experienced.

I force my gaze away from the perfect brown coffee and look at her, anticipating her judgment and disappointment. "I'm sorry," she says, reaching a hand to cover mine.

"Thanks."

This is the mother I remember from my childhood—always there, reassuring, loving us. I wonder what happened to send her off in the direction of disappointment.

She pats my hand, and I soak in the warmth from her reassuring fingers. "It'll be okay, though. You always land on your feet."

"I do? When? When do I land on my feet?"

"Always. You're very grounded. Steady."

"Exactly. I don't ever have to land because I never actually fly. I take the safe route, keep my head down, and work. And that's what I should do. Because every time I deviate, it ends badly."

Without a word, my mom scoots her chair closer to mine. The legs scrape on the wood floor, and I have a knee-jerk worry that she'll be upset. But she keeps dragging the chair, ignoring the noise, until it's close enough for her to wrap me in a hug.

"Don't think that. And don't think things with Tim have ended, not if you don't want them to."

The sentiment makes me uncharacteristically teary. Swallowing back the welling of emotion, I sip my coffee, which burns my throat. The cream barely tempered the boiling water.

"Both of us have to want it." My voice shakes at the reality that he hasn't made any effort to reach out this week. I need to come to terms with what our time together really was—him needing me to cover for him and me wanting it to mean more.

"I'm fine. It's fine."

My mother nods slowly. "You don't seem fine."

"I am. I'm great, actually. Relieved not to have to pretend to have a fiancé." My voice breaks on the last word.

She nods again and studies me. I do my best to maintain eye contact so she'll believe me and not ask too many questions. At the same time, there's that surge of tears again, and I find it harder to fight them, so I look away.

"But I'm sorry you don't get to plan the wedding of your dreams." Now I'm really sobbing—not for my mother's busted hopes but for my own. I realize how invested I was in our story of unrequited love.

She lets me cry it out, holding me in her arms until I've left a puddle on her shoulder. Needing a tissue, I finally unwrap her and go to the bathroom.

I look at myself in the mirror. Bloodshot sad eyes, hair falling out of its bun, not a stitch of makeup to hide the splotches on my skin. What a mess.

When I come out, my mom is there waiting, teacup in hand. Wordlessly, she signals for me to follow her into the living room.

The matching cornflower blue armchairs barely get any use, and the tulip wall sconces are reflected in the surface of a shiny antique coffee table. Other than gathering around the Christmas tree once a year, I almost never go in this room. So it seems odd that she's taking me from the comfortable kitchen gathering space to the one that feels the most stilted.

She points to the white slipcovered couch, and I stare at her. Really? She wants me to sit on it? "What if it gets dirty?" I ask.

She shrugs. "What if it does?"

I sit. She perches on the edge of the coffee table in front of me, and my eyes go wide. "Stop that," she scolds. "Did I ever tell you about my wedding?" she asks, apropos of nothing. Then again, it never exactly required prompting to get my mom to talk about weddings.

I comb my memory for the story I'm certain I've heard a few dozen times. She's told me about how she was the matron of honor at my aunt's wedding over and over again, and I've certainly heard about all of her friends' daughters' weddings and how beautiful they were.

But now that I think about it, I can't recall her wedding story. Clearly, she has one.

"No, I don't think you did. Tell me about it."

She looks at me for so long without moving I start to think something's wrong. "Did you ever stop to wonder why I never told you?" she asks, finally.

Of course, I didn't. I was probably just relieved not to hear about one more wedding event and how disappointed she was that I wasn't the bride.

I smile ruefully. "I imagine it was because I was always such a crappy pain in the butt when you brought up wedding stuff. So you spared me?"

My mother shakes her head and brushes some nonexistent dust from her lap. Then she smooths the legs of her pants, stirs her tea, and takes a leisurely sip. "I didn't tell you about my wedding because I didn't have one."

I wait for the rest—this is the part where she tells me that Page women don't have weddings, we have gala events. Or something like that.

But she just watches me. And waits.

"So…you…" I want to complete my thought, but it's stuck in the middle of my brain, unable to squeeze through a rat's nest of incomprehension.

I stare, willing her to crack a smile to let me in on the joke. This is my mother. The social queen of her tiny universe. Weddings and all the accompanying fluff and fanfare are the currency she trades in, to the exclusion of almost all else. "You're saying you didn't have a wedding?"

Shaking her head, she doesn't look upset about it. Which also doesn't make sense. "My parents couldn't afford it. And we didn't want to wait until they could."

"So you just…" I can't finish my thoughts. I can't make sense of what she's telling me.

"We went to the courthouse and got married. Just me and Dad." I startle at the last part. My mom is a stickler for grammar, and I've never heard her say "me and" anyone in my entire life. It's like she's drifting into a kinder, gentler place with the memory, and I like it.

I also can't believe it. Thinking back, I realize I've never seen a photo from my parents' wedding. I'd probably chalk that up to patent disinterest, given how I always resisted any talk of marriage from my teen years onward. Why would I seek out pictures of her in a white dress?

I glance around the living room, where various framed photos perch on top of the baby grand piano that my dad occasionally plays. There's no need to look at them one by one, but I do so anyway, confirming what I already know I'll find—not a single wedding photo amid the collection of posed family pictures. There are a few of my brother and me as kids, both of us with gaps from where we lost our baby teeth. There are more from our teen years, me in a cheerleading uniform, him in an artist's smock.

"You didn't have a big wedding?" I have to confirm it once more.

My mom, who's been watching me take everything in, shakes her head. "Surprised?"

"I mean, yeah. Kind of." I'm also kind of delighted. This gem of information makes me love her more, and it makes me curious about other things.

"So why is it such a big deal to you that I have a wedding? Obviously, you know from your own experience that it doesn't matter. You and Dad have been ridiculously happy for years." I ask the question even though I have a feeling I know what she'll say.

She shrugs. "I want you to have what I didn't. You're my daughter. I want you to have everything."

Tears erupt anew. Of course, she wants that. I just never understood that her enthusiasm was about giving me something she never had herself.

"Mom...I'm sorry. I wish you'd been able to wear the garter or toss the bouquet and do all the things."

"Oh, I did all of that. At the courthouse. Even though no one was there to catch my flimsy supermarket roses, I tossed them. And your dad and I had burgers for lunch and fed each other bites of a grocery store cake that sat in a hot car while we were inside the courthouse."

Recounting her story, she looks animated and happy. It makes me feel emboldened to ask her what I really want to know. "Mom, why don't you have a career? You're smart, you have tons of interests. You could have done anything."

Her face falls slightly, and she shakes her head. "I never found something I loved." She watches me absorb this information.

"That's it?" This can't be the entire story, so I cock my head like a puppy and wait for the treat I want. It doesn't come.

My mom shrugs. "I got married young, had kids, and that became my world. And it was enough. I loved being your mom every day, all the way up until you and Chet left home. And then I tried to find the next thing. I wanted to find a passion outside the house—maybe I'm missing a gene or something—but I bounced around a bunch of career possibilities, and nothing stuck. So I hover around, mixing into everyone else's lives. You may have noticed."

My jaw gapes wide. Of all the things I ever imagined my mother might say, this was not on any list. "Yeah, I may have noticed."

"Sorry. Not sorry," she says.

"Mom, seriously, you need to stop with the tweens on social media."

She dismisses it with a clink of the spoon in her cup.

"So is that it? All the pressure to get married is just so you can throw me the wedding you never had?"

She swats my arm and squints as though I'm being ridiculous. "No. Hardly. Though a wedding would be fun to plan."

"So what, then?"

She stops stirring and looks at me. "You were a smart girl, and now you've become a brilliant woman. I couldn't be more proud of what you've accomplished. But I watch you, and I worry. I've loved being your mom, and I want you to have that too. That's why I'm always bugging you about finding someone and settling down. It's not about the wedding. It was never about that."

I feel like a misbehaving teenager who's been grounded for staying out past curfew. I've misjudged my mom for all these years because I didn't understand her. I decided she had the wrong perception about me, and instead of giving her a chance to know the truth, I wrote her off entirely.

"Mom, I'm sorry." I swallow hard, expecting more tears, but they don't come. Maybe I'm empty.

"For what?"

"Thinking the worst when I should have seen you wanted me to be happy."

She nods. "You were happy, weren't you, with Tim?"

"I really was."

"I loved seeing you two together. The way he looked at you was exactly what you deserve."

"You sure about that? We weren't even together the day we were here."

"Oh, honey. I'm sure. He was so in love with you that I think he had cartoon hearts circling above his head and daisies in his eyes. And that doesn't end because of a fight. Do you think it's fixable?"

I shake my head. "I don't know. Maybe?"

Abruptly standing, my mom reaches a hand for me. "I'll take a maybe. A maybe could turn into a very beautiful wedding."

"Mom…"

"Or not, all I'm saying." She bounces her eyebrows and reaches for me again. I let her fold me into her arms. It's the best hug she's ever given me.

CHAPTER 30

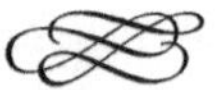

$\mathcal{J}$ ordan

"I REALLY WANT to give you a hard time about the shoes, but I know you've got bigger issues," Sofia says, a hopeful half smile on her face. She points to the pair of blue shower shoes I'm wearing over white socks. After two days in them, I've ditched the gray sweatpants for red plaid pajama pants and a purple hoodie, no bra.

I know I look hideous.

And I'm in no mood to laugh.

We sit in my living room, where I've been staring at Tim's succulent arrangement all weekend long. With the blinds half drawn, the yellow afternoon light makes my living room look depressing. I kind of like it. Good wallowing lighting. But those damn plants are thriving. A couple have even mysteriously sprouted flowers.

Sofia stares at me staring at them. "Did you bring me here to water your plants?"

I shake my head. "They don't need water. Or love. Or anything, apparently. I'm pretty sure we're soulmates."

"Stop it. The wallowing isn't a good look for you."

"I don't care. Tim gave me these. I tried to kill them, but now that they've proven themselves to be resilient, I kind of love them." The purple aeonium rosettes have sprouted some baby versions of themselves, the trailing green ones are a little longer, and the tallest plants still stand proudly above the rest.

She looks more kindly on them. "They're nice. Guy knows where to buy a nice arrangement, at least."

"He didn't buy them," I tell her, my voice sounding robotic and sad. "I mean, he did. He bought the plants at Trader Joe's, but then he arranged them."

"Seriously?"

I nod.

"The hot boyfriend has a boat and arranges plants? Okay, we need to right this ship."

"We can't."

"Not so fast, doubter."

She digs into her recyclable grocery bag and starts spreading food out on my ugly black coffee table. I know it's ugly without her having to tell me because everything in here looks ugly. When I remember how it looked when Tim sat on this couch and put his feet on the table, the absence of him looks barren and dreary by comparison. Guess I'm gaining some design insight after all.

Briefly tearing my gaze away from the succulents, I see she's set out three pints of ice cream, a bottle of gin, tonic water, limes, snickerdoodle cookies, a wedge of brie cheese, and a pint box of cherry tomatoes.

"What's with the tomatoes?"

She moves them back to the grocery bag. "I thought they might go with the cheese, but you're right. Let's keep the healthy foods out of this."

Going to my kitchen to gather glasses and plates, Sofia keeps talking. "So he hasn't called at all to tell you he was being a British twat and he loves you more than life itself?"

I shake my head numbly, not caring that she probably wanted an audible response. I don't care about much, so I curl into a ball on the couch and wait for Sofia to come back.

She appears a minute later with an ice bucket, glasses, a bowl full of cut limes, and small white plates I rarely use. "Okay, what'll you have? Sugary crap or sugary crap?"

"I'll take some sugary crap," I mutter, not uncurling from my protective ball.

Sofia puts two different scoops of ice cream on each plate, crumbles some cookies on top, and goes about making gin and tonics while I stare at her like I'm watching the Food Network.

"Sit up," she instructs. I feel my bones creak as I shift around, so I ignore her bossypants request. I think I've aged a year in a week. "Have you seen Tim at all?"

I shake my head. "I haven't gone to the practice field, and he hasn't come to the medical suite."

"So now he's playing without any medical supervision?"

"I don't know what he's doing." My exhausted response is half swallowed by the neck of my hoodie as I roll myself to sitting. "Can we not talk about him?"

She levels me with an eye roll that says I'm nuts. "It's why I'm here. Now sit. Up."

Obeying, I groan. Then I survey the plate in front of me. Even the pile of sugar doesn't tempt me. Neither does the drink she forces into my sweaty hand.

Settling into the pink overstuffed chair to my right, she sips her drink. "Mm. I did well."

"Good job."

"Wow. You're really determined to blow this, aren't you?"

I roll my eyes. Maybe I do need the drink. Taking a sip, I

wince at how strong it is. "I'm not determined to blow it. I just don't know what to do."

"Stop fighting fate, that's what you do."

She leans back in the chair and folds her legs underneath her. Continuing to sip her drink, she waits for me to figure out what the hell she's talking about.

"I give up. What does fate have to do with any of this?"

"Everything."

I'll admit to being mildly intrigued, if baffled. "Explain thyself."

Before saying a word, Sofia picks up her phone and tells it to play coffee house music. Within seconds, my apartment sounds like the place around the block where I get my smoothies. Remembering that first day in the parking lot when Tim threw my moldy drink in the trash sends a new gouging pain through my chest.

I miss him so much. "I can't believe I can miss someone this much after only being in a month-long relationship."

It doesn't even dawn on me that I've said the words out loud until Sofia responds. "Because you haven't."

"What?"

"Your heart has been in this relationship since you were sixteen." I start to protest, but she holds up a hand. "Maybe not all the time, maybe there were big gaps, but that's what I mean about fate. It's given you two chances. I wouldn't wait for a third, if I were you. You might not get one."

For the first time in a week, some thought other than abject sadness and pain worms its way through my brain. "I never really believed in fate."

"Because you're a scientist. I'm not. So indulge me." She waits for me to extend a welcoming palm before continuing. "Tim came to the US to play soccer. Of all the families he could have stayed with, he came to yours. The one that gave him something he was missing from his own home life. But he got scared because the thing between you was too big. Too big for you guys to handle. So he left."

I nod, even though I never thought of it that way. Because I'm a scientist.

"So fate tries again. Of all the teams in the US that looked at him, the Strikers was the one to make him an offer, one he couldn't refuse. And then you—you're finally ready to move to a job as a team medical director, and who has an opening? The Strikers."

"I don't really think that's fate. It's just…coincidence."

"Call it whatever you want. The point is…you have the chance now that you didn't take advantage of back then. Are you really going to risk walking away again? What if fate gives up on you because you're too dumb to bother coming around again for a third chance? Or what if it takes another fifteen years."

"Then I'll be as miserable as I am right now. For fifteen years."

"You love him."

I nod. No hesitation. I love him, and I want us to work. I don't want to take a gamble on fate giving us a third chance.

"Then you might have to do something a little bit impulsive."

She sits back in her chair like a lawyer resting her case after giving the closing argument she knows will win over the jury. And because she's my badass best friend, she downs the rest of her drink.

Pressing my lips together, I feel a grudging smile fight its way through. Being impulsive has gotten me this far.

"Okay, let's talk about this. Is there such a thing as being impulsive and also smart at the same time?"

Sofia shrugs. "I don't see why not."

"Because I do have one idea, but it's a little crazy."

"Bring it, sister."

So I do.

CHAPTER 31

im

THE FIRST TIME I walked away from Jordan, it wrecked me. At age eighteen, I told myself that going back to a rainy England spring was what had me in a horrendous mood, but it lasted well into summer. I stayed in a shit mood even though my good mate's flat was ten times nicer than my parents' house, and he let me live there for free. I stuck around even after the football season started and I established myself as a starter.

Because I knew I'd blown it with her, and now I was thousands of miles away. I'd had no choice, but that didn't blunt the sting.

If I'm honest, it took all four years of uni to get over her, and by then, I had a shot at coming to play in the US. It was the first time I'd felt optimism, even if I'd deny to anyone who asked—including myself—that my interest in returning to the States had anything to do with the hope of seeing Jordan again.

But of course it did.

Then I made it to the Strikers, practically around the block from where Jordan grew up, and I didn't reach out, didn't make any effort to see her again for a while.

Eventually, I did some digging and found out she went to medical school and headed up a sports medicine clinic in Oakland. Seemed like a perfect fit for the smarty pants I knew back then, always with her nose in a science book. Probably still too good for a bloke like me—at least, that's what my dad would have to say about it, and he never even met her. So I didn't reach out. Just played my game.

I don't know how I'm going to get over her a second time.

This is a new kind of pain that has no relation to the searing torture I felt on the field when I sprained my ligament. That was physical pain. My body has become well-versed in enduring physical pain over all my years in the sport. It's why I was able to keep showing up on the field, even with an injury barely masked by pain meds.

The way I've felt since Jordan walked out of the Strikers treatment room is pure, wrenching torture from the inside out. Like an icepick to the heart, stabbing over and over until it bleeds out. Slow, intentional, mean.

It's a pain like I've never experienced, an utter void that can't be filled.

I need to leave town. Or quit the team. Or leave the country.

And I know none of those will come close to blunting the agony because she won't be in any of those places, and the pain of losing her will follow me everywhere.

I hate my apartment. Every room reminds me of her. Staring out through the plate glass windows used to fill me up—that view. Now I only remember looking at it next to her, and the sparkling lights on the Bay Bridge bring no joy.

Swallowing the last gulp of my beer, I wince at the taste. I pulled a six-pack straight from the pantry and didn't even try to chill it in the freezer before popping the top off one of the bottles and filling a glass. It feels fitting that I've effectively ruined my favorite ale, along with everything else in my life.

I suppose I should have known it would come to this—if she needed to choose between her career and me, her career would come first. It's how she's built. She admitted it early on. It's hard to fight who you are. I know that firsthand.

I don't expect her to abandon the ethic she was raised with just to suit me. I guess I should be flattered she tried to step out of her comfort zone for my benefit, even for a little while.

I don't feel flattered. I feel flattened.

What's the point of playing the sport I love if I want her more?

I'd say I wish I'd never met her, but that would be a lie. I guess I'd take the few good weeks we had over nothing, but I'll spend the rest of my life regretting that it was all we had.

As I'm pouring my second pint of ale out of the bottle and into a glass, there's a knock on my door. It sounds as lonely and hollow as I feel and I debate ignoring it.

Then whoever it is knocks a second damn time, and I get the feeling it's a losing battle to pretend I'm not here. My lights are visible from the street, for one thing. For another, once I hear the voice on the other side, I know I'm up against a mate as stubborn as me.

"I know you're home, and I'm not letting you drink alone." Coach Jaynes doesn't make house calls. He told us as much on his first day with the team.

When I open the door, he shoves a bottle of whiskey at my chest and walks past, straight over to the broad windows I've been avoiding as I suck down warm beer alone. I hear him stumbling against walls until his aggravated voice rings out, "Where the hell's the light switch?"

Walking over to the switch plate and throwing one light on, I immediately wince at the brightness and dial it down on the dimmer. I do the same with a light in the living room because

Coach is already moving in that direction, and I know he'll just yell at me again.

"Hey, Coach. This a social visit?" I try to keep my tone light, figuring he just might bugger off if he's here for some kind of home check or whatnot. I look around and attempt to take in what a newcomer would see upon walking in.

Unfortunately, the past two days of slovenly living don't look good on me or my apartment. I haven't bothered to shower or put on a clean shirt, so there's a decent chance I smell horrible. I don't feel like dealing with contact lenses, so I'm wearing an old pair of glasses no one sees me in—ever.

"Nice specs," Jaynes says. Of course, he notices. It's why he's good at his job.

"What can I do for you, Coach?" Hands stuffed into the pockets of my gray sweatpants, I take a few slow steps in his direction, dreading whatever dressing down he's here to give.

He has his back to me because the view outside the windows is a whole hell of a lot better than the sorry state of myself, so I can't blame him there. He wheels around and looks at me. "I'm here to help you get your head screwed on right."

"Great. A new mum," I mutter.

"Only not half as nice, I'd bet. You need to get your thinking turned around right, or you'll sit on my second string bench for the rest of your career."

I tilt my head and study him. He comes across as thoughtful and measured, but when he needs to lay down the law with a player, he doesn't mince words. The difference is that those words have so far not been directed at me. I don't like the way it feels.

I start to cobble together some sort of answer, but he waves a hand to stop me, passing by me on his way to the kitchen. Then he doubles back and swipes the bottle of whiskey from my hands. "Do you drink scotch? This is a decent fifteen-year-old blend."

Following him into the open kitchen space, I wince at the fast food wrappers that tell the tale of the past few days. I only hit up Taco Bell and Wendy's when I'm deeply depressed, and come to think of it, I've never eaten at both of them in the same week before. Even during high school when fast food was a way of life.

Without comment, he moves the crumpled wrappers aside and puts the bottle on my countertop. He doesn't ask where I keep the glasses, just starts opening cabinets until he finds them. Pulling out two juice glasses, he shrugs at them and puts them on the counter. Then he opens and pours a healthy two fingers of scotch into each.

Gesturing with a tip of his head, he hands me a glass and goes back to my living room, sinking into one of the dark leather sofas. As the cushion swallows him up, its protesting groan sounds the way I feel. Why is he here drinking in my living room, uninvited?

Because I still don't know why he's here, I follow and sit in one of the uncomfortable white club chairs to the side of the couch. The designer I hired way back when didn't ask what I thought of the chairs, and I didn't argue when she said they were the right "look" for the room. I've never particularly enjoyed sitting in them, but I'm not about to cozy up next to my coach on the couch.

"Nice of you to stop by," I say, taking a sip of the drink, which is stronger but not necessarily better than warm beer.

"Not a social call."

"Okay."

He sips his drink. "You a scotch drinker?" Then he shakes his head. "Why am I asking? You were drinking beer. Typical Brit."

"It's ale."

"Tomato, tomahto. This is better."

"Matter of opinion." I take another sip. It's less heinous this time around. Maybe he has a point.

Jaynes inhales deeply, exhales in equal measure, and takes another sip. I'm beginning to think we made plans that I forgot about—dude plans to sit around sipping whiskey and talking about nothing. In another second, he's liable to pull out a cigar.

"You're either incredibly stubborn or just plain dumb. Which is the same thing, by the way."

Nope, no cigar. Daggers instead.

"What'd I do?" It's the wrong question. It should be, "Which of all the assorted dumb things that I've done are you referring to?" He can take his pick in laying them out.

"It's clear you're in love with Jordan."

His directness surprises me. And if he wasn't a hundred percent correct, I might tell him off. But a small sane voice in the back of my thick head tells me I should listen. "Okay."

"Okay. Now, I'm not an expert in that department, but I'm a good coach. Which means I have a large problem in you."

"I know I've been off my game. But I'll come back next season healthier than you've ever seen me."

"Get the surgery."

I roll my eyes. "I know. I will. After the season."

"Do it now. If you don't have the surgery, you're not playing for me at all. I'll let you ride out the bench until you either beg for a transfer or finish out your career."

"Jesus, you're a hard-ass," I grumble. "I can't decide if I hate you for it or respect you."

"Likely both. Don't worry, I'm not offended."

"Ha. I wasn't."

"Did she put you up to this?"

"She? You mean the woman who read up on FIFA bonus rules and found a way to get you that bonus you were killing yourself for? She went to bat for you with a medical waiver and got them to agree to pay you in full even if you sit out the playoffs on the injured list."

I close my eyes. Then I drink his stupid expensive scotch. "She didn't do that."

"She did."

I'm in denial that she loved me enough to do this after I walked away from her. Because it hurts.

Coach leans back on my couch and crosses his foot over his knee, makes himself comfortable. Even when he's intensely focused on the game, he has this vibe—comfortable, thoughtful, with an infectious love for the sport. He understands players because he used to be one, and he's gotten results in the few months he's been with the team. And obviously, that's what makes him a great coach.

So maybe I ought to listen to what he came here to say.

Raking a hand through my hair, I take a large breath of air into my lungs and get ready for the soul beating I have a feeling is coming.

"What did Jordan do exactly?"

"Went to Charlie and explained why she cleared you to play even though she shouldn't have. Explained why she didn't recommend surgery when she should have. Why she risked her job—her career—to keep you on the field. She turned in her resignation."

My stomach drops. I feel a surge of bile rise in my throat.

No. She wouldn't do that.

"What?"

"Admitted to a conflict of interest as your treating physician which jeopardized your health. It was an ethical breach. She took an oath, and you may have noticed she takes her job pretty seriously."

Which is why I don't believe she'd jeopardize it now.

She already did that weeks ago. For you. Because you asked her to.

"But Steiner said—"

"Steiner was lying. He was trying to needle you by telling you Jordan called you out. Don't you know that guy's ruthless? He'd say anything to throw you off your game."

"Jesus." I know he's right. Soccer is a game of consistency. I play every game with that in mind. But I trusted the wrong thing.

I banked on Steiner's consistency, when I should have trusted hers.

And now I've fucked up everything.

I can't come up with words. Should I explain, justify, apologize? He doesn't give me time to come up with an answer before hitting me with the rest. "She also told me about your fake fiancé arrangement." He says the words slowly, flicking the f's against his bottom lip before giving into a smile.

"Reilly never should have put her in that position," I mutter.

"Reilly's gone. Charlie sent him packing as soon as he heard. He has a zero tolerance for sexism and discrimination of any kind. She could have reported him and saved yourselves the whole charade." Now he's outright laughing at me. "But I get the feeling it hasn't exactly been a hardship."

The hardened dude in me wants to deny my feelings for Jordan. This is my coach—he doesn't need to think of me as a pussy-whipped player. When I look at him, the understanding in his eyes won't let me lie. "Maybe the best thing in my life."

"For a career player, that's saying a lot."

I nod. "And I accused her of going back on her word because I believed Steiner. Shouldn't have."

Coach Jaynes tips his head to the side. "There are guys like Steiner on every team. You know this. Circumstances were different, you had less raw talent, you might even be him."

I rub the back of my neck. Every inch of my skin feels like it's crawling with unease, realizing I'm the one who fucked everything up with Jordan. "So that's what you came here to tell me? That I'm to blame for my troubles?"

He shakes his head, a quiet laugh under his breath. "No, man. I came to tell you to stop beating yourself up, get the surgery, and make things right with Jordan. Charlie isn't firing her—he understands the big picture and what she was trying to do for you."

My jaw hangs frozen for a moment.

"She still has her job?"

Jaynes nods. "Assuming she wants it. That's for her to decide." He finishes his drink. "Anyhow, just thought you might want to know."

He stands, and I assume he's going for the front door. It surprises me when he walks into my kitchen.

He returns with two glasses of water. "No, I'm not leaving. I'm going to help you get your girl back."

That seems futile. I insulted her at her very core. I didn't trust her. "I'm not sure that's possible."

"Do you love her or not?"

I swallow hard because it's the only way to choke back the pain. Nodding, I slug down half the glass of water. "Yeah."

"Let's talk about that. I have some ideas." I worry he's going to produce a whiteboard from thin air and start mapping strategy. By his own account, Jaynes just got out of a messy divorce, and I'm not sure how much I trust his sense of romance.

But I have zero ideas, so I let him stay.

im

I SHOULD BE at my first pre-op appointment with an orthopedic surgeon. Instead, I'm in a window seat of a 747, staring down at the patchwork of green and gold squares of wheat or corn or whatever comprises the acres of farmland below.

With eight hours still to go, I have plenty of time to think.

My sisters practically got into a fistfight over Facetime, arguing over who would pick me up from the airport. They finally texted me to say they'll be coming together, so I'd best be bringing each of them a Strikers jersey with my name on the back.

I packed three in the hope that my dad might want one, but no guarantees there.

With Wi-Fi on the plane, I haven't even had much time to think because Linnie keeps texting me while she's on break at the pub.

Linnie: You should text her from the plane. So romantic.

Me: Why is that romantic?

I'm asking for real. If there's some grand gesture that can be done from a mile in the air, I'll do it.

Linnie: Because it feels like a movie. The plane's about to crash and as it's going down, the hero texts the love of his life and tells her how he feels.

Me: Hold up. No plane crash. Are you kidding with that while I'm in the air?

Linnie: Sorry.

Me: Is that your only romantic scenario?

Linnie: Hang on. Lemme ask Mare.

Fortunately for me, Mary must be helping an actual customer at her actual job while my other sister is busy playing plane crash cupid. So I get a few minutes of peace. It doesn't help me figure out how to make things right with Jordan.

My phone buzzes again, and I catch a glare from the woman next to me. She already rustled around under her sweater and took off her bra for the redeye flight, so all etiquette bets are off as far as I'm concerned.

Mary: Don't listen to Lin. Just apologize, be honest, and tell her you love her.

Me: Sounds simple enough.

Mary: Simple but not easy. We'll coach you when you get here.

Me: Both of you?

Mary: Maybe I can go it alone while she's on shift. Love you. Fly safe.

I take that as a sign I won't be bothered for a bit and put my phone in the seat pocket. Then I get to work thinking about what to say to my dad. No surprise, after about a minute of that, I fall asleep.

～

THE CHATTER DOESN'T STOP ONCE I get in the car. "You lot never quit, do you?" I grouch, my neck tweaked after a terrible few hours of sleep.

"We're just happy to see you." Linnie, who insisted we sit in the back seat together so Mary could "act like a proper Uber driver," kisses me on the cheek. For the sixth time. I'm not going to have skin left if she keeps it up.

"How's Dad?" I ask. The talking stops. "Whoa. That bad?"

Mary waves a hand, then honks loudly with the other one. "Bloody bastard, stay on your side of the road."

"He's the same. Not a lot of energy, but still stubborn," Linnie says.

"He know I'm coming?" I ask.

"He knows," Mary says.

"How's that seem for him? He gonna be glad to see me? Or what?"

"He'll be glad." Mary turns in her seat to smile at me, nearly hitting the mirror off a car in the process.

I shake my head and point her forward. "Watch the road. We can talk at the house."

"We're at the house," Linnie yelps as we turn down a paved road I don't remember.

"Was this road always here?"

She casts me a side-eye. "Um, yes. But they came and serviced it a while back, so now it's drivable. Dad says it's helped business now that people's cars aren't breaking down on the *way* to the shop because of the shit roads.

Ah, so we're not going to our actual family home, a brick house on Elder street, just over the Wales border. Instead, we've entered the small business district in Chester proper, a small walled city with a combination of bars and restaurants housed in traditional black and white buildings with pitched facades and a more workaday area of less touristy businesses. That's where the Cheltenham Garage has sat for nearly a century in a one-story brick building near the highway and a couple of inexpensive inns. The "house."

The tightness in my chest that set in when my plane landed begins to subside as we approach the shop. It feels familiar, a part of me I've pushed away unnecessarily. It's been a couple years—more than a couple, if I'm honest—and now that I'm here again, I'm having a hard time remembering why I stayed away.

Pride, hurt, ego.

Stupidity.

When Mary pulls the car into the service bay, I see my dad immediately. Normally, he'd be underneath a car or truck, but today he sits in a folding chair off to the side of a black Peugeot on a hydraulic lift. He's not working on it himself, just calling out orders in his raspy voice from the sidelines.

"This is how he does it now. Still working ten hours a day, just not doing the work himself," Mary says, sweeping her brown ponytail over her shoulder and unlatching her seat belt. Linnie unclasps mine and leans over to open my door. "Go on, now. He's been waiting on you since breakfast."

I highly doubt that. If there's one thing I remember about my dad, it's the dismissive tone in his voice when he told me I was a disappointment for choosing a game over a real job and an obligation to my family. I'm suddenly not sure why I'm here.

I mean, I know why, but it feels like self-torture.

From the outside, the auto shop looks the same, a large, red and white Cheltenham Garage sign hanging over the twin metal rollup doors, which are currently open. Taggers used to graffiti them on the regular, but once my dad stopped washing it off, they stopped bothering to paint new stuff there.

Inside is a different story. On the wall behind my dad is a row of Strikers posters, none framed, all tacked up with pushpins. And they're all different versions of me playing. Each year, the team puts out a new image for each of the players and retires the old ones, so there's no chance he loaded up on all of these right before my visit. He's collected over time.

The shock I feel is matched by the familiar comfort of being here, something I deny when I'm gone, but now it feels like time to be honest with myself. About everything.

I look from the posters to my dad and see my eyes matched in his exact color green. For the first time, I glimpse what I'll look like in thirty years if I'm lucky—sun-weathered, discerning, and content.

My dad is unsteady as he rises from his chair, and Mary reaches out a hand instinctively. He swats it away. "I've got it." His hands shake as he extends his arms toward me and pulls me into a hug. He's as tall as me and more solid, the product of manual labor and a few too many sausage biscuits, and he hugs me hard. Brings tears to my eyes.

I never knew a hug from my dad could elicit that response. I'm about to say as much when I meet his eyes and see the exact reflection of what I feel. Maybe after all this time, we can both let the past go.

"I've missed you. Glad you're here." His gruff voice is the same as a remember, but it sounds a little less fierce, the product of age and his declining health. My sisters filled me in on the ride over here. Dad has an assortment of ailments, Parkinson's Disease being the most prominent.

"Garage looks great," I tell him. My dad releases me from the hug but keeps his grip on my forearm, using me for balance.

"Whole thing's paid for? Land too?"

I nod. "Deed should be coming to you soon. You can transition to having someone else run the place, but it will always stay in family hands. Right in this spot."

"Waste of money if you ask me." He shakes his head, always disappointed. Then he laughs. "Proud of you, Tim. Thank you."

My throat feels caught in a vise, and I open my mouth but I

can't find words. Linnie elbows me and puts her arm around our dad.

"Okay, enough with the sentimental stuff. You coming to the pub or what? It's…" She checks her watch. "Two in the afternoon. Not sure what you all are waiting for. I'd have been there two hours ago if I didn't have to grab this one from the plane."

Mary rolls her eyes. "You begged me to let you come." Then she leans close to me. "Good to have you here, Timmy."

With my dad gripping my arm and shuffling like an older man than he is, we follow Linnie down the block to the pub. Been far too long.

CHAPTER 33

*J*ordan

MY EYES LIGHT up when I hear footsteps approaching my office. It's a couple hours early for the players to come to practice, but I'm hoping that by now, Tim has heard from the soccer federation, and maybe, just maybe, he'll come see me.

I had the same hope yesterday. And the day before.

The initial bold brushstrokes of hope fade with every day I don't see or hear from Tim. My heart fights with my brain, begging it to find a reason to hope he'll at least want to talk this through. Yesterday, I finally asked Danny Weston about Tim, hoping to hear he's okay, and Weston let me know he'd gone to England. My heart drums in my chest at the idea of him seeing his dad and the potential to put some of his demons to rest.

On a corner of my untidy desk sits a newly-minted stack of Strikers gear, courtesy of Charlie, who told me I'll need to start showing team spirit under my white coat. No more pencil skirts.

Today, I have on a black Strikers Henley with faded jeans and Chucks. Almost as comfortable as scrubs.

Turning in my resignation wasn't the way I'd hoped to get one-on-one time with Charlie, but things don't always go according to plan. As an inveterate planner, I find this lesson hard to swallow, but I'm working on it.

Once I attempted to resign, Charlie cleared his schedule, and we spent half a day talking about the team, my job, player health, everything.

He apologized for Reilly's behavior and assured me my relationship status has no bearing on a job he hopes I'll keep for a very long time. He couldn't have been more effusive in his admiration for the work I've been doing with the players.

Turns out that even though Charlie hasn't been here physically, he's kept abreast of player development, watched footage, read every medical chart, and seen the improvements in player health in just the month I've had my job.

Which is why he offered me a second chance if I wanted to stay.

At first, I couldn't say I definitively want to be here. Seeing Tim daily will break me. I have no doubt about it. It's not the kind of love a person can get over.

Charlie agreed to table that discussion until I take some time to think, so that's what I'm doing.

Also, once I explained to Charlie that I wanted to contact FIFA about the bonus clause, he put me in touch with the right person straightaway. Turns out that in case of injury, the bonus can still be paid on games played if the injury is reported to the federation and proper medical care is given. Tim probably didn't know about that because he spent his time avoiding the perception of injury instead of investigating the fine print in the bonus clause.

The upshot was that Tim was given his bonus and has his surgery scheduled for next week. I still haven't heard from him, and the hole in my heart is gaping. I doubt I'll stay with the team if he and I don't repair things. It's too painful, even for a dream job.

The person who appears in my doorway, however, lets the wind out of my sails as soon as I see his face. And not just because I'd rather see Tim. Steiner leers at me like he's preparing to have me for a snack.

"Hey, Steiner." I shuffle through the mess on my desk to find my calendar, which is useless because I haven't been writing in it. "What's going on?"

Nodding and rubbing his lips together, he looks like he wants something.

"Thought we should talk." He doesn't wait for an invitation before sauntering in and taking a seat in the chair in front of my desk. He pushes it back a few inches to make more room for his long legs. Then, with his hands interlaced diplomatically on his stomach, he hits me with another leering smile.

Whatever his game is, I don't like it.

But I give him the benefit of the doubt. "Do you have a medical issue? Happy to help."

"Not exactly. I have a Tim issue."

Here we go again. My heart starts beating faster, and I feel my cheeks heat at the mention of Tim. "Maybe you should talk to him about that." I hope he doesn't notice the shake in my voice.

He digs into his pocket, unwraps a piece of gum, and pops it into his mouth. His smirk stays as he begins to chew. "Nah, I'm talking to you."

"Okay, what's the issue?" Clearing my throat, I glance around my messy desk as though a bottle of water will appear. No luck.

He smiles, enjoying himself. "I feel bad about spilling the beans on your fake relationship. That's all. I'm here to say I'm sorry if it caused trouble."

I flinch. He notices. I pretend it didn't happen.

"Why are you really here, Steiner?"

"Like I said, I'm saying sorry. And with Tim injured and me taking over the starting spot, I need to know you're in my corner."

Ah. It's the "no hard feelings after I back-stabbed your boyfriend" visit.

"What does that mean, exactly? I'll give you the same medical attention as always."

"Right. Just making sure you won't look for reasons to bench me just because you're mad about what I said to your fake boyfriend."

He's taking his time, casting out his line and keeping it loose so I'll bite. I hate this. I hate that I need to sit here and play nice with a guy who ruined my relationship and is indirectly responsible for the fact that I almost lost this job. I hate that I need to be the good girl who lets guys like Steiner get away with the shit they pull. There's no way in hell a man would have to put up with this.

"In other words, you're asking if I plan to be ethical when it comes to you."

"Yup. Ethics are important, doc." He has the gall to wink. "So, we good?"

Something shifts.

And Steiner is the unlucky man on the receiving end of my tirade. He gets to experience what happens after I've minded my pile of sexism grenades for a decade, and someone pulls the pin.

I stand up from my chair and lean forward on my desk, so there's no mistaking the seriousness of my words. "No, Steiner. We are not okay."

Now it's his turn to flinch. "Um, o-kay..." His brow furrows, and he waits, suddenly looking less tall and intimidating sitting in his chair.

"I told you about the fake engagement, so that's on me. But what you chose to do with that information offends me on a deep level. I asked you to trust me when I started this job, but it's a two-way street. And right now, I don't trust you. I don't trust your motives, and I know you're ruthless and don't give a shit about anyone but yourself. That may be a winning attitude on a soccer pitch, but you made it personal, and I don't play that way. You're on notice, Steiner. I'll be watching that ankle of yours like a hawk. If I see the tenderness come back, I'll put you on the injured list so fast it will make you lose your lunch. That is, until Tim is back, at which point you will take your rightful place on the bench."

"You're not the coach. Starting lineup isn't up to you."

I tilt my head at him and give him a fuck-you smile. "Actually, it is. If I don't sign off on your fitness, you don't play."

He squirms a little in his chair, and I watch the machinations in his brain work to convince him I'm not correct. "I'll report you. Ethics, remember?"

"Yeah, I do. How about the ethics of lying to your competition right before he takes the field, trying to throw his game off, so he ends up injured? Because that's the manipulation I saw, and I have no doubt Coach Jaynes will see it that way too."

He shakes his head. "Jaynes knows it was just talk."

"Maybe. But I don't think he'll be happy to hear that one of his players showed up drunk in a female employee's office, closed the door, and threatened her job."

I watch Steiner's eyes shift back and forth as he thinks about what to say. He presses his lips together and runs a hand over his face. "Your word against mine." He has the nerve to grin.

"Except that it's not. Remember Reggie, guy who took you home that night? He'll corroborate exactly what I said."

His confidence finally wavers, and he scrounges up enough common sense to stop talking. Daggers shoot from his eyes, but he only nods.

"Your ankle looks a little weak to me. I'd be very careful." He starts to respond, but I don't give him a chance. "You can leave now." And because I'm not an asshole, I add, "Please."

He gets up slowly. He moves away slowly. Then, before he goes, he turns and looks back at me as if to make sure I really meant what I said.

Just to make myself perfectly clear, I smile and calmly take a sip of my coffee. Then I flip him off.

CHAPTER 34

*J*ordan

THE FIRST THING I see is the flowers.

A field of blooms fills the doorframe when I answer the knock and find Tim. Only I can't see him behind the orchids, the purple and orange tulips, the trailing white sweet pea.

It's Saturday morning, and there's a playoff game later, but for the first time, I'm not worried about Tim hurting himself because I know he's not planning to play. Coach Jaynes assured me of it.

"Are you back there someplace?" I ask, weeks' worth of pain and sadness slowly giving way to relief that he's here.

"I am." He lowers the vase enough that I can see his face. My chest aches with so many emotions. The residual hurt from all the things we still need to resolve. And a stronger pull toward him that I can't resist.

Questioning, his eyes roam over my face, never settling in one place. Searching. I don't know what he sees.

"I missed you." The words are out of my mouth before I can

edit them. If we have any hope of working things out, I need to tell him the truth. And this is it.

"Me too. Love..."

I pull in a jagged breath, remembering the first time he called me that. "It doesn't mean what you think it does." I hear his words come back, and I remind myself that we still have a long way to go from where we are. It's not until he answers me that I realize I said the words out loud.

"No. It doesn't. It never did. Because how the fuck could it? The way I feel about you is so much more than a word."

My eyes dart to his and stay there, pulled into a vortex of intensity. We stare at each other, locked in something only the two of us understand—that it's always been like this. And it always should be like this. But can it?

The flowers wobble a little in his grip, and despite how much I like looking at his strong hands gripping the vase and the roped forearm muscles holding it up, I can't leave him out here like this. "Why don't you bring those in?" I back up a few steps so he can cross the threshold.

"Thanks," he says softly.

He walks the vase to the kitchen table and places it in the middle. He doesn't turn around, and I wonder if he's admiring his handiwork. "So you've branched out from succulents," I observe. "They're beautiful."

"They're flowers," he says. "*You're* beautiful."

My tense, frozen heart starts to thaw. I hope he's here to tell me he did, in fact, pull his head out of his ass. It looks to be sitting where it belongs on his broad sexy shoulders, so that's something.

When he turns to where I'm standing in green striped pajama pants and one of his Strikers hoodies, I see something different in his face. His expression is firm, resolved. The muscle in his jaw ticks, and he grimaces.

Is this where we start or where we end?

Tim gestures to my couch, but the memory of his mouth on every part of me there makes me shake my head. We sit at the kitchen table instead in high-backed uncomfortable wood chairs my mother bought me as a housewarming present.

"I-I don't have a grand gesture." He rakes a hand through his hair, and the plaintive green of his eyes pierces my heart.

"What do you mean?"

"It means I don't have tricks. Some skywriter out there throwing hearts into the sky. Or your name on the stadium marquee asking for forgiveness. But I'm sorry. I fucked up, love. You didn't deserve what I accused you of, and I am so, so sorry for not trusting you of all people." He exhales hard after he gets the words out and wipes a hand over his face.

I nod and extend my upturned hand on the table, needing connection. He drops his over mine and wraps his fingers around tight. "I don't need tricks."

"No, but you need to know why I lost faith. It wasn't about you, but I took it out on you. I think…all the issues I've been holding on to for years with my dad…that was the breach in trust. And I needed to rectify that in order to get whole."

"You talked to him? I heard you went to England."

He nods. "Flew out to visit this week. That's why I haven't been at the stadium."

"How did it go? What did he say? Did he—?" Tim chuckles, raises a finger, and presses it against my lips.

"We'll talk about all of it. Maybe while I'm recovering from surgery. Bound to have some downtime after that, no?"

"Yes. But Tim—"

"No. Wait. Let me say the rest of what I came to say." His eyes close, and I watch him inhale a deep breath, preparing. I wait, a part of me worrying that in spite of the apology and the love, maybe we still can't work.

No. Stop allowing old hurt to color things.

Tim's eyes open and I see determination. And also love. "You risked everything for me, and no one's ever done that for me before. I shouldn't have asked you to do it, but I know why you agreed. And I'll never take that for granted again."

"I did it because I love you."

"I know. And I-I don't deserve you."

"Tim. Yes, you do. Trust. That."

He reaches for the flower arrangement, plucks out a single white sweet pea, and hands it to me. "I trust you, love. I do. I also know that if I don't fucking touch you right now, I'm going to lose my mind."

I nod. "Yeah. That too."

The conversation ends there because Tim is standing in a flash, the wooden chair falling over behind him as he moves toward me. Lifting me with an arm under my legs, Tim pulls me hard against him, and our mouths connect in a firestorm of apology and forgiveness. And I don't care if it's fate or luck or common sense and hard work that brought us here.

I just know I'm not leaving.

CHAPTER 35

*J*ordan
One Week Later

TIM LOOKS EDGY, perched on the edge of the couch in my office. Before he notices me standing in the doorway, he starts pacing in a circle. Then he sits again.

"Hey," I say quietly, not wanting to make him more jumpy. He jumps anyway. And starts explaining.

"I figure I have a fifty-fifty chance of getting thrown out on my head."

"What? Why?"

He gestures around my office, which I didn't notice because I was focused on him. In a corner is a mini-fridge with a top-of-the-line cappuccino maker sitting on top. He's nailed a rack of mugs on the wall next to a Strikers scarf hung like a banner with blue and black fringe on the ends.

And on the corner of my desk, an orchid with small succulents tucked into the soil. I smile because he knows this will survive, even if I forget to water it.

"What is all this?"

He shoves a hand through his hair in that nervous way I've come to love. "I wanted to do something nice for you."

"You decorated my office?"

He walks to the mini-fridge and opens the door with a flourish. "Got you some cold brew coffee, real cream, some fancy smoothies that will stay cold in here instead of rotting on your desk."

Pointing to the espresso machine, he shrugs. "This one is supposed to be as good as Starbucks."

"Tim, that's so sweet. Thank you." I pat the various piles on my desk. "I see you didn't clean up my messes."

"I'm kind of fond of the piles." He laughs. "Not nearly as fond as I am of you. I fucking love you, beautiful Jordan 'Danny' Page, and I really hope you like this."

He points to one more thing I hadn't noticed—an empty silver frame on my desk. "Thought we could put a picture of us in here, you know, like you wanted to have as proof of our fake engagement. Only now, it's just us the way we are. Irritatingly smitten with each other."

I laugh. "I love it."

My window shades are up, and I can see the practice pitch below, where the team is warming up on the fuzzy bright green turf. Tim skipped his first pre-op appointment with the surgeon when he went to England, so it's been rescheduled for this morning. I promised to go with him. "Is all of this a stall tactic because you're nervous about the doctor's appointment?"

"What? No."

"Okay, good." I walk over to my desk and open the top drawer. "I've been meaning to give this back to you, unless you want me to have a keepsake of the fake engagement nonsense."

I hold the ring out in the velvet box, but he doesn't take it. Doesn't take a step closer to me or even acknowledge that I'm trying to give it to him. So stubborn.

Shaking my head at his childish obstinance, I move to put the ring on the desk, but his hand flies up to stop me. "No."

"Why not?"

"Because I fucking love the hell out of you. Always have. And I want you to keep that ring."

His words warm me so thoroughly that I forget about the ring or the discussion. I step closer to him, and he folds me into his chest. I sigh at the fireworks that blast from my heart. Every damn time. "Tim…"

"Love." He tips my chin up and lowers his lips to mine so slowly it feels like I'm falling through air, waiting for a landing in a sea of down pillows. I've never been kissed like this—not by anyone but him.

Even for him, it's spectacular. So tender, so loving. My knees wobble and he holds me against him.

"Okay," I say when I'm finally able to draw a steady breath. "I'll keep the fake ring. You sold it with that kiss."

He laughs. And maybe that's why I don't take him seriously when he says, "It's not fake."

"I know. It has a certain charm to it. It symbolizes the beginning of us. It'll always hold a special place in my heart. Of course, I'll keep it." I place the ring back on my finger and wiggle it around in front of his eyes.

"And get some insurance. That thing's an antique."

I stop moving, not sure I'm hearing him right. "Hang on. When you said just now that it was real…" I don't dare finish the sentence. It's a crazy thought. We barely knew each other when he brought the ring to me at work. Why would he—?

"I bought you a real diamond." He pushes his hand through his hair, shaking his head like he doesn't understand it himself. "I know it probably seems crazy."

"Probably?!"

"I know, I know."

"Tim."

Tilting his head to the side, he looks at me. Those olive eyes, deep with promise and hope. I remember thinking it the first time I saw him, and I love that eyes don't change.

They're the window into who Tim was when he was young, and their depth and wisdom draw me in again for the story of what they'll see and experience as they get older.

All I know is that I want to be there for the journey. I want to look into those eyes every day for a lifetime and know they'll be my anchor.

When I think of it like that, buying a real diamond doesn't seem crazy at all.

With some things, you just know.

"Really?" I ask again.

He lifts my hand and examines the ring, which picks up the light and flickers as he gently moves it. "That day in the parking lot... something came over me, and when you agreed to the fake engagement, I guess maybe...I had a weird feeling we might be standing here like this. Or maybe it was wishful thinking."

"Magical thinking," I confirm. "Now, if you said you bought the ring back when we were in high school, that might be a little crazy."

He feigns a nervous look, but I know he's kidding.

I think he's kidding.

Tim drops to a knee and takes my hand. As his breath fans over my knuckles, my skin ripples with heat, and my heart starts thundering behind my ribs. He kisses my palm and holds it to his heart. "I want a whole lifetime with you if you'll marry me."

"Yes. Yes, please."

Since I've long since abandoned the two-inch heels for a pair of black Chucks that match my Strikers warm-up jacket, I'm back to my five feet, three inches. Which means Tim towers over me by a full foot, so I have to stand on my toes to wrap my arms around his neck and kiss him.

It also means that when he folds me into his arms, my head

tucks perfectly in against his chest. The steady thump of his heart grounds me.

"I couldn't love you more for believing. In us."

He nods. "I was crazy about the girl." He leans in for a deep kiss that I'll feel in my heart for days. When he draws back, he laughs, and I know it's because I have a dopey, pink-cheeked, just-kissed grin on my face.

He nods to confirm, "Still am."

EPILOGUE

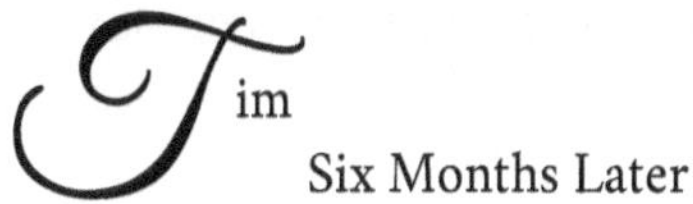

im

Six Months Later

THE TINNY TAP of silverware on dishes and indistinct chatter fills the restaurant on a tiny street in North Beach a few blocks from Grace Cathedral.

The weather is misty and cold this time of year, but Jordan and I walked here from my apartment anyway. Reminds me of England, and I already have another trip planned to see my family. This time, Jordan is coming with me.

"Five months post-op. To you, footie player." Jordan raises her glass in a toast.

I clink her glass. "To us."

We sit tucked into a table in the corner under a window. The bench seat faces outward, and there's a chair across from us for Weston, if he ever gets here. We've already poured wine into our glasses from a pitcher shaped like a chicken, but Jordan won't let me order food until Weston arrives. He's our sidekick tonight since his recent semi-steady jersey chaser gave him the boot. He's been a little down, so we invited him out for pizza at this place we like. "It's polite to wait for everyone to get here."

"It's just Weston. There's no everyone."

"Stop being crabby."

"I'm crabby because I'm hungry. If you let me order something, it'll solve both our problems." I reach for a breadstick from a glass jar on the table, half expecting Jordan to swat my hand away. "I never knew you were such a stickler for etiquette."

Jordan looks at her phone and shrugs. "He's kind of late. Has he texted?"

Digging my phone from my pocket, my hand brushes against the exposed skin of Jordan's knee. I check the phone. "Nope, no text. I'll give him five more minutes, then I'm eating." I drop the phone on the table and return my hand to Jordan's knee and rub circles on the skin.

"Mmm, I like that," she sighs contentedly.

"I still don't know why you wore a short skirt on a chilly night."

She waggles her eyebrows and gestures to where my hand is taking advantage of her bare skin. "Don't you?"

Which gives me an idea. Cocking my head to the side, I nod at her. "Okay, I'll make a deal with you. Set a timer on your phone. If I can give you an orgasm in under five minutes, you let me order dinner, with or without Weston."

Her doe eyes grow even rounder, but I can tell from the nervous drumming of her fingers on the table that she's at least a little bit into it. "Are you serious? At the table?"

I already have my arm around her, but I pull her in tighter, so the sides of our bodies are flush. "Yes."

She looks over her shoulder to where three chefs work in the open kitchen, which has a brick pizza oven at the center and a low enough countertop that they can definitely see us if they have any interest. I'm betting that pizza making is distracting enough that they won't notice. And if they do, they'll be fucking jealous, so what do I care? But Jordan still looks near-scandalized.

"What if Weston shows up before you're done?" she whispers even though the other tables are far enough away and there's enough ambient noise that no one can hear us.

I shrug, unconcerned about Weston. I can always text him to wait outside for five fucking minutes. Because we are doing this.

"What if—"

I stop her incessant worry and questions by putting my hand on top of her worried little fingers and letting her see the heat in my eyes, which I hope conveys how much I want her right now and how much she's going to enjoy the rewards of that. Judging from how her tongue darts out to lick her lips, I've succeeded.

Leaning in, I whisper against her ear. "Stop asking questions. Time to be a little impulsive, love." Her whole body shudders, and she nods. "Start the timer."

With shaking hands, she reaches for her phone and fumbles over the screen until she finds the right app. "Hang on a sec."

My nose grazes the side of her neck, leaving goosebumps in its wake. "No," I growl. "Fuck the timer. It won't even take me five."

The phone hits the table, and I slide my hand up under her skirt, taking my time to graze every inch of flesh on her inner thigh as I glide upward. Her hands drop to the seat, then one flutters up to rest on my arm. She doesn't know what to do with herself, and I'm getting off on her complete lack of grace.

"Love." I'm still whispering in her ear, and I'm not leaving this spot because I know how crazy it makes her. "Put your hands on the table. Hold on to your wineglass and sit still like the gorgeous, polite dinner companion you are. Can you do that?"

She moans in quiet agreement. I shift away to look at her, and what I see blows my mind. She sits perfectly still like a spring flower. No one would know the riot of heart palpitations that I can feel under my hands. It's so fucking hot. Who knew there was such a thing as etiquette porn?

I slide my hand higher, pushing aside the lace on her panties and delving a finger inside. She clenches immediately, and I hear her suck in a breath. "No one has any idea this is happening. This is all for you," I whisper. She doesn't move, but she's trying hard to keep her breathing steady. It's not working.

I can already tell it's not going to take me more than another minute to get her exactly where I want her, so I double down and start circling her clit with my thumb, still curling my finger inside and moving it slowly.

She gasps.

"Easy, love. I've got you." I nuzzle her neck, and I'm sure to anyone who glances over, I look like a besotted lover next to a woman who won't give me the time of day. I love the optics of that since every bit of her is trembling, and it couldn't be further from the truth.

My hand moves a little faster, pressing and pinching the little bundle of nerves until she moans again. I look at her hands and see the glass of wine shaking on the table.

"Tell me when. Tell me how close you are, love," I growl so only she can hear.

"So close," she whispers.

She swallows hard, and her head lolls back. "No," I tell her. "Sit up straight. You've got this."

She nods and inhales a deep breath. Then I slip in a second finger and take her over the cliff in about four seconds.

Her breathing is choppy, and I can feel her heart hammering. It takes a good minute before she can look at me. When she does, she's blushing a color pink I've never seen before. But you can be damn sure I'll be seeing it again.

I stare into her glassy eyes and nod. "Well done, love." Trailing kisses slowly down her cheek, I land on her lips. I'm about to dive in for the kiss I'm aching for when Weston shows up.

"Hey, sorry I'm late."

Jordan scoots a foot away from me in an instant and smiles like she has six canaries in her feline belly. Weston looks from her to me and back again.

"What's up, guys? Am I interrupting something?"

Jordan and I look at each other and laugh. "Nope, you're good," I tell him. "We ordered wine, but Jordan made me wait an extra five minutes to see if you'd show before ordering food."

Jordan starts laughing. I know she's been holding everything in for the past few minutes, and it was bound to erupt somehow. It looks good on her.

He scans our faces suspiciously as he takes his seat. "Why do I have the feeling you've sneezed on the breadsticks or something?"

Jordan laughs. "No, nothing like that. We've just been taking bets on whether you'd get here within five minutes." She picks up the chicken pitcher and pours wine into Weston's glass.

"Oh, okay. So, who won the bet?"

"I did," Jordan says quickly, her cheeks flushing pinker. She fans them. "Red wine. Happens every time I drink it."

"In that case, we ought to order another pitcher because I like the way that color looks on you." I take her chin in my hand and kiss her.

"All right, get a room or stop inviting me to dinner," Weston says, rolling his eyes.

"Fine, fine. Sorry, Weston." Jordan pats him on the hand before whispering to me, "Not that we need a room."

She settles in and starts reading the menu, but I keep looking at her, astounded I've gotten this lucky. And fuck Weston. If I want to kiss my fiancée, I'm going to do it. But for his sake, I keep it polite.

Like always, when I kiss her, it rocks my world off its foundation. That's what we are, what we've always been.

Fate.

Love.
Boom.

~

LINNIE AND WESTON'S story is coming next, a brother's best friend, forced proximity, grumpy-sunshine sports romance. You can reserve your copy of HE'S A WINNER now. Read on for a Sneak Peek.

EPILOGUE Two
Tim
One Month Later

"I'M SO CHUFFED to be here, you have no idea!" Linnie bounces along in the backseat of my car and tugs on the blond pigtails, which look lopsided as I regard her in the rear-view mirror. To be clear, she's not bouncing because I'm driving over potholes. My sister looks like she has a spring under her ass.

"I think I have some idea," I grumble, unapologetic about the grouchiness in my voice. "You're not especially subtle, Lin."

"Why are you in a mood?" Linnie asks, playfully swatting my shoulder and looking at my profile for answers. She's insisted on sitting in the backseat and treating me like a damn Uber driver. I even loaded her three pieces of luggage into the trunk while she settled in and checked her lipstick in a compact from her purse.

"Because it's one in the morning, and I'm going on a sixteen-hour day—half of it on the soccer pitch doing drills."

The bouncing continues, and it's giving me a headache to see her in the rear-view mirror, so I tip it away. "You really aren't a morning person," she gripes.

"I am, actually, but I don't think this qualifies as morning."

"It does where I live. It's practically tea time back home."

My brain hurts too much to calculate the time difference, even though I'm fairly certain she's off by at least a handful of hours. No point in arguing.

"And when did you ever drink tea?"

"Half past never. Not when there's a pint of beer as an option." Even without the mirror, I can see the grin on her face. What's more, I can hear it in her voice. And, like always, her enthusiasm is contagious enough to thaw my irritation.

"Glad you're here, Lin." The freeway is empty at this hour, save for the Silicon Valley diehards who are either heading to their ergonomic desk chairs or coming from them. "Now we've gotta get Mare and Dad on a plane."

I'd tried to convince them all to make the trip out, but Linnie was the only one who jumped at the chance for some time off work and a free plane ticket. Not surprising at all.

"Eh, just be glad you got me. Not sure those two are movable from the motherland, even for a vacation."

No point in arguing about that. She's right about my dad, at any rate. Even though he's taking more days off from the shop, his health isn't reliable enough to make the trip. And with Mary, it's more about getting time away from work, so I'll keep working on her.

I move the mirror back so I can make eye contact with Lin. Her mile-wide smile melts about half of my resistance, but it's still ridiculously early.

"Where's Jordan?" Linnie asks, leaning so far forward I take a quick glance back to make sure she's still wearing a seatbelt. She has it stretched forward in her hand, making it pretty much useless as she hovers over my right shoulder.

"Probably asleep. She wanted to come get you herself, told me to go to bed—"

"Of course she did. Because you're crabby."

"I am not crabby." I am getting crabby. I really need to sleep, and Linnie's energy is a lot for this time of night.

"I am so not tired. Are there pubs near your place where I can go hang out if you insist on going to bed like a ninety-year-old man?"

I shake my head, chuckling at her exuberance. She's a handful on a good day, but she's practically shouting, and we're the only two people in the car. "Right down the block. Knock yourself out."

We zip up the peninsula from the San Francisco airport, and before long, the Transamerica spire and the other downtown high rises come into view. "I love all the lights. Are we going over the bridge?"

Raindrops start spattering on the windshield, a winter storm that's been on the weather forecast for days.

"Not unless you want to be in Oakland."

"Tomorrow. I want to go over that bridge." She points at where the lights rain down from the spires of the Bay Bridge.

Linnie's face is about six inches from mine, sandwiched between the front seats. "You know, you could've just sat in front if you wanted to be this close to me."

She tips her head to the side and conks mine. "Nope. I like having a driver. Feels so proper since you're a famous baller and all."

I can't help but smile at the little sister energy, and I can't help loving that she looks up to me a little bit. "Hardly famous, and definitely not your driver after this trip."

As we enter the city, the skyline rises above us. We drive through the SoMa area, where people spill out of bars, and I worry Linnie might make a break for the scene, which is much more interesting than this conversation.

"Bollocks, are you kidding me with this weather? I thought I was coming to sunny California."

"It's sunny sometimes, but it *is* winter."

"I just left winter. I don't need more gloomy weather. So what do you have planned for me while I'm here, other than splashing in puddles?" Linnie asks, finally leaning back on the bench seat behind me and staring out the window as we enter the city.

I flip on the wipers as the rain droplets turn to a more steady rain. The city lights squint through the droplets, blurring in reds and yellows.

Now it's my turn to smile. I've been holding onto a surprise, and the words tumble forth before I can decide whether this is the right time to tell her everything. "Actually, we're taking you to Lake Tahoe. We bought a mountain place there, and with this storm, you're in for some snow. It's beautiful up there. You'll love it."

"Well, that sounds…nice."

I look at her in the mirror. "Nice? It'll be quiet and snowy, and we can build a fire and hang out."

She waves a hand and unwraps the fuzzy blue scarf from her neck, messing up her hair even more as she whips it off. "It sounds lovely and all, really it does…"

"I sense a 'but' in that sentiment."

"I was hoping to have fun in the city."

Of course, she was. This is my super social sister. "Right. Okay, well, we'll do that, then."

"I'm not saying I don't want to see your fancy mountain house."

"When did I say it was fancy?"

She waves a hand. "You're a soccer star. You probably have a fancy mountain house, is all."

I laugh. If she sees the house, it won't take long to disabuse her of that notion. It's pretty barebones, and that's the charm. But now that I think about it, I can see why my twenty-nine-year-old sister wouldn't think it was particularly fun to be cooped up in a mountain house on her first visit to San Francisco.

"It was just a thought. We'll just stay in the city."

Linnie crosses her arms and pouts. "Now I feel as if I've offended you." Then she points out the window. "Whoa, what's that, a giant penis, then?"

"It's Coit Tower. It was built as a monument to a firefighter. Supposed to look like a firehose."

"Firehose, my arse." Linnie's cackle is louder than appropriate for the small enclosed space, but it reminds me how glad I am to see her. She climbs over to the front seat. It's not safe, but we're about a block from my house, so I don't bother to reprimand her.

Linnie immediately picks up my phone. "How about some tunes? Look this way," she commands. When I do, the face recognition unlocks the phone.

"We're almost there. We have time for maybe half a tune."

But she doesn't play any music. "Tim, do you know you have a bazillion texts from someone named Claire? Stuff about a water main bursting?"

"What? No. Who's Claire?"

Linnie reads before nodding and summarizing. "Your neighbor at your fancy mountain house. She says a pipe burst. There's water coming into her property from your house."

"Nooo." I pull into my parking spot and slump over the steering wheel. "I'm gonna need to go there and deal with it. And I'm knackered."

Linnie is waving her hands and bouncing in the seat so hard I have to reach over and still her so she won't hit her head on the ceiling. "Stop. You're giving me motion sickness."

"I'll go! Let me deal with the pipe or whatever. It's daytime in England. I'm wide awake, and I slept on the plane. Plus, I've always wanted to drive on the wrong side of the road."

"I'm not sending you out to drive three hours in the middle of the night."

"But I want to do it! Please, Timmy. I swear I'll drive sensibly. And then I'll get to see your house and still have time for fun in the city. Please?"

Her pleading and my exhaustion somehow meld into something that seems like a good idea, even though I know it's a terrible one. "You really want to drive right now?"

"I really want to drive right now. Please?"

Shaking my head, I know what the right answer to her plea is, and I hear the words come out of my mouth before I can stop them. "Okay. I'll give you the directions. If you promise to be really careful."

"I promise."

Which is how I end up sending my sister out on a middle-of-the-night errand to fix a busted pipe in the mountains. Kissing her on the cheek, I try once more to talk her down. But Linnie won't budge.

I watch her pull slowly out of my garage and cross my fingers that she doesn't get into trouble on the way to the cabin. Then I drag my exhausted ass upstairs.

"Hey!" Jordan looks past me, then turns back and hits me with a questioning look. "Where's Linnie?"

I explain everything, realizing all the while that I sound like the most irresponsible older brother on the planet for sending my sister out on this mission. "I'll call her and have her come back. I don't know what I was thinking," I admit, willing Jordan's wide eyes to stop glaring at me in disbelief.

"She's never even been here, and you send her out into the mountains in the middle of the night?"

"I know. I'm awful. I'm just exhausted."

"Well, yes. Awful, for sure. But why didn't you just call me? I already dealt with it."

"What do you mean?"

"When Claire didn't reach you, she called me. So I called Weston. He's already halfway up there."

I feel a sudden shower of gratitude for my beautiful, incredible fiancée who just saved my bacon. Like she always does. "You, love, are the best thing that ever happened to me."

I cup her chin in my hand and kiss her, immediately pulled into the vortex of needing her in such an elemental way that I know I'll never stop feeling it. Reluctantly, I pull away.

"To be continued. Let me get Linnie back here before she gets too far."

We wait as my phone speed dials Linnie's number, but after four rings, it goes to voice mail. I try again. Same thing. "What do I do?"

"I guess, keep trying?"

I do. For an hour. Then two. But my stubborn, carefree sister, who loves loud music, doesn't pick up the phone.

BONUS EPILOGUE
Tim
Five Years Later

THE AIR FEELS different as soon as I cross the Bay Bridge and leave behind the Strikers stadium and all the tactical decisions that come with coaching a professional team. I'm not the head coach—Jaynes isn't close to relinquishing that job to me just yet —but working alongside a man I like and respect while offering expertise on a game I know well is just about the perfect job.

Not quite perfect, because nothing compares with playing, but it's damn near so. And I can work out every day and not get injured, which I've come to appreciate in my thirty-six years of age.

Hopping out of my car at the curb, I see the mass of auburn curls first. The sun catches the flyaway bits, lighting them up like wild flames. Then I hear the voice.

"Daddy!"

Eden races down the front steps of our house in the Berkeley Hills, and I hold my arms out wide to catch her as she careens toward me. At three years old, she already has some of my speed and all of Jordan's tendency to trip on things. She's the perfect combination of us—smart as a whip like her mom, beautiful like her mom, a little impulsive like her mom…okay, she doesn't have much of me in her, other than a whopping stubborn streak, but that's fine with me.

I can handle stubborn. In fact, I love it.

"Hey, moppet. How was your day?" Half my words get muffled as I lean down to wrap her in my arms and get a mouthful of her flyaway hair, which is damp and smells like tangerine sherbet.

"Terrible," she says, wriggling out of my arms and stomping a foot. It takes all my self-control not to laugh at her dour expression.

"Why terrible?" I reach for her hand, and she slips her small fingers in between mine. She pulls me toward the front door impatiently, as though I wasn't headed that way anyhow.

She shrugs dramatically, her shoulders dropping with an exaggerated exhale. "It just was. Can I come to work with you tomorrow?" Blinking up at me with moist eyes under her long red lashes, she has my heart served up on a platter.

"You want to come to work?"

She nods stoically, her hair bouncing on her shoulders as she does it. "I really, really do."

"Why?"

"Because I want to play all day."

"Don't you get to do that anyway?"

She shakes her head emphatically. "Nope. I have to go to preschool." She says it with a sneer on her face, even though I know she loves it. Or, she did…

"But…don't you play there?"

"Daddy, it's not the same." She blinks her round eyes at me, looking exactly like Jordan when she can't understand why I'm not seeing her point.

"Why not?" I ask because I don't see her point.

"Because *you're* not at school to play with. If I go to play at your work, I'll see you all day."

Well, I can't argue with that. I have no idea how it's going to work when I show up on the field with her and try to coach, but hell if I'm going to turn her down. She's never asked before, and it might be a problem if it becomes a habit, but I'm all for trying a "take your daughter to work" day.

"Okay, let's do it. Tomorrow?" I push the front door open, half expecting our sheepdog, Frisco, to come bounding outside, but he must be out back because I'm greeted with silence.

I wouldn't have thought her eyes could get any wider, but the deep brown of her irises dance while she presses her lips together and claps her hands. "Yay! I'm going to go pack all my clothes in a bag for tomorrow!"

She runs inside before I can tell her she won't actually need all of her clothes. I don't exactly intend to let her play soccer with a bunch of men bordering on two hundred pounds of muscle, but knowing her, she'll charm them all into playing hopscotch.

I'm not two feet inside the front door, when the scent of garlic hits my nose and I let out a contented sigh. I love my job, I love my daughter, and I love whatever garlicky Italian goodness lies at the other end of that wafting trail, but I still haven't hit the best part of my day. Not even close.

"Hey, footie player."

That's the best part of my day.

Jordan pads over to me in fuzzy socks, an oversized black Strikers hoodie and scrub bottoms because she spent her day at the surgical center. She still works fulltime for the Strikers, but she also does surgical procedures once a week at an outpatient orthopedic clinic.

Her arms circle my waist, and she buries her head in my chest the same way Eden did moments earlier. "I missed you, love."

"Me too."

"We're ridiculous. We saw each other exactly ten hours ago, but on these days when she doesn't work at the Strikers facility, I feel like a man starving by the time I get home. So I partake of what I'm missing, dipping to capture her mouth and indulge in the sweet taste of her lips, which I've been craving since I left the house this morning.

Wrapping a hand around her hair, I move it away from her face, so I can see her better, and also so I can access her neck, which I love kissing as much as her lips. It's the soft, sweet sounds she makes that sound like something between the purr of a kitten and the possessiveness of a tiger.

I will never get enough of this woman. Not ever.

She laughs at my exuberance because she knows all it would take is one quirk of her lips for me to tear the hoodie from her body and have my way with her.

"I made farfalle pasta and roasted broccolini. A little sorbet for dessert." She looks proud of her accomplishment, and I don't blame her.

"You did all that after performing surgeries all day?"

She nods, but then her tips twist into a guilty smirk. "Well, I purchased them from Scalini's and heated them up to a perfect temperature."

"I just fell a little more in love with you. If that's even possible." I steal another kiss before she playfully pushes me away. She leans her back against my chest and pulls my arms to wrap around her waist. My hands sit on her flat stomach, and it's all I can do to behave myself and not reach beneath the waistband of her scrubs.

"Are you ready for round two?" she purrs.

"I don't think we've exactly accomplished round one, love. Kisses don't count in my book."

I look between her and the staircase that leads to our bedroom, wondering if she means round two of what we already enjoyed once this morning before Eden woke up. Because that definitely counted.

Jordan shakes her head as though she knows exactly where my mind just went. Who am I kidding? We've been together for over five years. She knows where my mind is all the time when it comes to her. I'm not subtle.

She presses her lips together to suppress a smile. "No, not that." Then she takes my hand and pushes it underneath the Strikers hoodie she still loves to wear. Placing my hand on her stomach, I feel the same ripple of desire every time I touch her skin.

She presses my hand flat. "This," she says. "Or rather, what this will be in thirty-two more weeks."

I spin her to face me. This time it's my turn for the wide eyes. "Really?"

She nods, tears pricking the corners of her eyes, but her mile-wide smile making no mistake that these are happy tears.

We've been wanting to have another baby for about a year, hoping to have two kids relatively close in age. Like Jordan and her brother. Like my sisters and me.

Neither one of us wanted to put too much pressure on the situation, but I could tell Jordan was losing hope as each month passed without success.

"I am so, so in love with you, Jordan Page Cheltenham. And I'm going to fucking love this baby," I say, lifting her up until her legs wrap around my waist and her forehead tips against mine.

"Me too," she says, opening her mouth to say more, but stopping when I go charging up the stairs with her to our bedroom. "Hang on. What are you doing?" She knows damn well what I'm doing.

"What I'm going to keep doing until you're too big and pregnant to do it anymore."

She laughs. "We have a child in the house, you may recall."

I place her on the bed, wagging a finger. "She's in her room packing all her clothes. We've got at least another five minutes."

My eyebrows bounce because I know she knows what I accomplish in five minutes.

And maybe Eden has more clothes than we think. Maybe I'll end up with ten.

WANT a peek into Molly and Holden's future? Join my mailing list by typing https://BookHip.com/VMKKPXD into your browser to read an exclusive BONUS EPILOGUE. Mailing list subscribers only receive the good stuff—new release info, exclusive sales, and a monthly free romance from one of my author friends.

ABOUT THE AUTHOR

Stacy Travis writes sexy, charming romance about bookish, sassy women and the hot alphas who fall for them. Writing contemporary romance makes her infinitely happy, but that might be the coffee talking.

When she's not on a deadline, she's in running shoes complaining that all roads seem to go uphill. Or on the couch with a margarita. Or fangirling at a soccer game. She's never met a dog she didn't want to hug. And if you have no plans for Thanksgiving, she'll probably invite you to dinner. Stacy lives in Los Angeles with her two sons, and a poorly-trained rescue dog who hoards socks.

Facebook reader group: Stacy's Saucy Sisters

Super fun newsletter: https://landing.mailerlite.com/webforms/landing/c7r2g8

Tiktok: https://www.tiktok.com/@stacytravisauthor

Website: https://www.www.stacytravis.com

Email: stacytraviswrites@gmail.com - tell me what you're reading!

facebook.com/stacytravisromance
instagram.com/stacytravisauthor
bookbub.com/authors/stacy-travis
goodreads.com/stacytravis

ALSO BY STACY TRAVIS

The Summer Heat Duet

1. The Summer of Him: A Mistaken Identity Celebrity Romance

2. Forever with Him: An Opposites Attract Contemporary Romance

The Berkeley Hills Series - all standalone novels

1. In Trouble with Him: A Forbidden Love Contemporary Romance
(Finn and Annie's story)

2. Second Chance at Us: A Second Chance Romance (Becca and Blake)

3. Falling for You: A Friends to Lovers Romance (Isla and Owen)

4. The Spark Between Us: A Grumpy-Sunshine, Brother's Best Friend
Romance (Sarah and Braden)

5. Playing for You: A Sports Romance (Tatum and Donovan)

6. No Match for Her - an Opposites-Attract Friends-to-Lovers Romance
(Cherry and Charlie)

San Francisco Strikers Series - standalone novels

1. He's a Keeper: A Grumpy-Sunshine Sports Romance (Molly and
Holden)

2. He's a Player: A Second Chance Sports Romance (Jordan and Tim)

Standalone Novels - Adult Contemporary Romance

French Kiss: A Friends to Lovers Romance

Bad News: An Enemies to Lovers Romance